HIS SECRET HIGHLAND BRIDE

CLAN MACPHERSON SERIES

HIS SECRET HIGHLAND BRIDE

CLAN MACPHERSON SERIES

ALLISON B. HANSON

This book is a work of fiction. Names, characters, places, and incidents are the product of the author's imagination or are used fictitiously. Any resemblance to actual events, locales, or persons, living or dead, is coincidental.

Copyright © 2024 by Allison B. Hanson. All rights reserved, including the right to reproduce, distribute, or transmit in any form or by any means. For information regarding subsidiary rights, please contact the Publisher.

Entangled Publishing, LLC
644 Shrewsbury Commons Ave
STE 181
Shrewsbury, PA 17361
rights@entangledpublishing.com

Amara is an imprint of Entangled Publishing, LLC.

Edited by Alethea Spiridon
Cover design by LJ Anderson/Mayhem Cover Creations
Cover photography by Period Images and ColobusYeti/GettyImages
Interior design by Britt Marczak

Manufactured in the United States of America

First Edition May 2024

Chapter One

July, 1695 Scotland

Breathing in the scents of blooming heather and sunshine, Shane MacPherson allowed the first moments of his return home to sink in.

"Go away, you rotten whoreson!" A woman's shout rent the clean mountain air he'd been enjoying.

Not exactly the welcome he'd been expecting after being away for five years fighting in France. Though since he was still far from the castle, he hadn't expected any welcome at all.

"I'll split your skull until your tiny maggot brain falls out on your boot!" The woman's shouts were becoming more colorful in her distress.

Instincts, honed by war, had both him and his horse ready for battle as they headed toward the sound. Before he made it, the woman's scream shattered the still air. His blood went cold as he worried what he might find.

Memories flickered through his mind. A broken body,

pale skin, and dark eyes that seemed to search for him even in their emptiness. He'd let her down. He would not do the same with this lass.

Shane was out of his saddle before Hades came to a stop in the small clearing. The soldier in Shane had him pull his sword without thinking, as he assessed each threat separately. Two men, maybe only ten and seven, were being held back by a striking woman with raven hair and a large stick. The sleeve of her shabby, ill-fitting gown was torn and her dark eyes wild.

For a moment, he thought it was Maria, but he shook the thought away when she spoke again, for she didn't speak with a lilting Spanish accent. This woman was a Scot and much taller than his Maria. Plus, his wife was dead, buried back in Spain.

Once again, he shook himself to action. He would be no help to this woman if he couldn't get his head straight.

"Stay away from me, ye wee maggots," she spat out while poking the closest of the men in the stomach with her crude weapon.

The man bent slightly from the strike but managed to hold on to the stick and toss it aside. With no protection, she turned to run but was grasped by the other man and hurled to the ground. That was plenty for Shane to know what they intended, and he wouldn't allow it on MacPherson lands, especially not when he was now responsible for the clan.

He'd received word from his stepmother that his father had died. Shane wasn't any more certain how he felt about this news now than he'd been when he'd received the letter more than a month ago. Their relationship had been strained after the laird married Deirdre, his stepmother. The older man had become obsessed with his young bride to the detriment of the clan and his relationship with his children. Shane was the oldest, but his younger sister and brother were equally ignored by their father.

If his father was indeed gone, it would be Shane's turn to run the clan. And he wasn't ready. But as the new laird, he wouldn't allow these men to accost his people. "Hold!" he called, his deep voice grabbing their attention. "Unhand the woman. You are on MacPherson lands. Who are you?"

The men laughed and shook their heads. "Ye think we don't know whose lands we're on?" the taller man asked. "We are MacPherson guards, and ye don't belong here. Get on with ye, and let us to our business."

Shane hid his surprise. These vile creatures were MacPhersons? He took in their dirty clothes and thin bodies. These were warriors, these scrawny lads with no honor? Regardless, he'd not allow them to carry out their plans. "I said, you'll unhand the woman and leave her be."

With begrudging sighs, they pulled their blades. Though rusted and bent, there were two of them against Shane's single sword. For the past five years, he'd had Ronan at his back as he fought. He'd parted ways with his stepbrother the day before, as Ronan had business with his grandfather, leaving Shane to finish the journey. Together, they were unstoppable, but this battle would be fought alone.

Using proper strategy when faced with a single opponent, these scoundrels split up and moved out, leaving Shane exposed on every front. He pulled his dirk from his belt and flung it into the shoulder of the first man, dropping him where he stood, his sword clanging to the ground as he cried out in pain.

With the taller man down, Shane turned toward the other one, who, after seeing his friend bleeding on the ground, spun and ran away like a coward. At the sound of a loud thwack, Shane turned back to the man on the ground to see he was knocked out, and the Valkyrie was once again wielding her large stick.

She gripped it tightly as Shane slid his sword into the sheath strapped along his back. He held up his hands, palms out, to show he meant her no harm. "Ye are safe now," he told her, hoping it was true.

MacPherson soldiers armed with worthless weapons and no respect for women didn't bode well for the state of his clan. The clan he would soon be in charge of. Shame roiled through him at the thought. When Shane had last stood on MacPherson lands, he'd been barely a man at twenty. Now, he felt aged beyond his years. Unlike Ronan, Shane had managed to come back much the same as he'd left. At least in body. His mind, however, would never be the same.

"Who are you?" the woman asked, still holding out the stick in what she probably thought was a threatening manner.

That was a very good question. Who was he? A laird who wasn't ready to rule.

He didn't know if he'd ever be ready, but he planned to take a few more days regardless, especially since the letter he'd received included even worse news than the loss of his father. Before his death, the laird had negotiated a marriage between Shane and the daughter of another clan.

His father had no way of knowing Shane had already been married to a woman who had called his heart to pounding just to look at her. He'd lost her. And with her, his own soul. He would make a terrible husband to this poor woman his father had shackled him to. Not that she would expect any less. Alliances through marriage were common in the Highlands. Shane always knew he was destined for such a fate.

Making a match to strengthen his clan was one thing. Despite wishing to be alone, he took no issue with marrying to gain cattle to feed his people or land, or even an ally. But marrying to gain more riches for his conniving stepmother didn't sit well with him. Shane wondered who this woman was who would be sacrificed to gain coin for Deirdre's desires.

Embarrassed by his clan and the name he'd once felt honored to own, Shane offered a shrug and answered the trembling woman. "I'm just a soldier. Ye can call me Shane."

...

Lindsay Wallace frowned at the man. Shane.

He had possibly saved her life, her virtue for certain, but he was even more imposing than the two lads who had attacked her. He'd held the large claymore as if it were no heavier than the stick in her grip.

Actually, the stick was becoming quite heavy as she attempted to hold it out from her body. Her hand shook either from fatigue or the reality of the situation settling in. In the end, it wasn't the fact that he'd sheathed his giant sword, or that he was holding out his hands unthreateningly, or even that she grew too tired to hold up the stick.

It was the smile he offered that made her stand down and relax.

She instantly felt silly, for a smiling man could be as deadly as a sneering one. Perhaps even more so. But this man's smile, despite the emptiness of it, spoke of safety. *Shane.* His brown hair and moss-green eyes had disarmed her of more than the stick. She blinked rapidly, trying not to allow the tears building in her eyes to fall. She didn't want to seem weak, but if this man knew all the things she had endured in the last month, he could never think her weak.

Lindsay, daughter of the Wallace laird, looked nothing like she had when she'd left her home a month ago. Her mother had sent her to the MacPherson clan with a maid and a retainer to care for her mother's sister, who was ill. But when Lindsay arrived, she'd learned her aunt had already passed. Her uncle begged her to stay on to help him tend to his three motherless boys, but as soon as the retainer left to return home to Riccarton, everything descended into chaos.

Her maid ran off in the middle of the night, taking Lindsay's gowns and jewels with her. Her uncle's lingering gazes unsettled her. The boys were sheer demons who, like their father, treated her like a maid. When she wrote to her mother requesting safe passage home, she was denied for reasons she still couldn't accept. Her father planned to marry her to the heir of the MacPherson clan. She couldn't think of a greater disgrace than becoming a member of this horrid clan.

Except, perhaps, returning home to tell her father she had rejected yet another betrothal he had arranged for her. Last summer, she had refused Robert Fletcher, the heir to the Fletcher Clan, and caused great embarrassment for her father.

She shivered at the memory of seeing such disappointment in her papa's eyes. But, surely, he would need to understand why becoming the mistress of the MacPherson Clan was entirely unacceptable.

"Are ye a MacPherson?" she asked, her chin lifting as if she could tell if he offered a lie.

"Aye, though I've not been here in five years. I've only just returned today." He frowned at the man lying on the ground, who was still breathing but unconscious from the knock to the head she'd delivered.

"It appears my clan has declined in recent years, if these two are any testament to the men tasked with protecting the people here."

She sniffed. "I've not seen many better than these two."

"And yet you go about the forest unaccompanied." His frown showed his disapproval, but she saw something else as well. Worry. For her? Still, his reproach ruffled her feathers greatly.

She wished she hadn't tossed away her stick, for she

would have pointed it at him for greater effect. "Do ye think to judge me for taking a moment to sit on a rock alone in the middle of the woods? Why should I not be safe here? This is how the MacPhersons treat their women?"

Once again, Shane raised his hands in forfeit. "You have the right of it, Valkyrie. You should be safe to go anywhere you desire. I apologize for my clan that it isn't so. May I offer my escort?"

She looked back to where the village lay beyond the forest. She wasn't yet ready to return to the cottage with her uncle and the wee devils. She'd come to the woods for a bit of peace and had gotten just the opposite.

"I would request a moment to sit in silence before I return."

He gave a single nod and gestured toward the rock where she'd originally hoped to find refuge. It looked out over a river that was swelled and rushing from the melting snow flowing down the mountains.

"I'll wait until you are ready to depart and ensure no one bothers ye."

He took a seat on a nearby stump and seemed content to wait for her no matter how long it took.

Shifting on the rock to find a comfortable position, she allowed the July sun to soak into her back as it sifted in through the trees to warm her. She looked down at her hands, red and chapped from the work she'd been made to do.

She wasn't against labor. She enjoyed helping the Wallace women in the kitchens, and she took pride in what they accomplished by providing a hearty meal. The pleased grunts from her clan and the scraping of trenchers were her reward. But here, it was different.

Her uncle barked orders and forced her to do everything while he and his sons watched and made cruel jokes. They made her tasks more difficult for their entertainment.

Tripping her while she was carrying wood. Bumping into her and making her spill the water she'd collected to make their meals.

She was exhausted most nights but feared sleeping too soundly for needing to keep watch. Her uncle had made no move to act upon his glances, but Lindsay worried it wouldn't be long before he worked up the courage to do so.

"You would have been better not to have come here," she said, breaking the easy silence between them. "Wherever you were, it was surely better than this place."

He sniffed and frowned. "I don't wish to argue, but, as I said, I'm a soldier. I've been fighting in France and Spain for the past five years. These two mutts don't bother me compared to a line of French muskets."

She recognized the pain swirling in his green eyes and wondered at what horrors he must have seen. Still, he wouldn't find much peace here. "Ye haven't been in the village yet, I assume."

He laughed at that and then shook his head. "What is your name, lass?"

She rather liked the name he'd given her. After all, Valkyries were women of power and prestige. At least the Norse knew to respect their females. "Lindsay," she said, pausing before providing her surname.

This man, honorable as he seemed, was a soldier just returned from war and most likely hurting for coin. Would he turn his back on honor if he learned who she was? The daughter of the Wallace laird, promised to the MacPherson chief, would bring a high price in ransom if given the opportunity.

At the last second, her lips formed the name of her feckless maid instead. "Cameron."

The man winced. The Camerons were enemies of the MacPhersons. As soon as she'd spoken the name, she worried he might very well pull his sword again and bring it across her throat, but he made no move to harm her.

She held back a smile as he shook off his disgust and nodded.

"A Cameron," he whispered. "Even still, any woman should be safe on MacPherson lands."

"From what I've seen, the former laird and his lady care only for riches and allow their people to fend for themselves. The guard doesn't have enough money to care for themselves, let alone a family, so they find their comforts wherever they can, willing or no."

It was her turn to give him a look of distaste. Looking through the trees at the sun on the horizon, she sighed her reluctance to leave. "I imagine I must return."

Without answer, he stood, and at his command, his horse moved forward so he could take the reins. Rather than mount or suggest they ride together—something she wouldn't consider—he walked beside her through the forest. "Do ye mind if we make a stop here?" He nodded to a cottage at the edge of the woods. The roof was in good repair, but the building had an air of abandonment about it.

"Your home?" she asked.

"My brother's, but he said I could stay, since he is not using it."

She waited as he stabled his horse in the small building behind the house and then went inside. He left the door standing open and pushed out the shutters on the two small windows. She imagined he wanted to let the fresh air in.

He came out carrying a dusty bucket before returning to her side.

"Shall I see you home?"

"You may see me to the hovel where I am living at the moment, but I shall never call this place or this clan my home."

"I remember a time when it was not so bad. When the

MacPherson name was something to be proud of."

Shane looked so distraught it was as if he was responsible for his clan's disgrace himself. She might have said more, but the thought of being forced to bear the name MacPherson sent a shot of fear through her.

She couldn't allow such a thing. She needed to find a way to get home without disappointing her father yet again.

Chapter Two

Lindsay's face flamed with embarrassment as they approached her uncle's home. The roof needed rethatching, and the door wouldn't close properly. Even Shane's cottage, which had sat dormant for some time, was in better repair than the shack she was currently living in. It was little wonder why her aunt had gotten ill and died while exposed to the elements and vermin.

Lindsay knew she would be spared this life if she would only present herself to the new laird at Cluny Castle. But then arrangements would be made for her to wed the MacPherson heir, and she'd rather take her chances on the vermin in the cottage than become a member of this clan.

No, she planned to wait until her family arrived so they could see for themselves what they agreed to marry her to. She would write to them and tell them what happened here today. That she was attacked by the very men who were sworn to protect their clan. Surely, her father would see the error of his plan and take her home immediately. She only needed to wait until her escort arrived.

Except she had already returned home once before rather than marry the man her father had arranged, and at great cost to her clan. She didn't know if he would allow her refuge a second time, but she had to try. She couldn't stay here.

"Ye live here?" Shane asked as he stood beside her, a deep frown on his handsome face.

She hadn't been certain he was truly as attractive as she'd thought at first. Anyone would seem appealing when stepping in to save one from harm as he had. His face had not seen a blade in a while, but as they'd walked from his cottage to the village, she'd had a few chances to steal a better look at him. His body was large and honed by battle. His green eyes were kind, despite his displeasure at what he was looking at now.

"Aye, it's my uncle's home, but I'll not be here for long. I will be returning to my home soon enough." She prayed that was true.

"And how soon is that?" he asked.

Before she could answer, Doran rushed out of the house yelling at her.

"Do ye know what time it is? Ye're late making our supper. Da is going to be angry when he gets home and finds us wasting away because ye haven't fed us."

He was only fourteen, but he stood eye to eye with her tall frame as he yelled. It wasn't until Shane put a hand on his chest and pushed him back that the boy stopped screeching at her.

"Watch how ye speak to yer kin, lad." Shane's voice had turned low and threatening. Had she not already seen his kindness, she would have been alarmed.

"Who are ye?" Doran glowered at Shane, not seeming to realize the other man was larger than he. His narrow gaze flashed back to her. "Are ye selling favors to men now, cousin?"

Lindsay gasped at the crude comment made in front

of Shane. It was bad enough his first impression of her was with men pawing at her, but for her cousin to insinuate such a thing…

"Did I not just tell ye to watch your tongue?" Shane said, his words even more menacing for he had not raised his voice.

"And did I not just ask ye who you were to think to tell me what to say to my lackwit cousin?"

When Shane took a step closer to the boy, Lindsay stepped in. It wouldn't do for the boy to get murdered on their doorstep.

"Doran, please go inside. I will be in shortly to make your meal."

"You'd better," he said before offering a final glare at both of them and heading inside. The way he kicked the door shut made it clear how it had become damaged.

"I don't know if I can leave ye here." Shane looked at the other cottages near hers. They weren't much better than the one she was living in. Hard times had befallen the MacPherson clan, though from what she could tell, all their problems began in the castle.

Yes, she could walk up to the gate and tell them who she was, and it would spare her from having to make supper for her ungrateful family. But she couldn't help thinking it would be a terrible mistake. She might have food in her belly and a clean place to lay her head, but being married to the new laird would no doubt be worse than the way she lived now. He was surely just a much larger rat.

• • •

How was Shane supposed to leave this woman in such an unsuitable place? Every instinct had him wanting to pick her up and carry her away from here so she wouldn't have to look at such horror, let alone live in it.

He shook his head.

He thought himself a protector, but he'd neglected to shield the one person he'd made an oath to always defend. His failure had resulted in her death, a betrayal he would never forgive himself for.

Despite her rough clothing, Lindsay Cameron was a fine woman. Elegant and graceful. Educated, if her speech was anything to go by. She didn't belong here in this filth, and she definitely shouldn't be spoken to like a dog by a sniveling pup with no manners. It had taken all Shane's control not to tell the boy who he was when he'd asked.

It would have amused Shane to see the look on the lad's face to know he was barking at his new laird. But Shane wasn't ready for anyone to know he'd returned. After years of giving and following orders, he just wanted some peace. And maybe he was avoiding one order specifically—the one his father had given to come home and marry. He couldn't do that to an innocent woman. He couldn't bind her to him, a man who was empty inside and unable to love her. For he'd given his heart to his first wife, and it had died alongside her on a field in France. He could never love like that again; of that, he was certain.

His gaze flickered to Lindsay.

Would the bride forced on him be as lovely? Her dark eyes held secrets, and he wanted to learn each one. But she was not his. He'd found love with a woman and lost it. He didn't deserve to be happy when Maria was gone because of him.

"I must get inside," she said while brushing a lock of her midnight hair away from her face. "They get more unbearable when they're hungry."

"I can't imagine him being worse."

"They bluster about, but they've not struck me. I've made it clear I won't stand for it. They need me, so they will behave.

Besides, as I said, it's not for much longer."

He nodded, glad to know she wouldn't be forced to stay here beyond what was necessary. Though he felt something similar to regret deep in his gut to learn she'd be leaving and he'd no longer see her. It was a silly thought. It wasn't as if he was free to wed someone else. He was promised to whomever his father had arranged to be his bride. He could offer Lindsay nothing more than respect and protection.

His warrior instincts kicked in. Wanting to shelter this woman when he'd not been able to help his own wife caused his stomach to twist. Still, it wasn't Lindsay's fault Shane was broken.

"Ye know where I live now. If you need anything, come to me. If you wish to go walking in the woods again, I will escort ye." He would do better for Lindsay than he had done for Maria. He'd not allow another woman to die.

"I wouldn't want to take more of your time," she said, a smile hinting at her lips—lips he was now staring at.

An overwhelming ache gripped him. This woman was beautiful, but to think of her lips and kissing her was wrong. Her hair and eyes were dark like Maria's, but she was not his wife. And while his body had yearned for the comfort of a woman, his heart kept him from acting on those feelings.

"It is no hardship," he found himself saying, though he should have nodded and walked away, leaving her to her life so he could shut himself away with his pain in Ronan's cottage.

But Lindsay had been a welcome distraction. He'd enjoyed his time with her, even for the time they sat in the forest in silence. He found it was easy to be with her. He was grateful for the short respite from the guilt that had settled on his shoulders.

She didn't seem to be in any hurry, and after the chaos of an army, just sitting quietly was something he realized he had missed. She hadn't filled their comfortable silence with idle chatter. Instead, she'd seemed pleased to listen to the birdsong and the small animals as they scurried about in the leaves.

"Then perhaps I shall see you tomorrow. Good day, Shane."

"Good day to ye, Lindsay." He gave a short bow that made her smile grow, showing off her white teeth. As he turned and walked away, he realized he had a matching smile on his own face.

He felt that weight of guilt return as he left her. It was not fair that he would find a reason to smile with another woman after what he'd done, or hadn't done. The smile melted away. He stopped at the well to get water before returning to Ronan's cottage. The night was warm, so he didn't need a fire except for the light. The bed ropes would need to be restrung and the mattress filled with new straw before he could sleep there. After years of sleeping rough on the ground, he had no problem tossing down his plaid to sleep on the floor.

It had been a long day of travel, yet he didn't rest well. Perhaps it was because the floor was harder than the earth he'd made his bed upon all these years. Or maybe his mind was busy with thoughts of all the things he needed to do and the one thing he *wanted* to do: see a certain black-haired lass again.

"I'm sorry, Maria," he said into the darkness as he closed his eyes against the visions of Lindsay.

· · ·

He must've managed some sleep, since he woke with soft morning light and the sound of whispers coming through the open windows.

"I'm tellin' ye, no one lives here. We can take it."

"If no one lives here, who set the snare in the first place?" another lad responded, this one with the squeaking voice of a boy changing over into a man.

Moving quietly to the door, Shane opened it and stepped out on the small porch. "Bad things come to those who steal a man's spoils," he said when he could see the boys clear enough.

They screamed and looked at him with wide eyes before dropping the rabbit and running off.

"I might have shared it with ye, if you weren't yellow-livered," he called after them.

Shaking his head, he picked up the discarded rabbit and readied it for his morning meal. It would be a busy day, getting this place set up to be a home. He wasn't sure how long he could stay here. Frowning, he corrected his thought. He wasn't sure how long he planned to *hide* here, for he was hiding. From his future, from his past.

He got to work on cleaning out the cabin after breaking his fast. He enjoyed the work. At the sound of a stick cracking somewhere over his shoulder, he spun around prepared to face a French soldier, but it was Lindsay Cameron who stepped out of the woods with a smile on her face. He forced his breathing to slow as an easy grin pulled up his lips at her presence.

Damn his reaction. He had been a faithful husband, an in the year since Maria's death, he'd not wanted to be with a woman. But this woman…she tempted him. He had not been a green lad with women when he'd went off to Spain. The women that lived on the edges of the battlefields did not appeal. It was a hard life, one often ended by nasty diseases.

But then he'd met Maria. They hadn't spoken the same language, but they'd communicated all the same. A smile, the tilt of her head. Their love was a blazing passion. They loved hard and often fought harder. Or rather Maria did. She had a hot temper that amused him. He loved riling her up only to make up in a fiery lust. They rarely had need for words when a look or a touch told the other what they needed.

Lindsay didn't singe him with desire. Instead, he'd felt calm, at peace when he'd been near her. She seemed full of life and happiness despite the conditions she lived in. And he felt excitement rush through him when he saw her, even after he'd given up all hope of ever feeling that again.

"Good morning to ye."

"It is just past noon," she corrected.

"Is it? I've missed the noon meal. Have you eaten?"

"Yes." She pressed her lips together.

He hadn't known her long, yet her expressive face told him what she was thinking without hearing her words. And at the moment, he thought she regretted telling him she'd already eaten because her meal hadn't been enough.

He frowned, not liking that he could read this woman so well after such a short time. But he couldn't help his desire to provide. "I made rabbit stew. I'm used to cooking for two and have made too much. Would you have some?"

She nodded and followed him inside. He still had the doors propped open to let out the stale air. He'd dusted, or rather spread the dust about the room. But the small table and chairs were clean.

He took the chipped bowls down from the shelf and filled one for her first. She waited for him to sit before she dug in.

"Oh," she said, looking at him with wide eyes. "It's good."

He laughed at her surprise. "Ye thought I couldn't cook something decent?"

"I'm sorry. I don't mean to offend you, but, no, I didn't expect it to be full of flavor. I guess I assumed a soldier ate for the sake of strength and nothing more."

"You have the right of it, but I learned to use many spices from Spain." The smile on his lips faded at the memory of who had taught him. "And I'm not a soldier any longer."

"What will you do now?" she asked before taking another bite.

He tilted his head to the side and thought about what he would have wanted to do if he'd had the option. If he had been born with the ability to choose, he might have been a vicar, though he cursed too much. He might have owned a tavern, but nay, he wouldn't have had the patience for drunkards. Mayhap he'd been a crofter or a smithy. It didn't matter, since his future was already told.

He would be the laird of the MacPhersons, and a husband.

"I'm not sure," he said instead. "I have enough coin for now to set up this house and stay a bit until I decide." Whatever fate lurked at the castle, it could wait until he was ready.

He feared he might never be ready. It was a waste of time to wish for a different life when his path was set out for him. Right down to the woman he would be forced to marry.

When they finished their meal, she helped him clean up, and they went outside again. She bit her lip, and he knew she had a question. "What is it?" he asked, finding he enjoyed talking with her despite his desire to be alone in his grief.

"Ye said you were used to cooking for two." Curiosity shone in her dark eyes.

"Aye." He nodded and looked away. She wanted to know if he was wed. And he wanted to tell her, but he feared she would ask him more questions he wouldn't be able to answer, so he answered with part of the truth. "My stepbrother, Ronan, was with me in France."

Shane must have frowned, for she placed her hand gently on his and said, "I'm sorry."

"Nay, he's not dead," he corrected. "Though for a time there, after he was injured, I worried he would die. He had a bad fever. He's well enough now, though his leg pains him at times."

"You looked sad when you thought of him."

Except Shane hadn't been thinking of Ronan. He nodded. "Aye. I do feel responsible for what happened to him. He went to fight in France because I went. I don't know that he would have made the choice if I hadn't pushed him into it." He paused for a moment before sharing a small part of his greater pain. "I...I did lose someone else, though. Someone dear to me. It was my fault." He stopped speaking when his throat grew tight with the burn of tears. His jaw clenched as he tried to keep control over his pain.

It happened any time he tried to talk about Maria. Would there ever come a time he would be able to speak of her without his guts twisting?

"You carry a lot of responsibility on your shoulders, Shane MacPherson."

He nodded. She had no idea how much responsibility he felt or how much more was about to land on his shoulders. He could only hope he wouldn't be crushed under the weight of it.

Chapter Three

Lindsay cleared her throat when she caught herself staring at the man's full lips. Even pulled down into a frown as they were, she found them fascinating. She wondered if the dark-brown whiskers covering his chin and upper lip would be soft or tickle if she were to kiss him.

Except she wouldn't kiss him.

She blinked and looked away to the trees. He must have noticed, for he nodded toward the forest.

"I imagine ye wish to go off into the woods for some quiet?" Shane asked, those lips turning up again. But she saw the effort it took to keep the smile there. This man was dealing with a great amount of pain. She decided not to pry.

Lindsay shrugged. The truth was she didn't need the embrace of the forest around her, not when she was with him. He brought a different kind of peace than what she felt sitting on the rock and looking out over the river. The warmth she felt came not from the stone that had been touched by the sun all day but from his closeness.

"I did mean to escape, for Wee Robbie walked all over

the rugs with muddy feet. Those rugs are so thin they'd never stand a scrubbing. But while I was trying, Uncle Randall came in wanting his noon meal, while James—the middle boy—picked a fight with Doran and began wailing when it didn't go the way he'd wanted."

She shook her head and felt her cheeks go hot. "Here I am, complaining about a few stressful moments to someone who has been fighting in a war for five years. Forgive me and forget everything I just said." She waved a hand dismissively.

She'd been so grateful to have someone to talk to, she'd forgotten herself. She'd felt so alone this past month, even as she never seemed to have any time on her own. She didn't know how to explain how she could be lonely while also overwhelmed by the people around her. But that was what she'd felt.

However, it was clear from looking at him that this man was carrying around a great deal of pain and guilt. She was ashamed of her silly complaints.

He shook his head. "One person's plight doesn't make another's less."

"No, but it should put it in perspective."

"To tell the truth, after meeting your cousin yesterday, I might pick fighting a battle with the French over dealing with the likes of him. I think ye might have the worst of it."

It was kind of him to say it to make her feel better. But she couldn't imagine the fear he must have felt day after day for so long. Or perhaps it was worse. Perhaps numbness had taken over the fear and he no longer realized the danger.

"I doubt even Doran is worse than a French brigade, but thank ye for understanding."

"If you wish to sit in the woods for a spell, I'll sit with you and make sure you're safe."

She wondered why he winced on the last word. *Safe.* She didn't think he regretted making the offer, but maybe he didn't think he was capable. Did he think her to be too much trouble for the likes of a formidable Highlander? Despite the issue, she simply shook her head. "Nay. I have no need for silence now that I've spent time here with you. You have a calming way about you."

"I would gladly accept your praise, but I feel it's misplaced. Anyone would be better than those ruffians you live with."

She laughed as his cheeks turned pink. She guessed Shane wasn't accustomed to accepting praise. How different he was than the warriors at home who constantly expected to be admired for their strength.

"That may be true, but I thank you for inviting me to stay anyway."

"And not making a mess you'll need to clean up?" he added with a grin.

She'd noted how neat he was. And despite his large size, he was graceful when he moved. As if he'd thought through each movement before making it.

"That too." She let out a sigh. "But now I am keeping you from your work, and I have had my escape for the day. I must get back."

He looked around and gave an easy shrug. "I have time." He swallowed and said, "I'm taking time."

The correction seemed significant to him in some way, but she didn't understand and let it pass.

"Perhaps I can help you."

"If you're of a mind to stay, I'll not put ye to work, but I would enjoy your company. After years of being in the midst of a large group, it does feel strange to be alone so much."

She smiled, pleased to be asked to stay. He was right— she would've taken anyone over the monsters she lived with— but she actually enjoyed being with Shane. He wasn't simply a diversion.

"What of your family? Were you born here?" she asked

to get a conversation started.

"Aye. As were my younger sister and brother. Do you have any siblings?"

"Nay. Perhaps that's why I enjoy the quiet so much. Being an only child meant spending a lot of time alone." She recalled the times when her cousin Meaghan would come to visit. They often pretended to be sisters. And when she would leave to return home, how Lindsay felt the loss.

"I'm sure you were hoping for sympathy, but you never had to fight anyone over the last tart, so you'll get none from me." He was teasing her.

"Never," she conceded with a laugh. "The next time I make tarts, I'll bring you some so you won't have to share." It would be the least she could do after what he'd done for her the day before. "I don't know that I thanked ye properly for your help yesterday."

"I hope the events did not haunt your sleep last night," he said. His green eyes spoke of a man who had dealt with his own demons the night before.

Rather than tell him she'd hardly slept because every time she closed her eyes she saw those men, she pressed her lips together and tossed a piece of stick she'd picked up.

He shrugged and frowned in the direction of the woods. "A woman should be safe to walk about wherever she pleases without risk of…harm." His voice cracked on the last word, and he swallowed before continuing. "And ye shouldn't have had to worry about being set upon by the MacPherson guard—the very men who have sworn to protect the people on these lands. I'm embarrassed my clan has fallen the way it has."

"I don't mean to speak ill of the dead, but the laird didn't see to his people the way he should've. Leaving the clan to fend for themselves has turned them desperate."

He nodded in agreement. "I imagine you're looking

forward to returning to your own clan."

"Yes." No clan was without its problems, but at least she was safe on Wallace lands. She was careful not to say so—she didn't want to let it slip that she was a Wallace. She had no idea what the Cameron clan was like.

She felt bad for lying to the man who had quickly become a friend, but it was safer that no one knew who she was. She'd sent a letter to her parents explaining her unwillingness to marry the new laird of the MacPhersons and requesting escort back home until a proper match could be arranged. But until they arrived, she wanted to be safe.

Being a laird's daughter meant marrying for an alliance rather than love. She'd been raised for such a thing and knew her duty. But now she reconsidered having rejected Robert and the Fletchers. For the MacPhersons—with the exception of the man next to her—were completely unacceptable. Thinking of those unacceptable MacPhersons made her realize she'd been with Shane for too long.

"I must go. I have chores to finish before starting supper."

He must have heard the worry in her voice, for his gaze narrowed. "Do you wish for me to see you home?"

"Nay." That hadn't gone well the day before. It wouldn't be good for Doran to see Shane again and tell her uncle. "I'll be fine." But she wasn't fine.

After reluctantly leaving her new friend, she returned to the small cottage to find her uncle in a fit of rage that her chores were not done. "I'm here. I'll see to them quickly," she assured the man, picking up the cracked bucket that leaked more water than it carried. She had to make multiple trips to have enough to cook with.

"Where were ye? Sittin' about in the forest, staring off at nothing again? I'm not sure how things are on the Wallace lands, but here, laziness is punished."

At the word "punished," Lindsay stood straighter and

looked the man directly in his narrowed, bloodshot eyes. "And if ye touch me, you'll need to make your own meals so not to find poison in one of them," she threatened, and the man laughed, showing off his blackened teeth.

"Just do what you were sent here to do."

What she'd been sent there to do? She'd been sent to care for her mother's younger sister. And now…she was supposed to marry the MacPherson laird. She wondered if her mother had known before she'd left Riccarton. Surely, her parents had discussed their plans.

Had her father thought tricking her was the only way to get her to do what he'd bid? She shouldn't have caused such a fuss with the Fletchers. Robert wasn't a horrible man; he was just much older than her. But despite her rebellion and his blustering over the incident, he'd never touched her violently. Pain didn't always come at the sharp stab of a fist, though.

Lindsay had known all her life how disappointed her father was that he'd not been given a son. While Lindsay's mother did her best to make up for the lack of affection, Lindsay knew the only value she held for her father was to marry well. And now she'd begged him to go back on another betrothal agreement to find a more suitable arrangement. He wouldn't be pleased, but there had to be better options than the MacPhersons.

It'd be amusing to see her uncle's face if she were to tell him she was to marry his laird. And even more pleasing to see how quickly he changed his tune if she became Lady MacPherson. But she wouldn't dare. Whatever discomfort she faced with her uncle's cruel words was better than being married to the laird's heir. After all, her time here was temporary.

She only had to wait until her father's retainers came for her and saw her home. A month at the most, and she'd be out of this place.

...

By the time Shane returned from his hunt for supper, he'd had more than enough of his own company. He'd never tell Ronan he was missed. The information would go straight to the man's head. And as Shane considered it, he knew it wasn't Ronan he missed.

He thought of the meals he'd shared with Maria. How she could speak so quickly he barely understood, even when he'd learned a fair bit of Spanish. How quickly and efficiently she moved, using her skirts to grip the hot pans. The sharp scent of spices he knew would heat his tongue and make his eyes water. How she would laugh at him. But as he allowed the memories to flow around him, he realized he also thought of Lindsay and how nice it would be to share his meals with her.

He'd noticed she was bonny the day before. It had been impossible not to appreciate her striking black eyes and lovely dark hair. But he'd refrained from studying the rest of her. It felt like a betrayal to his dead wife. And after what Lindsay had been through, it would've been wrong to leer at the poor lass.

But today he'd noticed. In quick glances, he'd taken in her tall frame and perfect breasts. Not too small but not too large. He'd found himself wondering if her nipples were the same rosy color as her lips. Even now that she was gone, he still wondered.

It was all for naught, just idle thoughts he'd never act on. Or rather couldn't act on. His destiny was determined, and it wouldn't do to dally with a lass he had no way of properly caring for, especially one who'd already been mistreated by his clansmen.

It was useless to think that if it weren't for his duty, he might consider it. For his being married off was only one part of the problem. There was still the matter of his heart—that he no longer had one to give, it felt so shattered.

But, still, it was enjoyable spending time with her, someone he liked and felt comfortable with. Would he be lucky enough to feel the same friendship and comfort with the wife that awaited him? Or would it be a cold alliance, married in name only and otherwise remaining strangers?

Perhaps, expecting the worst would make anyone seem more pleasant in comparison. He laughed and finished preparing his meal. He carried a chair out onto the porch so he could enjoy the warm evening as he ate. Through the trees, he could see the orange and pink of the sun bending to the earth in the final light of the day.

He recalled the evenings he and Ronan had the opportunity to watch the sunset. How often they thought of the people at home and wondered if Tory or Alec was watching the same sky. A few minutes into his meal, he was joined by a small dog who trotted up on the porch as it sat next to him. "Aren't ye the wee beggar?" he said to the dog as he dropped a few bites, which it quickly snatched up.

When Shane reached out to pet him, the dog ducked away, eyes closed as if expecting something harsher than a scratch behind the ears.

"This clan…" Shane muttered. "Attacking women and hurting wee dogs. How am I going to fix this?"

Instead of dropping more food on the floor, Shane held the next morsel out on the palm of his hand. At first, the dog paced and whined, clearly wanting the food but unwilling to put himself in harm's way to get it.

Shane continued to speak soothingly to the animal, encouraging him to take the chance and see not everyone meant to harm him. It took a long while, possibly an hour, but Shane forced himself to be patient. After all, he'd need a great deal of patience to take on the work needed to make his clan one he could be proud of.

Eventually, both of them were rewarded when the little dog collected his courage and darted close enough to snatch the food from Shane's hand. "Ah, there you go now. What a brave one ye are."

He held out his hand again, and the dog only hesitated briefly before coming forward to get the treat. "See there? Didn't I tell ye you could trust me?"

The next bit of food was held high, and when the dog reached up, Shane chuckled. "It would seem I've won the heart of a lass after all."

She tilted her head to the side with her scruffy, gray ears cocked.

"Shall I call ye Treun, for you were a brave lass to take a chance at my door?" Again, when he reached out to pet her, she ducked away, but not so far as before.

He just needed time to earn her trust. Time.

He wondered how much time he had before he would have to give up this small life he was making and bear the responsibilities waiting for him at the castle.

"I'm not yet as brave as you, lass. I'm not ready. I fear I may never be."

Chapter Four

Lindsay found herself rushing through her morning chores after a restless night. She rarely slept soundly, sharing a one-room cottage with four men—some smaller than others. But last night she found she didn't wake from their noises as much as her thoughts of a certain soldier she'd been spending her time with.

She knew he was the reason she wished to finish cleaning up after the meal so she could steal away to his cottage and a bit of peace. In fact, she no longer counted down the hours waiting for word from her father telling her she could leave this place. She was glad to have some time before she'd have to leave.

Time with him. And would it be so bad if she kissed him, if she was to leave and not have to see him again?

Her thoughts of kissing were disrupted by her uncle's angry laugh.

"If you think to run off for most of the day, think again. I'll not have to wait on my supper tonight. You'll stay here."

"If you force me to stay in this house all day, you'll find

me gone before your supper to never come back again."

"Your father should have tamed that mouth of yours."

"Real men do not need their women *tamed*," she said, though low enough he couldn't hear her.

Her father had attempted to make her more docile. Or rather encouraged her mother to do it. Since Lindsay was not the son he'd wanted, he rarely had time for her. She wondered why she cared so much about disappointing him further by calling off another betrothal. "I've packed you a few bannocks and a bit of cheese for your nooning." She handed him a small bundle of cloth.

With a grumble of what she decided to think of as thanks, he and the boys left the cottage to head to the field where they'd spend the day gathering peat for a few coins. Hopefully, this time he wouldn't spend all of their earnings on whisky.

When the cottage was as good as it would get, she eagerly left for Shane's home on the edge of the woods. She had to focus on not hurrying her steps. It wouldn't do to break into a run just to get there faster. As she stepped onto the shaded path that would lead her to Shane's cottage, she was greeted by a scraggly, gray dog with a happy face.

"Well, hello there. Who might you be?"

"I named her Treun," Shane's voice called from the shadow of the trees, causing her to jump. "Sorry to startle you."

She offered a smile and crouched down to pet the little dog, who shied away but allowed a few pets as her tail wagged her appreciation.

"Hmph." Shane's grumpy sound frightened the dog. She ran a few yards away, where she felt safe. "She hasn't let me pet her."

"Are you certain Treun was the right name for her?" She didn't think of the word "brave" when she took in the skittish pup in front of her.

"Aye. She may be little, but she does what must be done even if it scares her. We should all hope to be as courageous." As was normal, she saw shadows of secrets and pain in his eyes.

"I thought bravery was not being frightened of things."

He shook his head. "Nay. Ye cannot be brave without fear. It doesn't take much courage to face something you're not afraid of."

She nodded. "I never thought of it like that."

"What are you afraid of?"

"Well, spiders."

"Of course. Only the daft don't fear the wee monsters." He added a shiver for effect, and she laughed. "Certain times of the year, I used to make Ronan check my bedding so as not to have one of the filthy buggers crawling on me while I slept."

She considered his question again. What was she afraid of? Her biggest fear at the moment was being forced into marriage to the new laird. She wouldn't know the man to see him, but she'd seen the old laird and the laird's youngest son, a large man with a fierce scowl who looked as if he'd sooner eat a person than speak to them.

But she couldn't tell Shane that fear, for then he'd learn the rest of her story. He'd know she wasn't a maid sent to help a family member but a laird's daughter promised in marriage to be lady of the castle. She no longer feared Shane would use the information for his gain. She didn't think he would tie her up and ransom her off for money. Yet she still didn't tell him the truth. This was better. They were friends, equals.

She smiled and answered with her second biggest fear. "Eels."

"Eels? You do not like to eat them?"

"Eating them is fine. I don't like to look at them. They

are horrible creatures."

He chuckled, though not in a way that made her embarrassed for sharing with him.

"What about you? What else are you afraid of? Surely, something more than spiders."

He seemed almost surprised by her question, but he should've assumed she'd have asked the same of him. He twisted his mouth as he thought, and she wondered if he was settling on something else as she had. Eventually, he answered. "Fire."

She didn't need to ask him to explain. He went on without her prompting him.

"When I was a wee lad, a fire started in my room. A spark from the fire on the rug, probably. I woke when the room was full of smoke and the fire cut off my way to the door. I screamed, and my da came in with a bucket to douse it. I was afraid to sleep alone after that. And I still dream of it, being trapped."

She looked up at the blue sky and shook her head. "I thought you would've said something about fighting in the war. Angry soldiers bearing down on you."

He shrugged. "I'm haunted by many things that happened over the last five years, but when I'm struggling with something, when I feel I have no control over a situation I'm facing, I always dream of that night with the fire."

Before she'd realized what she was doing, she'd reached out and placed her hand on his arm in an effort to soothe the sadness she saw in his warm, green eyes. She wondered what situations he faced that made him feel out of control. Whatever it was, it couldn't be as serious as the uncertainty she faced.

The uncertainty of being married to someone she didn't know.

...

Shane felt he'd missed a great opportunity as he and Lindsay walked in silence to the large rock she called her own. During their discussion of fears, he should have told her who he was, for no other reason than he could have confided in her about his concerns of taking over the clan. His worries over how he might make MacPherson an honorable name again. His concerns about taking a wife when he was nothing but an empty shell of a man. Perhaps she would have offered her thoughts and comforting words of encouragement. But he'd let the moment pass because of an even greater fear—that she would pull away from him.

She made it no secret she didn't care for his clan or the way the laird had taken care of his people. To admit to being the new laird would change her view of him for the worse, and he couldn't bear seeing her disgust. He was enjoying their newfound friendship far too much. It was a balm to his wounded soul.

Worse than disgust would be the pity he imagined to see when he explained how he'd lost his wife, followed surely by more distaste when she learned he was at fault. Instead, he kept his secrets and changed the subject to favorite animals. This time when they came to her rock, he took a seat next to her, enjoying the warmth of the stone where the sun had touched it. To his surprise, Tre jumped up beside Lindsay, and with her friend at her back, she allowed Shane to scratch her behind the ears.

"I feel betrayed. I shared my meals with ye, and yet you give your allegiance to a stranger over me."

"Ah, but you have won her trust. I will be nothing but a memory now that she has your attentions."

"You sound jealous," he said, finding it easy to flirt with a pretty lass even though he hadn't used the skill recently.

He'd always enjoyed women, but when he'd married Maria, he never had a worry he'd miss spending time in the beds of strangers ever again. It was the easiest thing to be loyal to her. He'd needed no other.

Now he was alone, his marriage vows severed with her death, yet the loyalty remained.

He was treated to a soft blush on Lindsay's cheeks as she glanced away.

"Perhaps," she admitted, and he felt he had made large strides with both of these females today.

He offered the smile that had won him the attentions of women in the past. And while she didn't swoon or go aflutter at the sight of it, he saw a response in her dark eyes as she caught her bottom lip between her teeth.

Realizing he had leaned closer to her, he bolted off the rock, making Tre yip in surprise.

What was he doing? He couldn't woo this woman to his bed or even so much as kiss her. He had nothing to offer her. He couldn't marry her. But she'd stirred something inside him. A tiny spark of life ignited in the pit of his stomach and began to thaw the ice in his chest.

He hadn't wanted this. Couldn't do this. Which was why he turned and walked away to a safe distance, before he did something he couldn't take back. Something he realized now he very much wanted to do.

• • •

At first, Lindsay was upset by the way Shane had practically run away from her. But as she lay in her makeshift bed—a pile of shabby blankets on the floor in the corner of her uncle's cottage—she realized Shane had saved them both from making a big mistake.

She'd wanted to kiss him. And while she'd not been

kissed before, she felt certain he was of the same mind when he'd moved just slightly closer with his gaze upon her lips. If that wasn't the way a kiss started, she didn't know how else it might happen. Her heart had nearly beat out of her chest as she'd waited for him to make what seemed to be an eternal voyage to her mouth. But he had put a stop to things before they'd proceeded too far, and she was both grateful for and annoyed by that fact.

Since she was a young girl, she'd envisioned marrying someone she loved. Her parents loved one another. She'd seen the way her father's gruff demeaner softened when her mother came near. Lindsay had hoped to do the same for her husband—a faceless warrior, until recently. But Shane had backed away from her, not unlike the little dog. But unlike Tre, he'd not been brave enough to trust her since.

Now, three nights later, as the night wore on and sleep evaded her, she felt frustrated by his rejection. She found she still wanted him to kiss her. Perhaps more each day. She was past the age to wed, which meant she was old enough for such experiences. And for her remaining time here with the MacPherson clan, she was free to do things she wouldn't do at Riccarton, where she'd been only the laird's daughter. But there in the darkness, she was forced to face the truth that maybe he had saved her from a great amount of pain by staying away for the last few days.

A kiss for the sake of a kiss would have been one thing, and she didn't think anything ill would come of it. But a kiss born of the emotions she was beginning to feel for Shane was a different matter. She might not be able to just leave with a memory of him. She could possibly want more. And as she was destined to leave and he was destined to stay, it wouldn't work between them. It could only ever be temporary.

Nay. This was better, to stay apart from Shane, as it meant no risk of something happening that would lead down a treacherous path. To make sure she didn't drift into dangerous territory, she planned to stay clear of the man. At least until she was certain she could keep him at a proper distance.

A friend and nothing more.

With that settled, she must have dozed off for a time, because she was woken by the sound of her uncle stumbling into the shack. He hadn't been home for supper, and Doran had mentioned his da had been paid for their work in the peat fields. She'd been with them long enough to know what that meant.

She winced at the sound of a loud smack followed by a wailing cry. Jumping to her feet, she found Wee Robbie on the ground, curled into a ball as his father stood over him yelling. She looked around for the other two boys, but they were nowhere to be found. Hiding, no doubt, the little cowards. Didn't they realize the three of them would've been able to overpower their drunken father and save their wee brother? Apparently, saving the child fell on her. She would step up to defend him. She wouldn't look away while a child was beaten.

"Uncle, please. Whatever ye think Robbie has done, I'm sure we can take care of it in the morning. You are tired and should lie down. Things will be better tomorrow."

"Tomorrow? How will they be better tomorrow? I still have no wife to warm my bed. No mother to my children." He waved toward the boy crying on the floor and thrust his hand out when he started to tip over.

"I'll help ye," she offered, rushing forward to bear his weight and steer him away from Robbie. She led the man to his bed, turning her head away when she needed to draw in a breath, for his stench made her ill. She continued on by grasping hold of one single fact: it wouldn't be long now.

In fact, the Wallace retainers should have arrived by now.

She'd counted out the days for the letter to get there. For the men to pack and ride to the MacPherson village. She'd sent off a second missive to ensure at least one of them made it to her father. Why hadn't he sent for her?

At her uncle's bed, she slipped out from under his arm, hoping he'd fall onto the sagging straw mattress, or close enough to it, and be out until the late morning. But, instead, he swayed toward her, his eyes a bit more focused than she'd expected.

"Ye are a bonny lass."

She said nothing. She may have stopped breathing, as still as she stood. He wasn't falling over; he was looking her over and was missing nothing from as slow as he was doing it. This was not good. She'd seen the way his gaze lingered on her breasts as she worked. It made her uncomfortable, but he'd never touched her. She'd made it clear she wouldn't stand for such a thing. But now he was stepping closer.

"I need ye. I've gone too long without a woman's touch."

She shook her head. "No. You're in your cups and not thinking straight. I'm here to help with the boys, nothing more."

"You could be more. We're not blood. I can take ye as my wife. Let me give you a try to see if you'll do."

She turned to flee the room, but he grabbed her hair with more strength than she thought he could manage in his state. He twisted it in his fist, and Lindsay cried out as her head—and her body with it—was pulled to the bed.

When she screamed, he smacked her across the face. As her mouth filled with the coppery taste of blood, she pushed him to the side enough that she could roll off the bed to the floor, hitting her head on something on her way down. Her skull throbbed, and light flared at the edges of her vision. But two swift kicks had her gasping for breath and pulled her from the tempting darkness.

Despite the spinning, when he reached down to pull her up again, she grabbed a piece of wood from the pile next to the small hearth and swung it with all her might.

Her uncle fell heavily to the floor, and Lindsay didn't spare a second to see if she'd killed him. She ran from the house. She'd warned him she would only stay so long as he didn't touch her. But now he had, and she had no other choice. She had to leave before something terrible happened.

Where could she go? She knew no one here. No one except for the man she'd just moments ago pledged to stay clear of to avoid getting too close. Regardless of what her heart thought of the matter, her feet took her in the direction of Shane's cottage. Despite the struggle to see where she was going, she kept running until she stumbled and fell.

And there she stayed.

Chapter Five

Shane tossed for what felt like the hundredth time that night. He half expected to hear Ronan's grumbling voice telling him to stop moving about like a fish out of water.

So often his brother had woken him from his nightmares of past battles and close calls. Of the evening they'd arrived back at camp to find Maria staring blankly up at the darkening sky. But tonight, Shane wasn't haunted by the years spent at war. And there was no one there to save him. Had Ronan been there, he might have told his brother how badly he'd mucked things up with the raven-haired lass. Staying away from her wasn't helping things as much as he'd hoped.

But being with her wasn't an option. Not only was he not ready to love again, if he ever could, but he was the new laird, a man she already hated, and he was set to marry by arrangement. After his near mistake on the rock days earlier, he'd thought about her endlessly. Most often he wondered why he was so drawn to her when she was so different from his Maria. He didn't know what to think it meant. And what did it matter? For somewhere there was a woman waiting to wed the new laird of the MacPherson clan.

He shifted in his bed again. The last three days had been difficult. Instead of facing the woman who tempted him, his only company was a small dog who had taken a spot in the corner of the room. "Do ye think I should have kissed her?" he asked his companion, who didn't bother responding. "I was afraid if I kissed her, I'd have wanted more, and I couldn't do that because I'm broken inside, as well as promised to someone else."

It felt good to speak the truth to someone, even if that someone was a dog who seemed set on ignoring his late-night confessions. "I'm to marry someone my da chose for me with no mind to what I wanted, I'm sure. He would have seen to pick the bride who offered the most dowry. Probably a Campbell or a Wallace, I imagine."

The dog finally responded with a sniff of sorts.

"Aye. I'm not pleased with the thought, either. Ye never met my wife. She was beautiful and full of spirit. She made me feel alive in a place surrounded constantly by death." He let out a sigh. "You've seen Lindsay. She's bonny and sweet. And talking with her is easy enough. I don't feel as though I have to be more than who I am. She seems fine with me being a soldier. I could find peace and happiness with a woman like that. Yet, I'm to marry someone else and take on my duties as laird."

As if she understood and wanted him to go to the castle that instant, Tre shot up from her resting spot and ran to the door, barking for the first time in his presence. Was she tired of hearing his ramblings? He couldn't blame her.

Shane chuckled and shook his head at his silliness. "Do ye hear something out there that needs investigating?"

As soon as he opened the door, she shot out of the cottage. Her gray coat blended in with the darkness, but her shrill bark spoke of alarm. At the sound of Hades's unrest in the small shelter behind the house, Shane slid the strap with his sword on his back and stepped outside. If someone thought to take his horse, they wouldn't get very far.

Even if Shane didn't stop them, Hades wouldn't have it. He'd toss the thieves and return home.

But that was not the way Treun had gone. It sounded as if she was on the trail that led to the village.

"What is it, lass?" He came closer, then paused when he heard a whimper that had not come from the dog. Moving quickly now, he saw a lump on the ground. It was cloudy that night, but the moon gave enough light for him to see it was a person.

Not just a person but Lindsay.

He rolled her over, seeing blood at the corner of her mouth as well as her temple. The wetness glistened in the low light, even in her dark hair. Something darker than a shadow crossed her jaw.

For a moment, he froze with memories of another lass, injured and broken with blood still wet in her shiny black hair. But Lindsay's eyes were closed, not staring up at him blankly. Her body was warm, not still and cold in death.

With a curse, he lifted her from the ground and carried her inside, setting her on his bed. Another whimper escaped when he shifted her, but her eyes didn't open. As much as her sounds of pain worried him, they were better than no sound at all.

"Lindsay? Can ye hear me, lass?"

She didn't answer. She needed a healer. He knew where to find one. But doing so would expose him. He would have to swear her to silence. Lindsay's care was more important than his secrets.

He looked down at the woman in his bed and didn't need even a full breath to decide there was no other choice. His aunt would help, and he'd deal with whatever happened after

Lindsay was safe.

...

After making sure Lindsay was settled, he left his home and slinked through the woods to the other side of the village. He came around to the back of Bess's cottage, which sat up on the hill closest to the castle. Looking in her window, he saw her in her bed, where any person should be this time of night.

He knocked and then knocked louder when she didn't stir. She grumbled as she headed toward the door. He left his place at the window to be at the door when she opened it. She was no stranger to being pulled from her bed, as many people took a turn for the worse over the night hours.

"What's wrong? Who's ill? How long—" She stopped her usual litany of questions to stare at him. Putting two fingers together, she poked him in the shoulder as if to confirm he wasn't a specter.

"Shane," she whispered a moment before she clenched him in a fierce hug.

"Ye still have more strength than an old woman should," he said.

"And ye're still ill-mannered to speak of a woman's age. Ye wee brat."

"I may be a brat, but I'm your favorite brat, aren't I, Auntie Bess?" He forced his best smile.

She smacked at him and gestured for him to come in. But now that she was awake and knew he was real, he needed to get her moving toward his cottage and Lindsay so his aunt could help the woman he'd left in his bed.

He knew well that the smallest injuries on the outside could sometimes be the result of mortal wounds inside one's body. He'd thought she suffered a few broken ribs, which could lead to death.

"I canna come in. I need ye to come with me. Someone needs your help."

With a nod, she donned a cloak and pulled on her shoes. He had picked up her basket of medicines she always kept by the door, ready to tend to someone at a moment's notice. They fell into silence until they got to the lane that split, one path leading to the castle. As he turned for the one that went to Ronan's cottage, she stopped and peered up at him with green eyes much like his own.

"We're not going up to the castle?"

"Nay." He shook his head once and then looked away. "I'm not staying there. We should hurry."

In the cottage, he found Tre up on the bed, huddled next to Lindsay as if using her tiny body to warm the woman. He patted the little dog on the head as she jumped down. He lit a lamp and brought it to the stand next to the bed so Aunt Bess could see her patient more clearly.

"Who is this?"

"Lindsay. She's staying with her Uncle Randall to tend to her cousins after her aunt died." Shane didn't want to give her last name of Cameron. He didn't think his aunt would care, but the Camerons and the MacPhersons spent much time raiding each other's lands. It was not an easy name to have in these parts, though at least she wasn't a MacColl. No manner of beauty would wash that name clean.

"Bless her soul for spending any time with that worthless heap and his demon lads." Bess frowned. "What's happened to her?"

"I can't say. I found her outside like this. She hasn't woken or said anything. She did cry a bit when I picked her up."

"Very well. Let me see to her. Ye can wait outside."

For whatever reason, the idea of leaving Lindsay alone even in the care of his aunt brought a twist to his gut. He'd left Maria, and she'd died alone. He wouldn't leave Lindsay to the same fate.

"Nay. I'll stay here." He stood straighter, prepared for a fight he'd see to winning, but his aunt only smiled.

"Ah. It's like that, is it?"

He let out a breath and shook his head. "Can ye heal her instead of jumping to conclusions?" He'd forgotten how much the woman could hear things that weren't spoken. "I think folk might be right when they call ye a witch," he said with a smirk.

"She's lovely," his aunt said, ignoring him, and then frowned. "But she's taken quite a beating."

Shane's fingers gripped into a fist. He would break Randall MacPherson for touching her rough. He opened his mouth to speak the threat, but another thought made his words catch in his throat. He swallowed before managing the quiet words. "Was it just a beating, or did he…" Shane swallowed, unable to say or even think the worst.

"As you'll recall, I asked ye to step outside."

He understood now. With a quick bow, he rushed out of the cabin. Tre looked to him and back to Lindsay for a moment before following him outside as if somehow knowing he needed her company more than it would benefit Lindsay. "Thanks, lass," he said while sitting on the edge of the porch. He was surprised when the dog came to sit close to his side. "She'll be fine. My aunt will see to it."

But as he said it, he couldn't be certain it was the truth. He was sitting out in the dark so his aunt could inspect the damage done to this strong, sweet woman. He'd seen what happened to women who had been violated in that way. The fear that never left their eyes.

Restless energy and anger had Shane standing and pacing on the path in front of the cottage. Tre kept up with him. He knew if he went to face Randall, he would end the man. He recalled the rage he'd launched on the French soldiers after he'd found Maria. Instead of risking such a massacre, he stayed where he was. It was more important to be there for Lindsay than to sate his anger.

A few minutes later, his aunt came out. A nod of her head communicated he could return inside.

"She's not been touched," his aunt confirmed.

Shane nearly fell to his knees in relief. She was not his, but still, he never wanted her to suffer such a thing.

"I don't think her ribs are broken, just badly bruised. It looked to be a boot print."

They shared a frown before she went on.

"She has a knot on her head that most likely put her into this sleep. She shouldn't be moved. She needs to rest and will wake up when she can. I got some willow bark tea into her and left some on the table for you to give to her when she needs it for the pain."

Tre hopped on the bed again and snuggled in at Lindsay's hip.

"It looks like you have someone to help tend to her."

Shane patted the mutt on the head. "Aye. Thank ye, aunt."

She nodded.

"I'll see you home."

His aunt crossed her arms as her brows raised. He was foolish to think he could take her home without answering any of her many questions. This was the price he'd pay for her help. He glanced at the woman in his bed and took a settling breath.

"From the looks of this cottage, I'd gather you've been here for at least a week."

He blinked. "Are ye asking me a question or speaking your observations?"

She laughed. "Very well. How long have ye been home?"

"You had it right. It's been almost a week."

"And no one at the castle knows."

"Ye know well what awaits me at Cluny. I'm to be named laird and married off. Is it so much to want a reprieve from that? To want a bit of peace after being away at war for years?" He'd not tell his aunt of all he lost in France. He couldn't talk about it.

"Nay. It's not. I understand."

"You do?" He tilted his head and narrowed his gaze. "And you'll not speak of my being here?"

She shook her head. "It's not my business. Besides, who would I tell? Deirdre?" She made an incredulous noise and a face to go with it. "We don't sit for chats, she and I."

That was certainly true. The women hadn't been friends. Aunt Bess was Shane's mother's sister. As such, she didn't care for the way Deirdre tossed away his mother's things to make room for her more expensive tastes. Deirdre insisted on fancy gowns and jewels. She dressed more like a queen than the lady of the keep. She acted as a queen as well. Expected everyone to bow to her wishes.

"Thank ye for keeping my secret."

She waved a hand. "As I said, it's not my business. But know ye can't hide away here forever. Eventually, everyone must step into the role they're meant for."

"I know. I want a little more time." It would never be enough time.

"With her?"

He nodded. There was no sense in trying to hide his feelings from the old woman. She'd known the answer before asking the question. She'd seen the panic and worry in his eyes.

"Maybe you shouldn't return to the castle alone." Bess winked.

It was late and Shane was too exhausted to follow along, so he shook his head. "I'm not taking your meaning, aunt."

"If you were to arrive at the castle already wed, that would certainly upset Deirdre's plans to marry ye off for coin."

Shane smiled. "You would enjoy that, wouldn't you?" Leave it to his aunt to stir up trouble for Deirdre.

She nodded toward Lindsay. "I think it would help the lass as well."

"Perhaps." The idea sprouted like a seed dropped into fertile soil. As he escorted his aunt home and returned to the cottage, he thought of how it might be to have Lindsay as his wife instead of the faceless woman his father and stepmother had chosen for him. Marrying her would offer her protection. She wouldn't need to fall prey to her uncle's abuses again. It seemed the right thing to do.

He and Lindsay were well suited. They were content to simply sit and talk to each other. But would it be fair of him to take a woman like that and force her into the role of Lady MacPherson? Her days would be taken up with the running of the castle instead of quiet walks in the woods.

She was barely managing her rowdy cousins. How would she handle her duties as the laird's wife? He imagined one of those duties more than the other. Her nights would be spent with a man who might eventually be able to give her his body but never his heart.

It wasn't the first time he'd thought of taking Lindsay Cameron to his bed. But it was the first time he'd thought of her as his wife as he did so, to have the blessing of the church if not the blessing of their families.

If she were his wife, he could protect her. Except he'd not been able to protect his last wife, had he? He could only imagine what his clan would think of him marrying a Cameron lass. They may never accept her, but he could force their obedience if not their loyalty.

He laid out some furs by the low fire and settled in to sleep as dreams of Lindsay *MacPherson* played about in his head. The two women, Maria and Lindsay—past and future— intertwined as he slept. Memories he had with Maria were taken over with Lindsay's smile, while he imagined Maria in the cottage playing with Tre. He woke at light, still tired from spending what was left of the night wrestling with what he was to do next.

He didn't wish to marry, and if given the choice he'd not do it ever again. But he would have to marry. Why not at least choose a wife he cared for?

He went about breaking his fast, making enough for her as well. When she didn't wake in time to eat, he gave some to the dog and then ate the rest of her share, too.

"If ye don't wake soon, you'll be responsible for making me soft in the middle," he threatened playfully before brushing a bit of hair back from her lovely face.

"Wake up, lass. We have important things to discuss."

Chapter Six

Lindsay opened her eyes to darkness and confusion. She was lying in a comfortable bed, which meant she wasn't at her uncle's cottage. Was she home? Had her father come for her? Regardless of where she was, she wished she could remain there despite the great discomfort she was in.

She lay still, trying to decide which part hurt more. Her back was stiff. Her face and head throbbed. Her side felt like fire, but, most of all, she needed to get to a privy. Sitting on the edge of the bed brought stars to her vision. She caught her breath with shallow pants as she took in the room. Enough light came from the moon and the low embers in the hearth for her to recognize it as Shane's cottage.

"How did I get here?" she whispered to the little dog by her side. Why was she here at night? Where was Shane? The answer to that final question was answered by the slight snore coming from the large lump next to the fire. He was sleeping on the floor while she had taken up his bed.

Touching her face, she felt the swollen, tender bits. Her lip. Her eye. She stood slowly, giving her battered body the time it needed to straighten, but as soon as she was upright, she pushed through the pain to get out the door and behind the nearest bush.

Of course, Treun had followed her and was now coaxing her back in the house by running and looking back at her as if it were a game. She hobbled back to the cottage to find Shane looking at her as if she were a ghost.

"What are ye doing out of bed?" He gestured to the bed where she'd been sleeping.

"I had pressing needs," she answered and smiled when his cheeks seemed to grow darker. She wished for more light to see better. Was the soldier blushing? She'd seen him look at her. Not leering stares like her uncle but rather with appreciation.

The thought of her uncle brought back an unpleasant memory, and she swayed where she stood.

Shane was quick to put an arm around her waist to support her, and she enjoyed his warmth and closeness. "You should have woken me. I would've helped ye."

She looked around the cottage, noticing the herbs and things that hadn't been there when last she'd visited. "It appears you've already helped me a great deal. How long have I been asleep?" Her mind was muddled, but more memories were coming now. Uncle Randall had come home in his cups and said he wanted to make her his wife. After trying her out first.

She slumped on the edge of the bed, unsure if she could remain standing even with his help.

Shane took the opportunity to guide her back. Her head sank into the soft pillow as he tucked her legs under the blanket.

"You arrived about this time the night before." She'd slept through the day. In his bed.

Even now, she could smell the scent of him on the

bedclothes. Leather, woodsmoke, and the forest where he seemed to spend much of his time.

"Did your uncle do this to you, lass?" he asked, his jaw tense.

What would he do if she told him what happened? A small part of her wanted to see her uncle punished for what he'd done, but not at the cost of Shane's life. If he killed her uncle, he'd pay the price at the end of a rope.

"Do you promise you'll not do anything foolish if I tell ye?"

That made a smile pull up on one side of his mouth.

"Aye. I'm not one to be foolish. And I guessed it was him, for the little ones wouldn't cause this much damage."

She nodded and remembered poor Robbie. "The boys aren't monsters. They haven't been given the chance to be raised with love. I'm worried about them alone with him. Robbie was hurt as well."

"You see to healing. I'll take care of the rest. Now tell me what happened."

"He was drunk. But this is nothing compared to what it could have been. He plans to wed me so he has…a wife." She swallowed, remembering the vulgar way Randall had said he wanted a wife to warm his bed. "And someone to care for the children."

Though that would never come to pass, the thought still frightened her. Even if her father didn't send for her or offer her a reprieve from marrying, she would surely take her chances at the castle before ever allowing her uncle to touch her.

Shane frowned and paced about the room a few times before he came to sit on the bed. His weight on the mattress caused her to roll toward him. "I have something to say to ye, and I want you to sleep on it and give me your answer in the morning."

She waited silently as he seemed to struggle with this question.

"I think ye should marry me, Lindsay."

She shook her groggy head. "Marry you?" she asked, wanting to be sure she'd understood correctly.

"Aye. If we married, you would be protected from your uncle. You'd not need to toil away in his cottage. Instead, you would stay here with me." He paused and ran a hand over the bristle of his chin. "Or wherever else I may go."

She wanted to ask him about that last part. Where was he thinking to go? But he distracted her by speaking again.

"Don't answer right now. Go back to sleep and let your mind work things out while ye rest. You'll have your answer in the morning, and we can't act on anything tonight anyway." He tucked the blanket around her and winked. She heard his heavy footsteps as he crossed the room and saw his shadow as he settled back on the floor.

"Rest well, lass."

That was easy for him to say. She had much to think about. She ran her fingers through Tre's coarse fur and pondered what to do. How did she want to answer his question? That was the problem. What she wanted to do didn't align with what she ought to do.

He was offering her yet a third option. To not marry the laird *or* go home. She could stay here with a kind man she'd come to admire. Her father had promised her to the new MacPherson laird. Her sire wouldn't be pleased to find her married to a soldier. He'd be angry for sure. And after she'd already broken a previous marriage contract. Would he ever speak to her again? Would she be disowned? But would that matter? She wouldn't see her parents if she married the MacPherson laird anyway. Still, the thought of displeasing her father didn't sit well with her. She'd been nothing but a disappointment. Marrying the laird might make him look upon her with pride.

What was she willing to sacrifice for only the chance to win the man's approval? Surely not the rest of her life, her happiness, her heart. Marrying Shane would mean she wouldn't have to marry the MacPherson laird. She'd have Shane instead. She'd know his touch and finally understand what happens between men and women in the night. And maybe, most importantly, she'd be shown by a man she cared for. A kind, gentle man with intriguing eyes and a naughty grin, despite the shadows and secrets. Would he ever trust her enough to tell her what still caused him so much pain?

She thought through the things she wanted and didn't want. She didn't want to ever see her uncle again. That was first and foremost. She didn't want to marry the laird. She realized she'd made the man to be a monster in her mind. She didn't know what he might look like, but his younger brother, the war chief, was called Beast because of his large size, scarred face, and constant sneer. She shivered and then winced when doing so pulled at her sore ribs. Recognizing the things she *didn't* want, she focused on the things she did and only had one answer. Shane.

With her mind made up, she drifted off to sleep but was woken a short time later by someone calling for help. She sat up too quickly, thinking she needed to help Robbie, but as the pain faded, she recalled where she was. In Shane's home. It was Shane calling for help. Was he dreaming of fighting the French, or was his nightmare filled with the flames from his childhood? Either way, she wanted to help him.

"Maria! God, no! Please. Maria." Her earlier fear turned to soul-shattering agony as she wondered who Maria was.

Struggling with the stiffness of her sore body, she managed to get to her feet, but when she reached the place where Shane slept on the floor, she couldn't bend over to wake him. A plan came quickly as she went to the small larder and claimed a piece of dried meat. Waving it in front of the dog, she carried it over and dropped it on Shane's bare chest, where Treun jumped on him to snatch it up. When the treat was gone, she licked the place it had been, which roused Shane from his bad dream.

"What—?"

"You were having a night terror, and I used her to help wake you."

He closed his eyes a moment while petting the dog. "I guess I should warn you, it is common for me to call out while I'm sleeping. Something to consider as you think over my earlier offer."

She wanted to tell him she'd already made up her mind, but she wasn't sure either of them was awake enough for serious conversation. Instead, she shuffled back to the bed and held in a whimper as she pulled herself up on the mattress.

This time, she dreamed of her and Shane at the rock by the river and that near kiss. Only this time the kiss happened. The scene was foggy, as dreams often were when one didn't know the details.

She woke again, later in the morning. From the bed, she watched Shane go about making their morning meal as he hummed a happy tune. She wondered if his proposal in the dark had been a dream, but when she moved to sit up, the pain in her head proved it had been real.

Shane MacPherson had asked her to marry him, and she was going to accept. It was her only real option, one that at least had some hope of offering a bright future.

Her arranged marriage would have been important for her people, an alliance between clans. Her father wouldn't be pleased.

• • •

"You're awake," he said with a smile that warmed her to her toes. "Are you hungry?"

"My stomach thinks my throat's been cut," she said, making him laugh.

"I'll bring you something to eat."

"Nay. I must get up and move around."

He came to assist her to her feet, and with one arm around her back, he led her around the small cabin so she could work out the stiff parts, Treun quick on her heels.

"The wee one guards ye," he said of the dog. "If it hadn't been for her, I might not have known you were lying out there on the path."

She was moving more easily, but when she attempted to bend to pet her small friend, she realized it was too soon for such things. She sucked in a quick breath, and Shane hurried to support her. She nodded toward the chair. He helped her settle in, but before he'd taken his seat across from her, she blurted out a question.

"Did you ask me to marry you, or did I dream it?" If she had dreamed it, he would now know he inhabited her dreams. But she didn't have time to be embarrassed, for he nodded.

"Aye. I hoped you would pick me over your scoundrel of an uncle." He frowned as she shook her head.

"There is no question of who I would pick between the two of you."

"Then the question is: Will you marry me?"

She studied him for a moment, trying to see if he wanted this as much as she did or if his proposal came only from a sense of protection, but his expression was well guarded, and she looked away knowing little more than she had. It seemed like such a question should take more thought, but answering him was one of the easiest things she'd ever done.

She nodded while catching her sore lip between her teeth briefly. After nodding more vehemently, she answered.

"Yes. I'll marry you." Whatever happened when her father found out, Lindsay would manage it. But she could not let this opportunity pass her by. She had the chance to find happiness, and maybe someday even love. She couldn't let it pass.

She hated to disappoint her father, but she thought being with Shane would be worth it. She would have to apologize to Shane eventually for lying about who she was, but for now, she would have this time for herself first.

As Shane's wife.

• • •

Shane hadn't expected the wave of emotions that crashed over him when Lindsay agreed to marry him. The largest being guilt. How dare he move on with another woman after what he'd done to Maria? Because of him, she had died, yet he planned to marry another.

Lindsay didn't have many choices before her, but he was glad she'd agreed so he could protect her despite having forsaken Maria. He would not fail again. This marriage would not be like his first. He'd not be the eager groom waiting for the priest to declare them man and wife. Yet this wouldn't be the cold ceremony he'd expected with an arranged wife who didn't know him well enough to want him, either.

This would be a necessary agreement and friendship. It was the most he had to offer. He would need to apologize for lying about who he was. He'd hope she would adjust to her duties. He remembered the interest he'd received before he'd left. He knew the lasses may have liked the way he looked, but they liked the status he offered even more.

But Lindsay had said yes to *him*. As far as she knew, he was nothing more than a soldier returned from war. She wasn't marrying him to become the laird's wife or to make an alliance. Yes, she was also marrying him for the protection he offered, but he saw the smile on her face and knew it was due to more than just safety. "As soon as ye feel fit to stand, we'll see it done."

"Today." She swallowed and smiled shyly. "If it suits you, I will be ready to marry you today."

He wasn't prepared for it to happen so soon. But he understood her haste. Every minute she was unattached was one her uncle could show up and claim her back. As her kin, he'd have the right to take her home. Not that Shane would allow that to happen. Even if it meant claiming his title and giving up his quiet peace in the woods, he would never allow an innocent lass to fall into the hands of such a man.

"Aye. It suits me. But you need more time to heal. I have some things to see to in the village. I'll help you back to bed to rest before I take my leave." He did have things to see to in the village before they left. But he also needed a moment to himself, to make sure he could go through with such a commitment.

She frowned. "You will come back, though?" He could guess what she was getting at. If he attacked her uncle, he could be carted off to the dungeon.

"Get some rest. I'll be back," he said before he turned to the dog. "You stay here and watch over her." He slipped out the door and went to find the coward who'd hurt her.

Chapter Seven

Shane rapped quickly on the shabby door and waited for the yelling inside to quiet down. Randall opened the door, blurry-eyed and with a sickly tinge to his skin. It was clear the man was not well and the drink was making things worse.

"What do ye want?" he spat at Shane. "The girl's not here."

"I'm aware."

He stood straighter at Shane's comment. "If you know where she is, you'd better bring her back here. I'm seeing after her."

"As to that, I've witnessed the way you saw after her. Much the way you see to your boys, from the looks of it." The littlest boy had a blackened eye, and the eldest's lip was split and scabbed over.

"And what business is it of yours?"

Shane bit his tongue to keep from revealing exactly who he was and why it was his business. There was another way that wouldn't reveal his identity to the lout. "I am acquainted with the new laird and know well what he thinks of men who abuse women as you have done to your niece."

Shane took a slow breath to calm the rage that bubbled up. He knew what he was capable of when he allowed his anger to take over. He'd not be able to stop himself from killing the frail man.

Fortunately, his threat stilled the man's tongue. Shane decided to go further. From his father's letters, he'd learned his brother Alec had become a formidable war chief. It was difficult for Shane to believe, remembering Alec as a gangly lad of five and ten who only came up to Shane's nose when he'd left. But if Alec drew fear into the hearts of men, it was worth mentioning him. "Do you know of Alec, the war chief?"

The man's eyes went wide as he muttered, "The Trow?"

Shane didn't know of the name, but it was clear he'd managed the fear Shane had been hoping for. "Aye. I know him as well, and he will see you're punished properly for what you've done."

"Please. I'll not hit her again. I did offer the lass marriage."

"You mean you threatened marriage." The idea of someone as lovely as Lindsay having to be married to such a creature… He swallowed down the bile the thought brought up.

"If she took it that way…" His words drifted off as Shane took a step closer. A warning not to put any of the blame on Lindsay. "Please," the man begged again, which was exactly what Shane had wanted.

"Hear me. I make only one offer, and you will take it or face the castle for your crimes." He held out a few coins. "Take this money and leave the MacPherson clan today. You'll leave the boys with me so I might find a good home for them where they'll be raised properly into men this clan can be proud of."

Shane barely got the words out before the man grabbed

up the coins and gave a nod. The man seemed eager enough to be done with his sons as he ran back into the cottage to grab a few things, not sparing so much as a parting word for them. What kind of a father walked away from his children without so much as a hesitation?

"I'll be on my way, then. Thank ye." He took off and didn't look back.

The boys stood there watching as their da rushed off before turning to look at Shane.

He was not accustomed to being with children. There were some about the camps, but he and Maria had not been blessed with children in the year they'd been wed, so he'd never been a father himself. "When will he be back?" the older one asked, though Shane thought the lad knew the answer.

Robbie, the littlest boy, who was maybe eight, had tears in his blackened eye. Was he sad to learn the man had left them or was he afraid of what would happen to them? The man, coward that he was, was still the boys' da.

"He will not return. I've sent him away for what he did to your cousin. He was facing punishment from the castle, so it was best he leave." If the boys felt any way about that, they didn't show it. Shane didn't give them time to start worrying. "Doran, you're old enough to join the guard. If it is your wish to do so, I can start your training myself."

Doran's eyes went wide, and he nodded excitedly. "Aye. I would like to be a warrior." He looked down at his thin body, and the excitement waned.

"Worry not—you're tall enough and not done growing yet. With proper food, you'll fill out into a fine warrior. I was not much bigger than you when I was your age."

His eyes went wide as they moved, taking in Shane's size now.

"Very well, then. All of you gather your things and come

with me."

The smaller boys spared a second to look to Doran, who gave them a nod, which spurred them into action. They came out a minute later with small bundles of their things, then without question followed Shane deeper into the village. Shane took a breath before stepping up to the smithy's shop. He'd already had to reach out to Bess to see Lindsay was tended to, and now he would reveal his return to another old friend.

"Munro, how have you been?" he asked the large man with huge, work-worn hands. It took only a second for Munro to recognize him. White teeth showed in the depths of his thick beard.

Shane had worked with the man in the forge as a lad, learning the skill. His father hadn't known at first and afterward did not like having his heir working in the village. But he allowed it only so long as Shane learned how to make swords and other weapons.

Munro had lost his wife years ago in childbirth, and Shane knew his heart still burned for their loss. Shane knew that pain well himself and wondered if years from now his loss would still show in his eyes the way it showed in Munro's.

Shane didn't mean to take advantage of the man's loneliness, but these boys needed someone to help mold them into good men. And only a good man could do that.

"It's nice to see you whole and hearty. It looks as if you brought everything back with ye from France." The man patted his arms.

"Aye. I did." Except for his heart, which was buried in Spain with his wife.

"What can I do for ye?"

"Two things. If we may speak in private." Shane nodded toward the door to one of the bigger houses in the village.

Munro waved for him to come into his home as Shane

turned to the boys.

"Stay right here. I'll be back shortly."

Inside, Munro offered him some ale, which Shane took as he sat at the scarred wooden table. Shane spared a look around the clean cottage. The loft above the bed would be large enough for the boys.

"What's on your mind?"

"The lads out there need a home. Their mother passed a month or so ago, and their father left this morning." Shane hesitated to mention the reason he'd left but thought it might help Munro in dealing with the skittish children.

"I told him to go. He had taken his fists to them and spends his money on whisky instead of seeing them fed properly."

Munro's bushy eyebrows pulled together. He wasn't one who would stand by while a child was mistreated.

"They are strong from working in the peat fields, but we both know that work does not bring much challenge of mind. Doran, the older boy, will be training with me to become a warrior, but when he's not with me, I'd like the boys to stay with you. To learn your trade and, more importantly, learn to be honorable men."

Munro snorted and looked away.

"If it's the expense, I can assist—"

"It isn't the expense. I can feed three scrawny lads on my own," the man snapped.

"If you don't want to do it, say so. I just thought they would have a better chance with you. The path they're on now, they will see nothing but the end of a rope or drowning in drink like their da."

Munro ran a palm over his beard. He was considering it. Shane felt the need to disclose all the information he knew. "They aren't afraid of work, but they have a strong mouth on them for not being taught differently. They've been wronged by nearly everyone who's cared for them, so it might take some time to earn their trust."

"I've never shied away from a tough job, and you know it."

"You'll do it?"

"Aye, I'll take them in. What is your second request?"

Shane leaned closer to look him in the eye. "I've not told anyone at the castle I've returned. I'd like you to keep it to yourself that you've seen me."

Munro chuckled at that. "You're still hiding in the village from your duties in the castle as you did when you were a lad."

Shane laughed. It seemed that was indeed true. "Perhaps. It won't be for long. I do know I need to take on the title of laird eventually." With his father gone, he guessed Alec was seeing to the running of things in the castle. It was good for him to see how it was done. If anything ever happened to Shane, it would fall to Alec as Shane's heir. This would be good practice.

"As with anything, it's always better to make a choice to do something rather than it being forced upon ye."

Shane nodded, for this man understood many things. Shane's brows pulled together as he considered the man's words. "You do not feel I have forced the boys upon you, do you?"

"Nay. Ye gave me a choice. And I'll allow you to make the choice as to when you claim your birthright. I'll not tell anyone I've seen the new MacPherson laird in my shop. And not just because they wouldn't believe it."

They shared a laugh and rose to go back to the boys. Shane turned to them, thinking about what Munro had said about making a choice to do something rather than it being forced upon you.

"I have arranged for the three of you to stay here with Munro. He can teach you his trade in the forge. You won't have to work in the peat fields anymore. But you would need to mind what he says. He'll see your bellies don't go hungry. Is that agreeable to you?"

They shared a silent conversation between glances, and finally Doran answered for the lot with a nod and an "Aye."

Shane figured the offer of food and an honorable trade was too good to pass up.

"Good. I'll check in on you. And, Doran, I'll come for you soon to start your training." He turned back to Munro, who set to his new duties straightaway.

"How about we go inside for some bannocks with honey and get to know one another better?" he suggested, and the smaller boys rushed forward at the offer of food.

Doran looked back to Shane.

"You have a choice to be a better man than your da. This is your chance. Munro is a good man. He'll not raise a hand to any of ye—you have my word on that."

Doran nodded and went inside. Shane didn't expect gratitude or excitement. This was a big change for them and a scary one. Shane also faced a big change. Marriage. The thought stirred his stomach to knots.

In the year since Maria had died, he'd not once thought of ever marrying again. But here he was, planning to take on another wife, even if for some kind of convenience. He'd give her his name, but she could never have his heart.

• • •

Rather than marry Lindsay in the village near the castle, where someone might question his name or recognize him, he took them to the next village to find a priest.

She rode with him on Hades, and he took things slow so as not to jostle her injuries. It had been two days since he'd proposed marriage, and she insisted she was fine. Still, he didn't so much as rest his hand on her for fear he might press on something that would cause her pain. Instead, he sat behind her, breathing in the smell of sunshine and lavender in her hair and wishing he could touch every part of her. Not that he would. He was marrying her to protect her and would do so no matter what he or his body might wish.

They crossed over a sparkling river, and he shared stories of fishing there when he was a lad. When they broke through the dense grove of trees, he shared that this had been the field where he'd been blooded. "I took my first life here at the age of six and ten, and I thought I'd lose my stomach all over the body. My da was proud, and I tried to be as well, but mostly I remember how easy it was. How warm the man's blood was when it ran over my hand. I thought I was ready. I'd heard many stories. But the stories don't allow you to feel it like doing it. The smells and sounds…" He shook his head. "I tried to think of ways to never have to do it again." He smirked at the thought.

He, a soldier, who had been paid to end lives every day for the last five years.

"I assume it didn't work, as you ended up in France."

"Nay. It didn't. And it became easier after that first one. Knowing what it would be like helped with the fear. I'd never say it has become easy, for I do still claim a soul. But every life I've taken was to protect my own or someone else's. I would never kill for the sake of it."

Death was common enough at war, and Shane had become almost numb to the sight. Except for one death that still haunted him with every breath he took. He may not have drawn the sword that ended Maria's life, but he'd abandoned her when he should have stayed and protected her. His wife's blood was on his hands.

"I have never killed a man," Lindsay said. "But after those two mongrels attacked me, had I sword instead of a stick, I think I would have done what was needed."

"I shall hope you never need to know. I will protect you, always."

Heaven help anyone who thought to hurt her now. They would know his wrath. It was one thing to make sure she didn't come to harm. He would do the same for any in his clan. But he would defend Lindsay as he wished he'd protected Maria.

The blue sky faded to gray as they rode into the village just across the border with the Gordons.

When the cleric saw the bruises on Lindsay's face, he frowned, but Lindsay explained the situation and why she wanted to marry as soon as possible.

Shane barely heard the words they spoke as he did his best to keep the memories of his first wedding at bay. He may not be able to love Lindsay as he should, but he could at least honor her by not thinking of another as they took their vows. He watched her, almost expecting her to change her mind at any moment. Instead, she smiled up at him as best she could with her swollen lip.

His chest clenched. He managed to smile back through the pain and guilt coursing through his body. This was wrong. This wasn't the woman he'd pledged to love and honor the rest of his life. But he stood his ground and swallowed back the memories. It wasn't fair to Lindsay. This woman thought she was marrying a whole man, and she'd soon find out she'd gotten only pieces. And the parts that were left were shattered and broken.

He realized how selfish his act of selflessness was. He pretended he married her for protection, but he knew as he stood there looking into her dark eyes that it wasn't true. He'd wanted her soothing calmness to take some of his pain away. He'd not wanted to bear this hurt alone. He'd wanted to make amends by saving the woman he hadn't saved.

He had offered marriage for him, and she didn't even

know who he was. She wasn't marrying the MacPherson laird. She was marrying a soldier who had been kind to her. He realized when the priest looked at him expectantly that he didn't even have a ring for her. He'd carried his mother's ring in his sporran and had beamed with pride as he'd slid it on Maria's finger. She'd been buried with it still in place.

"I'm sorry. I should have thought of a ring."

Lindsay shook her head. "It's of no matter."

After they signed the register, the strangers he'd paid to be witnesses did likewise and the deed was done. He was married to another woman. It was as if his marriage to Maria had never happened.

...

He and Lindsay shared a meal at the local tavern before riding back home.

"You can ride a little faster. I'll not break," she said.

"You are already broken. I don't wish to do more damage."

"I may be a little raw, but I am not broken. That man doesn't have the power to do so."

He leaned closer so she could hear him when he whispered, "I know you are strong, and these injuries will heal and be easily forgotten. But for my part, I don't want to cause you even the tiniest amount of pain, so we will continue on at this pace."

"It will take forever for us to get home."

Her last word struck him in the chest. *Home*. It may be their home for now, but at some point, he would need to move to the castle and do his duty for his clan. To accept his birthright as laird, whether he wished to or not. Would she gladly move to the castle and call that her home?

As she continued to fuss about his slowness, she

unintentionally shifted against him in an enticing way. He knew she hadn't meant to, but his body didn't care what she'd meant and what she didn't. All his body knew was that there was a warm, soft woman in his lap where there had not been for many, many long months. He searched for the feelings that should have accompanied the physical urge and found nothing but emptiness.

He had made a terrible mistake.

Chapter Eight

Lindsay leaned back against her husband as he reined the horse toward home, but she was anything but relaxed. She was married, and that meant a wedding night. She understood some parts about what happened between men and women but had expected her mother to tell her the details before her wedding.

Now she didn't know what she was supposed to know before such an event. Would Shane be disappointed if she didn't go about it the correct way? Lindsay was known to babble when she was nervous, and she didn't think she'd ever been more nervous than she was right then. In an effort to keep quiet, she began shifting about in the saddle where she sat in front of Shane.

"Stop your squirming about, woman," he said, sounding as if he were in a great deal of pain. She stilled immediately after feeling something stiff prodding her in her backside.

Unable to move around, she had no other choice but to speak. "Thank you," she said quietly.

"You're welcome."

"Do you even know why I'm thanking you?" she asked after a moment.

She felt rather than saw him shrug. "For taking our riding at a slow pace so your head doesn't become dislodged from your body?"

She laughed even when he didn't.

"I was thanking you for caring for me. I was beginning to think no one did. Which sounds rather petulant, but I wrote to my parents to beg them to come for me, and they have not returned for me. Or sent word."

"Are you known to spin tall tales?"

"Am I the boy who cries wolf, where the wolf is my uncle?" She shook her head. "No. Never."

"I didn't think so. As it were, your uncle turned out to be a wolf, indeed."

"I'm also thanking you for what you did for the boys. Freeing them from that man will be the best thing for them, even if they might not realize it yet." When he'd told her what he'd done, she'd felt a rush of relief that they'd be cared for. Shane said he trusted this Munro, so she did as well. It wasn't as if he could be any worse than their own father.

"It was the right thing to do," he said easily, as if everyone chose to do the right thing. Her experience in the short time she'd been with the MacPhersons was that not many she'd met cared about right or wrong.

"I want you to know I will care for you, too. I'll make sure you don't regret having married me," she said quietly.

"I won't regret it."

She couldn't believe her good luck. To have found a kind man to marry, rather than an ogre of a laird. When her father found out, he'd have no choice but to support the match, for he would not have found a better man to marry her.

Shane didn't expect her to do all the chores. He hadn't married her to have a servant, as her uncle had treated her.

He had married her to protect her, which wasn't the best reason, but it wasn't for the exchange of cattle or land, so she was pleased enough.

"How can you be sure you won't regret it?" she asked after warning herself to be quiet. Some questions one didn't really want answers to. "You hardly know me. This marriage could turn out to be the biggest mistake you've ever made."

He made a sound. Not one that made her think he didn't agree with the possibility of their marriage being a mistake. Her worry intensified as they rode on, but she managed to stay still and quiet, if for no other reason than that she was terrified of what came next.

...

Shane was glad when Lindsay stopped talking and more importantly stopped wiggling around while her arse was settled on his cock. He didn't think he'd make it back to the cottage otherwise.

He needed time to think, and he couldn't do that when her enticing body was shifting against his. Or when she was talking about regrets. The truth was, he already had regrets, but it was too late now. They were wed. He'd do his duty to provide and protect her, but that would be all. Hopefully, she wouldn't expect more.

He didn't think she needed much. After all, she had no family there except for a couple of rowdy lads who'd not cared for her as they should have. As for the rest of her family, he would have a few words to say to them as well, if ever he met them. He didn't expect much from Camerons, but he didn't care for the way they sent their daughter off into the lion's den unprotected.

His censure would have greater impact if they knew he was the laird of the MacPhersons. He should tell her. He hadn't lied, exactly. He'd been careful to word things in a way so he wouldn't have to. After all, he wasn't the laird until he went to the castle and claimed the title for himself. But despite his success at twisting his words in such a way, he was traveling a thin line of what was not a lie and what a person should have shared with a woman before claiming her as his wife, no matter the reason he married her.

Guilt tugged in his stomach, as had been happening since he'd offered his hasty proposal. Yet he didn't speak until it faded away again. For as much as he wished he could tell her the truth, he needed this time with her, like this, quiet and calm, even more. She healed some of the broken bits of his heart.

Unfortunately, there was naught to be done about the chunks that were missing.

In the distance, a hawk screeched, and she turned to look for it. Even that quick movement had her luscious arse shifting in his lap, stirring him to arousal once more. He growled, and she muttered an apology. He didn't blame her for his body's reaction. It wasn't her fault. But he couldn't think of being with her physically when his betrayal was so firmly on his mind. He had not imagined he take on the life of a monk the rest of his days. He was a young man with many years of empty nights ahead of him.

He'd assumed he'd go about it the way he'd done before marrying Maria. During the years he was at war, before he'd met her, he'd seldom taken a woman to his bed, mostly because he didn't have a bed. Instead, he and Ronan generally found a place for their bedrolls away from the other men. They would talk of home and speculate as to what their siblings were doing.

Early on, they always assumed their sister and brother were doing mundane chores he and Ronan had been spared from having to do because they were men while Alec and

Tory were children. As men, they were eager to fight a path through France and claim the glory.

Unfortunately, their eagerness dimmed before the first year. Soon, they were looking at the stars above and wishing they were back home in Scotland. They would talk of things such as Lizzy's meat pies and berry tarts. The cook at Cluny had chased them from her kitchens more times than they could count, but remembering her meals made them think of home.

And then there was the issue of the women who followed the drum being well worn, often carrying with them diseases he and Ronan wanted no part of. While Shane had tempted fate a few times over the years, his brother—to Shane's knowledge—never had. When Shane had asked him about it, he'd only said he couldn't.

Shane wasn't sure what he'd meant by it and didn't ask further. Ronan never had a problem sharing something when he wanted to. Shane had met the woman who'd changed everything for him. She'd not been like the other women, who used sex as currency. She'd been carrying water in her village when he and his men had come through. He'd stopped to help her, and when he'd looked into her eyes, he'd simply known she would be his.

When he left the next day, she went with him, and a few weeks later they had married. The next year had been both the hardest and the best, for he'd spent the days fighting and the nights in her arms, loving her.

Now, with Shane's new wife nestled against him, his body had come alive, and the absence of company of the feminine nature was taking its toll. Lindsay was beautiful. It was a natural reaction, if one he had no plan to act on for some time.

"Shane?" she said, bringing his attention back from the discomfort of his cock. "Will you tell me about your family?"

He'd avoided questions about his family, but he would tell her the truth as much as possible. "My ma died when I was a lad. My da died recently, while I was away."

"That's too bad. You didn't get to say goodbye."

"Nay." He would have had some other words for his father in addition to "goodbye." Mayhap something like, "Do not think to marry me off to some lass just so you can buy useless baubles for your wife while your warriors' swords look like they would bend in a brisk wind." He kept that to himself. Instead, he said, "I told you of my stepbrother."

"Aye, but he's not with you now."

"He's a Grant by name. His grandmother was a MacPherson, though, and he came to live with us when he was only ten. For that, he thinks himself as much MacPherson as Grant."

He expected his new wife to make her disgust known. The Camerons and MacPhersons were enemies, but not like the Camerons and Grants were. They'd sooner kill one another than have to look at each other. But she said nothing.

"And then there is my younger brother and sister." He didn't mention his stepmother because he'd rather pretend she didn't exist.

"Have you seen them since you've returned?"

"Not yet. They were not pleased with me when I left. Especially my younger brother. He was left behind, just a gangly lad of five and ten. And then my sister was certain I'd get myself killed."

He went on to tell her of the things they'd gotten up to when they were young, until he felt Lindsay's weight against him. She'd dozed off. He held her loosely so as not to hurt her, but to support her as the horse continued on.

It was late when they arrived back at the cottage.

She woke when the horse stopped. Her head snapped up, and she groaned from the quick movement. "We're home already," she said.

"Aye." *Home.* He'd wanted to be home for several years, yet he hadn't realized once he'd arrived, he wouldn't be ready to take those final steps. For now, this cottage was his home and this woman was his wife.

He didn't know what would come, but for now he was content. He assisted her into the house, and they stood there. Nothing had changed within these walls since they'd left. The bedding was straightened from where she'd been asleep these past few days. And yet, everything was different.

They were married. Married couples shared a bed. They shared a lot more than that. But they had married for a reason that didn't include such liberties.

"You will, of course, take the bed, and I'll remain on the floor," he said stiffly.

"I don't mean for you to be uncomfortable."

"It's actually better. After years of sleeping on the ground, the soft bed is strange." It was a strangeness he was becoming accustomed to, but he wanted to reassure her that he was fine with the floor. The floor was safe. He wouldn't be tempted to touch Lindsay while he dreamed of Maria.

Lindsay nodded. She was exhausted. "I'm sure you're in pain from our ride," he said. "I'll brew you some willow bark tea and settle you in bed for the night. You still need your rest. Bess will be after me if I don't make sure you get plenty of sleep."

He went about starting a fire in the hearth and pushing the kettle over the flame as he sorted out the herbs his aunt had left for her. He sweetened the bitter concoction with a bit of honey and took it to where she was sitting on the edge of the bed. She still frowned at the taste. "I know it tastes awful, but it does help."

She nodded and gulped it down as if wanting the task over with as quickly as possible. He pulled off her shoes and helped her back on the mattress, tucking the blanket around her. She closed her eyes, and he thought she had already fallen asleep as he settled in on his makeshift bed by the wall. He closed his eyes and was hoping sleep would come for him quickly so he'd not spend the rest of the night lying there thinking of her in his bed.

But the stillness of the room was interrupted by her soft voice.

"Shane?"

"Aye?"

"Who is Maria?"

Air hissed past his teeth as he breathed in. Just hearing her name spoken aloud in the darkness caused a flood of memories to sweep him away. No one had spoken her name in months. Ronan knew how much talking about her pained him and did his best to keep their conversations on other things. Perhaps that was not the best way to have handled it. He'd thought it was getting easier, but hearing Lindsay whisper her name tore the wound open again, and he feared he would not be able to stop the bleeding.

Still, Lindsay was waiting for an answer. She'd most likely heard him calling for Maria in his sleep. It was the only time he said it. He thought about snapping at her that it was none of her business. He wanted to tell her to leave it alone and never speak the name again.

Maybe it was all the truths he was already keeping from her that forced him to answer this one.

"She was my wife," he said, surprised he'd managed to get the words past the lump burning in his throat. When she said nothing, he swallowed and continued. "It was my fault she died. I will never forgive myself."

When the silence went on, he assumed she'd fallen asleep. Part of him hoped she'd fallen asleep as soon as she'd asked the question. He didn't know why he'd shared so much. He'd not admitted his guilt to another soul until tonight.

While his insides felt raw and tender for saying the words aloud, he also felt stronger for having said them. When he fell asleep that night, he didn't dream.

• • •

Shane had been married before. Lindsay lay in his bed still thinking of his words hours after his breathing had evened out and a soft snore drifted across to where she lay in shock.

He'd been married before, and he'd not mentioned it to her. His new wife.

It was clear from the strain she'd heard in his voice as he spoke the few words about Maria that Shane had loved her very much. And he'd been responsible for her death. Lindsay had not had the courage to ask anything else. She'd instead allowed the stillness of the room to grow until he'd fallen asleep.

She was exhausted from traveling and the excitement of the day, but sleep wouldn't come now. She was busy thinking a hundred questions she wanted to ask him but feared she wouldn't.

What had happened to Maria? How long were they married? How long ago did she die? Had they married for love? Did he sleep on the floor while she slept in his bed while they were together?

Lindsay thought she knew the answer to that. She hated the jealousy that wound up her spine at the thought of Shane loving this woman. His first wife.

It explained the shadow of pain and regret she sometimes saw haunting his face. He'd lost his wife, and he missed her. Hurt for her loss. Yet he'd married Lindsay to protect her. How much pain had she caused him today?

Tears gathered in her own eyes when she realized

she'd married Shane hoping they might find more than an arrangement between them. She'd hoped, in time, they'd grow to love each other. But now she realized that could never be. For her husband was still in love with his Maria.

Chapter Nine

Shane woke to a dog snuffling around his face. He batted Tre away and rolled over on his side. No doubt she wanted to be let out to do her business. He realized he needed to do the same. Rubbing sleep from his eyes, he got to his feet, pulled his boots on, and grabbed up his plaid before heading for the door.

As he passed the bed, he saw Lindsay sleeping, her dark hair spread across the pillow like a banner flying in the breeze. How many times had he woken and seen Maria's hair in the same way and thought the same thing?

Shaking his head and the thought away, he trudged for the door. As soon as it was opened wide enough, Tre burst through and dashed down the path. Shane went the opposite direction toward the river. After relieving himself, he tugged off his shirt and shucked his boots to wash. The water was frigid, as only snow melt can be. He'd grown soft while in the warmer climes of France and Spain.

Only as he stepped out and was shaking the water from his hair did he remember the fragment of a conversation last night between him and Lindsay. She'd asked him about Maria. And he'd told her. His body went even colder, and not because of the water. What if she asked him other things? Things he couldn't speak of? Things that would break him completely?

He wasn't ready.

Instead of going back to their cottage, he belted on his plaid and went the opposite direction. He was a coward. He knew it as he knew his own name. But he couldn't face Lindsay. She didn't know how broken he was.

His feet stopped moving when he thought of Maria and the last day he'd left her. A skirmish had broken out on the edge of camp with some French soldiers. Shane had left Maria to go stand with his men. Usually, when he went off to battle, he'd put one of the lads in charge of watching over the women, but this time he hadn't, for it had risen up quickly. He'd thought only of getting to his men. To have Ronan's back as his brother had looked after Shane's since they'd first arrived there.

The battle went on until evening, when he'd moved wearily toward the tent he'd shared with his wife. He blinked the rest of the memory away and turned back toward the cottage. He would not leave Lindsay the way he'd left Maria.

While he wasn't ready to speak to her, he would watch over her as was his duty as her husband. He climbed a nearby tree that offered a view of the clearing where the cottage set and settled in to stand guard. From his perch, he saw clearly when she stepped out of the house and went to the stream to wash. He averted his gaze, wanting to offer her the privacy she deserved while also making sure no one came upon her unawares.

The dog met up with her, and the two of them had a nice chat—Lindsay asking the mutt where Shane was, and Treun barking her answer. Fortunately, Lindsay didn't understand

and went about breaking her fast and tidying up their small home.

When she went inside, he got down long enough to gather some berries to eat, all the while keeping watch over the woman who'd trusted him to keep her safe. He kept his distance until the sun sank over the horizon and the warm light of the lamp dimmed. He waited a few more minutes before deciding it was safe to go inside.

As he settled on the furs, he wondered what he would do the next day and the next. He couldn't carry on in this way, forever avoiding his wife because he didn't want to have a conversation. This was not the way lairds behaved.

He'd just decided he would do better the next day when, like the night before, she surprised him with his soft voice.

"There is more than enough room in the bed for the both of us," she said.

And damn if his body didn't urge him to take her up on her offer, but he took control and he shook his head, even knowing she couldn't see him.

"I'm fine here, lass. You'll heal faster with plenty of rest." It was true enough, but even more importantly, she'd heal faster without a man tossing and turning in the bed next to her for being so close to her.

And he'd not be tempted from where he lay on the floor.

It would suit them both better to keep their distance. He understood that a marriage was forever. Or was supposed to be. The priest took measures to make that clear in his message and the vows Shane had spoken. But at the time, he was only thinking of what she needed then. She'd be living with him and needed the protection of his name to do so; otherwise, she'd be ruined. And without his name, he'd be unable to stop anyone else from claiming her and forcing her to leave.

But for the rest of his life, he'd be tied to this woman.

And he'd surely not want to spend all his days living like a monk.

He just needed more time.

...

In the morning, Lindsay stayed quiet as Shane gathered his things to leave the cottage. But she stopped him before he could run away for another day.

"Will you come back?" she asked, her voice rough with sleep.

"Aye," he answered with a nod as well. "I'm going to wash and check my snares, but I'll return."

She nodded. It was a new day. She'd spent the day before allowing her mind to run wild. She thought of all the ways she might not measure up to Shane's first wife. But, eventually, she realized it was all for naught. She couldn't change anything. Nor would she, if she had known before they wed.

When she'd been hurt, Shane had helped her, even married her to make sure she was safe and cared for. Shane was hurt as well. While his injuries weren't easily seen, they were there. Deep wounds that might never heal. But Lindsay would stay and help him and make sure he was safe. If that meant listening when he wished to speak and not asking questions when he didn't, that was what she would do.

When he returned with a rabbit to break their fast, she took it from him with a soft smile and went about cooking it for them. She talked about other things. Easy things. And soon she felt him settle and calm.

Over the next few weeks, she and Shane settled into a peaceful existence. The bruises on her arms turned from purple to yellow and then faded into nothing as she healed. She moved around as she always had without wincing or gasping.

Every morning, Shane went to check his traps as she gathered water and started their morning meal. She'd found a few bushes that supplied enough berries for tarts, and she laughed when he ate them down quickly from years of fighting his siblings for the sweets.

They spent their days working side by side, making the small cottage a more comfortable home. Some days, Shane would go to the village to meet with Doran for his training. And in the evening, they'd sit by the fire and read from the few books they owned or share stories with each other.

They never spoke of Maria except for the nights when Shane woke her while calling out her name in pain. Lindsay waited for him to explain, but he never did. She couldn't have asked for anything more. At least until night came and it was time for bed. Then a strange awkwardness fell between them. Uncomfortable silence slithered in as she went behind the screen he'd fashioned for her to change.

From there, she'd slip into the bed while he doused the candles. In the darkness, she could hear him unbuckle his belt and was taunted by the soft sound of his plaid hitting the floor. She listened for the hiss of linen as he pulled his shirt off but didn't hear it. She imagined he slept in his shirt and wondered if that was how he preferred to sleep.

Nothing about their nightly arrangement was how she preferred. She hated to think of Shane sleeping on the hard floor after everything he'd done for her. He'd given her his name, his protection, and now his bed.

And perhaps that wasn't the only reason she wanted him to sleep next to her. Her new husband was pleasing to look at, and she was curious about what it would be like to kiss him—and do more. She'd gathered all her courage to mention the room in the bed that night, insinuating she'd like him to join her.

But in the silence that practically smothered her after

his rejection, her heart had pounded so loud she wondered if he could hear it from across the room where he lay. She'd assumed he was waiting for her to heal. But in the last few days, she'd mentioned many times how wonderful she felt to be back to her old self. And yet, each night she slept alone on the bed that should have been theirs.

It could only mean he had stayed away not because of her injuries but because he didn't want her. She imagined he must still have a loyalty to his first wife and how lying with Lindsay must seem like a betrayal of his vows with Maria. But she couldn't be sure that was how he felt.

Tonight, Lindsay was ready to try again. And she started her plan at dinner by pouring them each a second glass of wine with their meal. She was careful to stand close as she poured and gathered the dishes. She'd seen the way the maids in the Wallace hall had flirted with her father's retainers. She did her best to mimic their ways of flirtation, even going so far as to drop something to the floor so she could bend over to pick it up, giving him a clear look at her breasts.

When they took their seats by the fire, he picked up the book to start up the story he'd been reading, but instead she asked him a question. "Have you lain with anyone since your wife?"

He nearly choked, such was his surprise, and she cursed herself for her impatience. She'd promised herself she would not speak of his first wife and would hold on the conversation until he spoke instead, but she had grown curious. She waited until he collected himself.

"Nay."

"Did you lie with many women before her?"

He cleared his throat and took a large sip of his wine before answering. "I wouldn't say many."

"How many would you say?"

"More than a few, but not many."

"I'll not be angry to know the answer."

"If ye don't plan to be angry, why do you ask?"

"I just wonder of your experience with woman is all."

His brows pulled together. "Do you question my abilities?"

She almost laughed at his disgruntled response, but she held it in. She shrugged. "Nay, I have nothing to go on. 'Tis why I asked the question."

"Six," he said shortly and opened the book again. This time he went so far as to clear his throat and start reading the next passage, but she interrupted.

"Were you in love with any of them before Maria?"

"Why are you asking such things? I don't wish to speak of it. It is irrelevant now."

With another shrug, she answered. "It is relevant to me, your wife. We've asked each other all manner of things as we've been getting to know each other. This is just another thing I wish to know about you. If it is too private, you've only to say so, and I'll let it lie for now. But I do wonder if…she is the reason you don't want me."

He let out a breath and snapped the book closed, setting it on the stand next to his chair. He leaned over, and for a moment she thought he might simply get up and leave, but after another minute or two he sat back and looked at her.

"I imagine it is a natural thing to wonder about. Yes, I loved my wife. Yes, I miss her. Yes, I feel as if being with you in that way would be a betrayal of Maria, which is why I've avoided you. And, yes, I know it might seem silly for me to still feel such things for a woman who is not here when a very beautiful and *alive* woman is within reach, but I can't help it." He ran a hand over his chin. The stubble there rasped against his palm, and once again she wondered what it would feel like against her sensitive skin. "I don't know if I'll ever be ready to move on. Some days it feels impossible, and some days it feels within my grasp. I would hope knowing it's nothing you've done that has kept me from you would help, but it doesn't matter, does it? I'm hurting you, I can see it, but I can't make myself…"

"I wouldn't want you to do something you don't want to do."

"I do want it, Lindsay. I just can't allow it. It feels wrong. You, me, this—it wasn't supposed to happen. I am happy to offer what I can, but that part, I simply cannot." He stood to pace around before shaking his head.

She could see how deeply tortured he was over this and didn't want to push him further. Reaching out, she took his hand in hers and smiled up at him. "This is not something we need to decide tonight. We have time to become comfortable with each other. For you to become comfortable with being with me." She bit her lip a moment before going on. "I want you to know you can speak about her with me."

"I don't wish to speak of her." He ran his hand over his face. "Now, perhaps we should ready for bed. I plan to work with Doran in the morning."

"Very well," she said, not yet ready to give up but knowing she couldn't force him to open up to her. She hummed a tune as she changed for bed. But instead of going straight from the protection of the screen to the bed, she went to the fire to check on the clothing she'd hung there to dry earlier.

She knew her shift was thin and felt her nipples draw tight when she turned away from the warmth to the cooler room. A glance in his direction proved he'd noticed as well, as he stared at her chest. Feeling encouraged by his reaction, she leaned over again to blow out the candle next to the bed. This time she knew he could see everything, for she had no stays on.

He gasped as she crawled across the bed to blow out the other candle, leaving them in darkness that felt almost heaving with the tension running between them. She was smiling as she listened to him drop his belt and plaid, just as he had every night they'd spent together. But tonight, when he settled on the furs, he let out a most unsettled sigh.

"Good night," he said, putting an end to her efforts for the evening. But she was not defeated. They would have years to work things out between them.

Her smile faded as a thread of doubt began to tug loose.

If her father forced her to abandon Shane and marry the laird as promised, they may not have so much time after all.

...

Shane lay still on the floor, despite his urge to move around. He knew well that moving wouldn't settle the unrest, so there was no use of it. It was becoming clear as every day went by that his new wife would not be satisfied with a marriage in name only. She wanted more from him.

He wasn't certain he had more to give, but in the last few days since she'd spoken up about Maria, Shane had begun to feel things when he'd not been able to feel anything but guilt and grief the last year.

It was at this time when he searched for sleep to claim him that his thoughts collided. He had loved Maria. Her free spirit, the way she wasn't afraid to say what she was thinking and call him out to tangle with him. He'd not once seen her back down. He wondered now: if she had run and hid when the French attacked the camp, would she have been spared? He imagined her shouting at the leering soldiers when she should have looked for an escape.

Lindsay had a spirit as well, but it was more reserved, and he thought that would do her well in a violent situation. Not that he'd ever abandon her to face such a thing alone. He'd learned that lesson too well. The quiet continued, but he knew Lindsay wasn't asleep. He could almost hear her waiting for him to reveal some small piece of himself, as he had the past two nights. He'd told her small things about his previous life. He'd even smiled last night at the memories he'd shared.

She'd been right. It did help him to talk about Maria. He found himself eager to tell Lindsay something more significant in the hopes of lifting more of the weight he carried.

"It was my fault she died," he heard a voice saying before he'd given himself permission to speak.

"People often carry guilt for things they feel responsible for, even when there was nothing else that could be done."

He nodded, though it was too dark and too far for her to have seen him. He understood, but that wasn't the case now. He decided to tell her everything and let her judge him.

"A smaller battle broke out at the far edge of camp. It didn't take long for word to spread that the French had come looking for trouble. Ronan had gone to get water, and I knew he would have been close by when the battle broke out. My only thought was to get to my brother and have his back as he had mine the day before. It had grown impossible to remember who had saved whose life the most, but Ronan had saved mine most recently, and I could only think of the debt that needed to be repaid."

"Debt or no, your brother was in danger. That is reason enough to have gone."

He thought about that for a moment and realized she was right.

"Normally, when I went off to battle I paid one of the lads to watch over Maria. To help her carry things and see she was safe. But this came up quickly, so I grabbed up my weapons and ran. I can't recall if I even kissed her in my haste."

He felt a hot tear roll across his temple to be lost in his hair and cleared the pain from his throat.

"It was a ruse. A distraction to pull our attention away so they could raid the camp for food, weapons, and horses. Maria was fierce and wouldn't have given up our meager goods so easily. She paid dearly for it. I shouldn't have left her unprotected. I chose my brother and my men over my wife."

A soft sniff came from the bed, and he realized his wife was crying. He didn't think; he only knew he needed to go to her.

He climbed into bed next to her and pulled her against him. "Shh. I'm sorry. I upset ye," he said while rubbing her back.

He felt her shake her head. "I'm to be comforting you."

He laughed, a real laugh that sounded strange after he'd been so close to those awful memories just moments ago.

"You're doing a fine job of it, lass." It may have sounded like a jest, but it was true. He felt needed and useful as he held Lindsay. And for the first time since Maria died, he felt not so very alone.

He pressed a kiss to the top of her head and felt his heart trip as he breathed in the floral scent of her hair. It seemed the broken thing was not gone after all.

Chapter Ten

Lindsay brushed the tears away, feeling like a goose. She'd wanted to help her husband through his pain, but here he was, helping her. She couldn't even find something to say to ease his guilt, for telling him it wasn't his fault was insignificant and useless.

Somewhere in his heart, he knew the truth—that he'd made a mistake. He'd never have left Maria if he'd known it could have been a trap. But he had convinced himself he was at fault, and she would not change his mind until he was ready to believe it.

The best she could think to do was hold him a bit tighter and hope he understood.

As was common after he'd shared such an intimate part of himself, he faded quickly and drifted into a peaceful sleep. She imagined it would be exhausting carrying around such anger for himself with nowhere to put it.

Except he had found a way to punish himself. He'd rejected her and what happiness they might have by keeping his distance. She'd thought to be patient, to wait for him to eventually drop his guard so she might have the chance to win his heart.

But now she realized the error of this tactic. For he may not ever forgive himself enough to love anyone. Talking with her at night seemed to help him, but a person could not be as open with a stranger as a loved one.

She woke earlier than him the next morning and slipped from the bed to gather her cloak and boots. With Treun by her side, she took the path to the river and gathered the things she needed before going to the rock she had claimed as a special place for thinking. Crushing the berries with a stone, she used the juice to carefully paint the words on the pale stone.

"What do ye think?" she asked the dog, who offered no opinion beyond a cocked ear. But Lindsay realized Tre was responding not to her question but rather the panicked sound of a man yelling her name.

. . .

Shane had woken alone in his bed, and for a moment he had forgotten someone else was supposed to be lying next to him. As soon as he realized Lindsay wasn't there, he sat up and saw she was not in the cottage at all.

His worry began to grow as he stepped out on the porch and looked about their small yard.

"Lindsay?" he shouted and headed for the river, thinking she might have gone to wash and gather water for their morning meal. But when she wasn't at the river, fear took hold.

He recalled the day they'd met, the scrawny lads who'd meant to do her harm. As he rushed through the woods, with branches whipping at his face, he was reminded of what he'd found when he'd returned to camp that day. Maria's body, the blood covering her gown, a smudge of it at her face.

"Lindsay!" he screamed again as he stopped and spun around, listening for her quiet voice and hearing nothing but the pounding of his heart. He'd thought the thing was dead, but it was surely alive once again.

Finally, he heard it. Barking. Treun would be with her.

"I'm here," Lindsay called as he got closer to the rock where she liked to spend time thinking.

Upon seeing her, hale and hearty, his temper took hold. "What caused ye to go off on your own like that? You know well enough what can happen when you wander off alone. Are ye daft, woman?"

"I thought to do something for you, and once I decided, I couldn't wait. I wanted to…help," Lindsay said while using the back of her berry-stained hands to wipe away the tears.

He followed her gaze to the rock where he often found her sitting and saw there were words written.

Maria MacPherson. Beloved wife and friend.

Dear God.

"You said you had to bury her in France with no stone. I thought she should have a proper place so you might come to talk to her. This is the most peaceful place I've found."

She'd given up her own favorite spot for him to mourn his lost love? He turned to ask why she would do such a thing, but she had scooped up Treun and was walking away, leaving him there to grieve.

He took a step closer and then another until he could reach out with a shaky hand to touch the letters Lindsay had carefully applied to the rock. He closed his eyes and imagined Maria standing behind him, waiting.

He took in a deep breath and began speaking.

• • •

Over the next week, Shane spent many mornings away at the rock Lindsay had painted for him. She was glad he was finding good use of it, and she thought it was helping, though she did often find herself wondering what he said to his wife.

She hated that she suffered even the smallest jealousy of the woman Shane had loved—still loved—but she couldn't deny it.

She shook the thought away as she stepped out on the front porch and stared out at the rainy morning. Shane had already gathered water, so she went about breaking her fast. She heard a twig snap and smiled.

"Ye may come have a bite to eat," she called to Doran, who had been set to guarding her while her husband was away. Doran stepped forward with a frown on his face.

"I thought I'd been quiet."

"You were, but Tre gave ye away," she said to ease the young warrior.

"It sure is boring having to watch ye when you don't do anything of note and there's no danger."

"I'm pleased to be boring," she said while handing over a bannock for her cousin.

"I'm sorry," he said quietly while staring at his bread in his hands.

"I don't take offense," she said, but he shook his head.

"Nay, not for calling you boring—for the way I treated you before. When you lived with us."

"I imagine you were only doing what you'd seen your da do with your mother." Bless her aunt's soul for the harsh life she must have lived.

Doran nodded. "My da was a bastard, to be sure, but my ma loved us. I think I was angry at ye for coming to take her place."

She let out a sigh. It seemed she was doing a lot of that lately. Taking the place of someone who was deeply loved.

She wondered if she might ever have her own place.

Later that day, when Shane returned, she noticed a change in him. He was smiling, and his eyes were not so haunted as she'd come to know them.

"Are you well?" she asked.

He smiled wider and nodded. "Aye. I'm better than I have been in some time. The rain washes things clean."

"That's good." She pointed to the pot on the fire. "I've already collected the rabbits and started a stew for our dinner."

"I didn't wed ye to make you my servant," he said as water dripped off the ends of his hair.

"I know. You married me to protect me. I am fully aware of that. But I might as well be of some use. I know you do not want me. I am not a suitable replacement for what you once had. I am not like her. I am… I'm nothing but rabbit stew."

His eyes went wide as he dropped his hand to his side.

"You are…*rabbit stew*?" Of course he was confused—she was making no sense. But she couldn't stop herself.

"I am boring. Something you are grateful for because it is all you have at hand, but not something you truly desire. Not something with flavor and…spices."

His brows smashed together for a moment, and then, as she watched, he seemed to understand.

"Ye don't seem to know how much I enjoy rabbit stew. Coming home, the scent of it relaxes me. Makes me happy to be home, where I'm safe and comforted. And I would gladly have it every day and never tire of it." He rubbed his chin. "I'm running out of things to say about stew, so might I just tell ye what I like about you?"

She hung her head, embarrassed for leading them into this ridiculous conversation.

"I like that you are here when I wake up in the morning and come home in the evening. Seeing you gives me peace.

Talking with you gives me comfort. You are warmth."

"Warmth when you once had heat."

"It was wrong of me to tell you about Maria."

She didn't think it was possible for her to feel worse, but she did. She shook her head. "Nay. It was not wrong of you to tell me about her."

"You're upset and making comparisons when the two of you couldn't be any more different."

She did not feel the bite to his words she'd felt when he'd said as much earlier. She was not Maria and never planned to be. She was herself and was generally pleased with that. She knew Shane had loved his wife, while Lindsay was no more than an obligation. She didn't begrudge him his feelings for Maria. She looked him in the eye and did her best to explain.

"I don't wish her to be less to you. I just wish I was… more."

...

Shane felt her words in the center of his chest as if he'd just taken a hit with a club. She wanted to be more to him, when she was quickly becoming everything. So much so, it frightened him.

Earlier in the day, when he'd been sitting in the rain in front of Maria's stone, he'd told her about Lindsay and how she'd helped him start to heal. How Lindsay had given him a sacred place and encouraged him to remember Maria. And sitting there drenched and a bit chilly, he realized he was smiling as he spoke of Lindsay.

Lindsay.

Every response and reaction seemed the exact opposite of what he would have expected from Maria. To the point he wasn't sure how he could have loved Maria as fiercely as he'd thought when he enjoyed Lindsay's steady patience so much.

He thought he had a preference, but he'd come to realize while talking to a stone in the middle of the forest that he could enjoy both extremes equally. Perhaps he'd needed different things at certain times in his life. When he was young and reckless, he'd embraced Maria's spirit. And now that he was more mature yet unsure of his place, he needed the calm confidence of Lindsay.

He could love Maria and still care for Lindsay. But Lindsay just told him in her own way that caring for her was not enough. She wanted more. He didn't know if he was capable of such a thing, but he was certain it couldn't happen if he continued to keep this distance between them. He'd thought to punish himself by not allowing himself to be happy with another woman, but it was Lindsay who was hurting. He owed it to her to do better, to try.

And that night, he decided to do just that. As was becoming common, his wife changed behind the screen and walked out wearing only her thin shift that did nothing to hide the slight curves of her body from the light. Rather than glance away, he watched her.

She was tempting him. What he didn't know was if she was doing it on purpose or was just naturally alluring. Or perhaps it was knowing he didn't plan to deny himself anymore. Once she was settled in bed, he got in next to her but didn't turn down the lamp to go to sleep. Instead, he looked at her, studying every detail of her face. He'd been near her every day over the last weeks, but now he was actually seeing her.

"What caused that scar there under your left eye?" he asked randomly, wanting to get to know her better.

"Is it unsightly?" she asked, brushing a fingertip over the perfect imperfection.

"Nay. Not at all. I only wonder how you came by it."

"My cousin Meaghan and I were chasing each other in the woods, and I fell. A stick got me on the way down. It could have been much worse."

"Aye." He nodded and realized that their conversation had come to an abrupt end. Perhaps he could ask her about the type of stick it was? Or about her cousin. Why was it so difficult to try to navigate this space between them?

"Is Meaghan older or younger than ye?"

"She's a few months younger. My father's brother's daughter."

Another Cameron. He managed not to frown this time.

"She's recently married."

He nodded and realized once again they'd run out of things to discuss.

"What about your scars?" she asked, seeming as desperate as he to keep their conversation going.

He laughed. "There are too many to count, let alone remember how I received them all."

"Then tell me of the ones you can recall."

He nodded and went on telling her tales of his awkward youth that caused a number of marks upon his skin as he grew into his larger frame. About the line across his chin where he'd been thrown from a horse. When he nearly forgot himself and pulled up his shirt—the only clothing he wore—he realized this path was fraught with problems.

They fell into silence once more. Eventually, while he was grasping for things to talk about, her breathing slowed in sleep and he released a sigh and outened the light.

He'd made a fine start tonight, but there was still much work to be done.

Like many nights, his pleasant dreams turned to the war, finding Maria, and eventually to that night in his room when he woke choking on smoke, unable to breathe. The feeling of being trapped gripped his throat, cutting off whatever air was left until he woke up gasping for breath, Lindsay's hand on his shoulder.

"You're having a bad dream," she said.

He coughed a few times as if clearing the imaginary smoke from his lungs. "I'm sorry I woke you."

"Do you want to talk about it?" It was nothing they hadn't already discussed, so he shook his head.

"Nay. Go back to sleep."

"Very well." But instead of pulling away, she came closer. "Sleep well," she whispered.

She leaned in to kiss him on the cheek, and in a moment of weakness he turned his head so her kiss found its home against his lips rather than his face. The shock of it caught them both off guard, but rather than pull away as he felt he should, he leaned closer and took her lips once more.

A niggling voice in the back of his mind scolded him for taking such pleasure from a woman who was not Maria, but he pushed back, knowing the truth. Lindsay was his wife. He wasn't doing anything he shouldn't.

He questioned whether or not it was fair for him to be allowed to move on with someone else, but he only pulled Lindsay closer to fend off his worries. When that wasn't enough, his hands found their way to her hips and held her tighter to him. She willingly went where he guided her as his tongue slipped into her mouth. She let out a small gasp of surprise before doing the same and meeting his touch with her own.

It wasn't until her thigh touched his cock that he realized how close he was to losing control. "Lindsay," he said with a voice he barely recognized.

"Yes," she answered, though he didn't think she was answering to her name so much as a question he hadn't asked aloud. She was caught up in the same desire he was. He wanted to keep going, to take what she offered, to lose himself in her body. But his guilt reared up, stealing his breath.

He pushed her away as he gasped for air much like he

had in his dream. He couldn't breathe. He grabbed up his kilt and boots and rushed for the door, leaving her in their bed. Outside, he looked up at the starry sky and cursed. He felt he was being ripped in two, wanting to honor the wife he'd lost and respect the wife he had.

What he was doing may not have been wrong, but it didn't feel entirely right, either.

Chapter Eleven

Lindsay woke to an empty cottage. Well, empty except for Treun, who was patiently waiting by the door to be let out. She guessed Shane was already in the village working with Doran or out visiting the rock.

Memories from the night before rushed in at the thought of her husband, and her face went warm as she remembered the kisses they'd shared. It had been wonderful. So much so, she'd wanted more, but he'd stopped and left as if something were chasing him.

Likely, it was guilt.

She didn't know what else to do for him. It would take time for him to be ready to move on, and she would need to be patient, even if she wasn't certain how much time they had.

After finishing the cleaning of their home, she decided to go into the village to see if any of her things were still at her uncle's cottage. She only had the one dress, and while the other dresses hadn't been much better than the one she wore, they were better than nothing.

Her mouth pinched in anger when she thought of her

maid. If she ever got her hands on the girl… The dresses were one thing, but the jewels were much harder to replace. They'd belonged to her father's mother and were a gift from her father. One of the few times he'd seemed pleased to have a daughter to dote upon. When he learned they were lost, he would be very disappointed in her.

But surely not as disappointed as he'd be when he found out she was married to a soldier.

The cottage she'd shared with her uncle and cousins was dark and quiet for once. She threw the fabric back from the window to let the light in and took in the dusty room. The table stood in the center of the space, with a stub of a candle and knotted bundle of twine upon it. In the far corner, where she'd kept her things, she found nothing. Not even a scrap of fabric.

Feeling a familiar sense of dread, she quickly left the cottage, almost desperate to get back to the sun, where the light would scatter the ghosts of that place. Hearing the cracking of wood against wood, she found two familiar men in the field next to the village. She stopped to watch as Shane and Doran sparred, distracted by the way her husband moved out of range of Doran's practice sword, as well as the way his brown hair curled at the ends when dampened with sweat.

At the sound of a throat clearing, she turned to a smiling woman she'd seen with the butcher.

"Good day to ye, miss. A letter arrived for Randall, but I wasn't sure what to do with it."

"I will take it," Lindsay said, knowing when she spotted the seal that the letter was for her rather than her uncle anyway.

The woman nodded. "Well, then, I should be getting back."

Lindsay thanked the woman absently as she flipped the letter over and recognized the writing as that of her father.

When she was alone, she broke the seal and opened the letter.

Dear Daughter,

I will arrive after harvest to see to the matter of your marriage to the MacPherson laird. I will bring your belongings at that time.

I received your letter requesting passage back home to Riccarton, but there is no reason to make the trip. Make your way to the castle to prepare for the festivities. I will join you soon.

Until then,

DW

He'd signed the letter as he always did, with the larger-than-life *D* for Donald and the swooping *W* for Wallace. She read it again and a third time. With each pass, she realized how thoroughly trapped she was.

"What have I done?" she muttered to herself as she looked around, almost confused to find she was still where she'd been standing when it seemed everything in her life had suddenly turned upside down.

She was promised to the MacPherson laird, but she was already married to one of his warriors. What would the man do to Shane when he found out? They were only starting to know each other. She tossed the letter into a nearby fire and turned for home. She would need to tell Shane the truth and let him decide what they should do. They hadn't consummated the marriage. It wasn't too late to have their vows annulled.

Perhaps she could make her way to the MacKenzies. Her cousin Meaghan lived there with her new husband. But wouldn't her father simply track her down and bring her back to face this problem? With more anger for his efforts?

She considered her options as she made her way to the path that led to her new home. She found her husband coming in from the field in which he'd been sparring with her cousin moments ago. He held out a small bouquet of flowers he must have picked as she'd stood there reading her father's missive. With his full lips pulled up into a dashing smile, he held out his gift.

"I'm sorry for running off as I did last night," he said. "I am trying, Lindsay. Please, give me more time."

All thoughts of telling him what waited for her or ending their marriage drifted away as the scent of heather and daisies surrounded her. It was wrong. She didn't belong to him because she was promised to another. What would happen if he managed to care for her only to have her taken away from him? He'd lost so much already. But she wanted to be Shane's wife a little while longer. While it was still her choice to make, she was choosing him. Harvest was still a few months away yet. She had time.

"Are you well? You seem pale," he said, concern pulling his brows together.

"Aye." She nodded and then let out a sigh. "We have time."

"What were you doing in there?" He nodded toward the shack.

"It seems my uncle must have sold the rest of my dresses. I'm afraid I only have this one."

He tilted his head and winced. "It's not much to speak of."

She laughed and nodded in agreement. There was no defense of the tattered garment that showed her stocking-clad ankles. It was most indecent.

"I was off to the village to purchase cheese. Come with me so ye can pick out some fabric to make new gowns," he said as if it was the easiest thing in the world.

"I couldn't ask you to do that," she said quickly while shaking her head. It was one thing to marry a man she wouldn't be allowed to keep; to allow him to spend his money on things for her was another matter altogether.

"Am I your husband, Lindsay?"

"Aye." She couldn't help the bit of sadness that colored the word. He was her husband for now.

"As your husband, it is my responsibility to keep ye fed and clothed, is it not?"

This would have been the perfect opportunity to tell him everything. Spare him from this grave mistake she'd gotten them into. Tell him he was destined to lose another wife. But when he smiled at her in that way, she was unable to speak. He had only begun to smile; she wouldn't steal his happiness. She was weak. She was selfish. She was falling for this man.

He selected a blue fabric as well as green. "I can't decide which will look better on you, so you'll have them both," he said as he paid the merchant.

She opened her mouth to protest, but he pressed his finger to her lips.

"Unless the words out of your mouth are a simple thank-you, you'd do better to keep them to yourself. I'll not argue with you again over this."

"Very well. Thank you."

He bought them a bit of cheese and led them back to the cottage. She set the beautiful fabric on the chair where she would start working on the gowns after the evening meal.

"I planned to see about catching us some fish for supper. Would you like to go with me?"

"You don't wish to be alone to visit the stone?" she asked in surprise. He'd gone every day since she'd painted it.

He shook his head. "Not today."

She fairly beamed at him. It was silly to think he had

chosen her over Maria, but she couldn't help but feel she had won some precious gift. Every second she spent with him made it easier to forget about her future. The letter was gone as if it had never existed. She wished the butcher's wife hadn't found her to deliver it. She would've been free to go on not knowing what fate awaited her.

She smiled at her husband. "Aye. I would like to join you."

Tre followed along and hopped up on a log with her as they looked out at the river. Shane caught three trout, and she went about fixing them after he cleaned them.

What they didn't finish became a nice meal for the dog after she'd made sure there were no bones. She began working on her gowns, cutting the first pieces of fabric and sewing them together. Shane read from the book while she worked, and though it was a nice way to spend the evening, she knew what waited for her at bedtime. Or rather what did not.

He'd said nothing else about the kisses they'd shared. He'd apologized for leaving so abruptly. She knew he must feel a great amount of guilt in being able to move on when his wife could not. While Lindsay didn't agree that he was to blame for what happened, his opinion was what mattered.

He'd asked her for time, and for as long as she could, she'd give it to him. She did hope it wouldn't take too long, for she wanted whatever happened after kissing.

Sometime later, Lindsay blinked hard, trying to get her tired eyes to focus on the small stitches, but she could barely keep her eyes open. "I believe I'm done for tonight. I should be able to finish tomorrow," she announced as she stood and stretched her stiff back.

"Aye. We shouldn't do such things in the low light." He stood as well, and as they moved to pass each other, they ended up getting in each other's way instead. They laughed and moved only to find their paths blocked once again.

"I'll just go this way." She announced her plan to end their bumbling. But this time he stood in her way with intent green eyes studying her face. She reached up as he bent to kiss her, and like the night before, he placed his hands on her hips, guiding her body toward his.

They kissed for what felt like hours before he set her away from him.

"Pardon me." And with that, he moved around her toward the door. "I must take the dog out," he said.

When the door shut, she turned to the little dog by her feet. Treun looked up at her, blinking.

"It seems he forgot ye in his mad dash to escape me."

The door opened again.

"Treun! Come!" When the dog was through the door, it shut once more.

Lindsay sighed. She didn't know how much time they had together, but she hoped it was enough.

• • •

Shane frowned at the little dog, though it wasn't her fault he'd made such a fool of himself in his hurry to get out of the house. Away from his wife, to where he was safe from temptation.

"She certainly isn't making it easy for me," he said to his furry companion. "And I don't have the strength to fight my own passions and hers as well."

But giving in before he felt comfortable would only bring more guilt and regret. He didn't know if he could bear even more guilt heaped upon his shoulders.

Tre looked up at him but offered no suggestion on what to do. But that was the crux of the problem. It wasn't necessarily the wrong thing, was it? They were married before God and the church. It was expected of him to take his wife to his bed.

One might even say it was his duty as her husband. But they hadn't planned to have a real marriage. He'd given her his name to protect her—and to ease some of his guilt by helping a woman who needed him.

He liked Lindsay more each day he was with her, which was why he'd run away from her kisses yet again. He'd first avoided being with her because he didn't think it would be fair to her to do so while thinking about Maria. But now… now he feared the guilt he'd feel if he didn't think of Maria at all.

Anyone hearing his worries would no doubt think him mad, the way his thoughts flipped back and forth. Fear he wouldn't be able to care for Lindsay, guilt when he did.

"I only promised protection. Nothing else," he said to no one, for the dog had run off, leaving him to his fretting.

When the sky opened up and poured down upon him, Treun made a run for shelter back at the house. He'd faced lines of French muskets and the worst pain a person could endure; he shouldn't be afraid of one Scottish lass. With a sigh, he turned to head back to the cottage. It was best to have this conversation and get everything out in the open.

"You sure picked a bad time for a walk," Lindsay said with a smile as he came in and shook the rain from his hair.

"Aye. I wouldn't say I picked it. But I'm back now, and I think we should see to straightening some things between us."

She nodded, and as he watched, she caught her bottom lip between her teeth, nervously calling attention to the soft flesh he still remembered vividly against his mouth.

"I am trying to do the right thing," he said. "And you…"

Are too tempting by half.

Will be the death of me.

Make me want to carry you off to my bed and keep you there for days.

Bring me joy when I don't deserve to be happy.

He didn't say any of those things. He waited for her to join in the conversation, but she remained silent.

"And you're making it difficult for me to know what is right." As soon as the words were out, he felt like an arse. Was he blaming her? He tried again. "I don't mean to make it sound like you've done anything wrong. You certainly haven't. I'm just not…ready."

She nodded. "I'll be here when you are, however long that may take." She looked away from him. He was no stranger to guilt, which might be why he saw it so easily in Lindsay's eyes. He didn't know which part of her statement was untrue, but he was sure she'd just lied to him.

Chapter Twelve

Lindsay didn't say anything else as she readied for bed. She worried if she spoke at all she might not be able to stop herself from telling him everything. She wasn't a convincing liar, and she didn't think she'd convinced Shane.

She lay there in the darkness, trying to hold in the truth. Rather than think on what might happen after harvest when her father arrived, she focused on how it had felt to kiss Shane. It was truly the most enjoyable thing she'd ever done. But she would do her best to avoid those heated glances that had them reaching for each other.

She knew she wasn't alone in wanting. Shane had been equally as eager as she to continue. But she also knew her husband was healing from a great loss. She'd thought herself brave in leaving her home with only a maid and a few outriders. How many young women preferred to stay behind the safety of their castle walls?

She'd learned soon enough that her adventure was not as exciting as she'd planned. That the world was filled with danger. But this man made her glad she'd taken the risk. She couldn't go back behind the wall now.

When her father came and demanded she marry the laird, she'd need to change his mind. Even if her da hated her, she'd fight to keep Shane. To stay with him, so they would have enough time to be the couple she believed they could be. Have the love she knew was brewing in them.

The very thought of standing up to her father made her stomach twist into knots.

She knew well enough how one stern look from him would send her to tears. She'd earned his ire last summer when she didn't marry the Fletcher heir. That had been the silly fears of a girl, while this was so much more. But to her father it would seem the same. His rebellious daughter causing him disgrace yet again.

Unable to sleep when her mind refused to settle, she tossed off the coverlet and sat up.

When he sat up as well, she jumped. "I thought you were sleeping."

"Nay," he said sadly as he went to the fire to light a rush. With two candles burning, he turned to her. "Do you ever feel you think too much about something? And that it would be best just to stop thinking altogether?"

For a moment, she wondered if he knew what she'd been worrying over, but of course he couldn't. She considered his words and thought he must be referring to the time he'd asked for. How he'd told her he wasn't ready.

"Do you wish to stop thinking about whether you're ready for more with me?" she asked. When the only answer was a low groan, she spoke again. She didn't want to push him into something he might regret, but she also didn't want to lose her only chance to be with him because they waited too long.

"I'm not sure of everything that happens between a husband and wife further than kissing, but I would like to know that pleasure with you. I think whether you're ready or not, you want it as well." There. She'd not minced words. She'd stated what she wanted clearly, and if he turned her away because he needed more time, she would find a way to respect that.

"I lie here next to you and think about what is right and wrong, but I find no answers. And all the thinking doesn't stop me from wanting you."

He wanted her. Taking her hand, he drew her fingers to his lips, where he placed a soft kiss upon them. For all her courage just moments ago, she shook with nervous excitement. With the lightest of touches, he traced his fingertips along her cheek, across the edge of her bottom lip, over her chin, down her throat to her collarbone, then lower to circle the nipple that was peaked through her thin night rail. She drew in a shaky breath and looked up at him again. They shared a small smile, and she relaxed.

There was nothing to be afraid of. Whatever happened next, it would be amazing because it was with Shane. Her husband.

He leaned down slowly as if he was afraid to startle her, but now that they had confessed their desire for each other, she didn't want to wait or go slow. Instead, she leaned up to meet his lips.

With a groan of happiness, she opened her mouth to allow his tongue to delve inside as she explored with her own. It wasn't a sweet peck on the lips. He pulled her close, her chest pressing against his, and wrapped his arms around her. His hands rested below the small of her back and drifted lower.

Rubbing her hands over his chest, she eased her arms to his shoulder so her fingers could play in his long locks. She loved the way his lips trailed over her neck and decided to do the same to him, touching his skin with her tongue and even her teeth. When she caused him to gasp, she embraced her power. This wasn't just about him seducing her. She'd tempted him until he could no longer resist.

He pulled his shirt over his head and tossed it aside. She stepped back to look at him, noticing the sculpted lines of his chest and stomach. His nipples, though smaller than her own, had responded similarly into tight nubs. Wondering if they might be as sensitive as her own were, she reached out and caressed one with the tip of her finger. He sucked in a quick breath and kissed her again.

Her shift was thin, but at the moment it felt like the fabric was keeping them too far apart. She needed to take it off, but her hands and arms got tangled in the sleeves. Stepping back, Shane helped free her from the gown, and then he just stood there holding it in one hand as he stared, his gaze traveling from her toes up her body to stop when he was looking into her eyes.

The green in his gaze burned brighter than she'd ever seen. She took her turn to look him over. She'd seen his chest, but this was the first time she got a good look at the part of him that had been nudging her in the stomach. She must've looked distraught, for he chuckled.

"What is that look?" he asked. "You don't seem impressed."

She felt her cheeks flame with heat. They were standing before each other, naked; she didn't know why she would be embarrassed now. "I'm sorry. I wasn't sure what to expect. I thought it would seem threatening, but it's not." She shook her head and closed her eyes. "Forgive me. I'm being ridiculous."

He smiled and rested his hands on her bare hips, his touch sending a different kind of warmth through her body. "You're not ridiculous. I'm glad you didn't feel the need to run from the cottage screaming because you were terrified."

He was smiling when he kissed her, and her own lips were still pulled up in a grin, making the kiss more exciting with the intimacy of the moment. She wouldn't have thought laughter or smiles would have played a part in such a serious situation, but it went a long way to making her feel more at ease. But the kiss didn't stay light and fun—it transformed into a heated fusion between them. This time, when he pulled her against him, her nipples grazed his bare skin, and she trembled with excitement.

His hands gripped her arse and pulled her closer still. The rigid member throbbed between them. And she felt some part of her, low in her stomach, flutter as if in answer. He leaned on the bed and pulled her down with him, and she was relieved she no longer had to worry about how she would remain standing. It was an easy thing to run her legs over his as he kissed her neck, her collarbone, and finally her breast.

She didn't feel like she could get enough air into her lungs when his tongue traced around her nipple a moment before his lips surrounded it and he sucked her deeper into his mouth. She may have said something or made some noise of appreciation, but she couldn't be sure, for her blood was rushing through her body and all she could hear was her heartbeat.

She squirmed and moved, unable to stop herself. She didn't know what to ask of him, but fortunately she didn't need to. He kissed lower, to her stomach, and then lower still, his lips following his touch. When his fingers moved between her legs, she was surprised to realize she had grown wet in the area she was most in need. As if hearing her thoughts, he rubbed his fingers in the very place she ached. Each caress both soothed and ignited her desire for more.

That was the word she repeated unknowingly. *More.*

His fingers slipped inside of her, first one and then another when she cried again for more. But still, it wasn't enough. Then he kissed her in the place where his fingers explored, and she jerked up nearly into a sitting position only to sag back down to the mattress as he continued flicking and rubbing his tongue over her most sensitive places.

She tossed her head restlessly for a few more moments before she felt herself settling into a rhythm that matched his. Anticipating each touch, she was able to expect it, and the growing desire continued to build until she could no longer contain it. She wanted to ask him what was happening to her, but she was beyond words. And as she drifted over the edge, everything fell silent, and she was lost.

• • •

Shane smiled smugly as Lindsay succumbed to her pleasure at his touch. She was beyond beautiful with the flush on her cheeks, the moisture on her lips from his kiss, and the sheer bliss on her face as she throbbed with her climax around his fingers. He wanted to be inside her, but he waited until she returned to him, her eyelids fluttering open.

"I had no idea I could feel so…" Her words trailed off on a contented sigh as she blinked again and smiled. "That was what I had been aching for. But I didn't know."

He watched as her brows creased into confusion. She looked down at his body where he was still hard and aching for her and shook her head.

"I don't understand. I thought what was to happen was to be with…" Rather than say the word "cock," she merely nodded toward it, which made him smile.

"Yes. That is how it is done. What you experienced was the prelude."

Her eyes went wide. "There's more? More than what I have already experienced?"

"More of the same. Only better."

"Better?" She shook her head. "I'm not sure how anything could be better than that." She tilted her head. "Though I'd certainly be willing to try."

She reached for him, and he went willingly into her arms, placing kisses everywhere his lips touched her skin and making her giggle in certain areas. When he was poised at her warm entrance, he kissed her slower, more tenderly.

"This first time might cause a bit of pain. I'm sorry for it. I can only promise to be quick about it and then make it up to you."

She nodded and squeezed his shoulders as if she was bracing herself for attack. He hoped it wouldn't be as bad as that. He was eager to push his way into her body but just as unwilling to hurt this trusting lass who had given him patience and understanding when he needed it most. He kissed her slowly until her breathing came as quick as his own and she was as aroused as she had been earlier.

She made a soft sound of encouragement, and her legs tightened around his hips, pulling him in. He didn't need any more of a welcome than that. He pressed forward and held when she gasped and hissed in a breath. He fought his body's impulse to move until she relaxed and met his eyes, silently telling him she was well enough to continue. She even graced him with her beautiful smile when he moved out and back in.

"Has the pain gone?" When she nodded, it was as if she'd given him permission to let loose his reins. He clasped her closer as he moved in and out of her body, claiming her as his own, until he thrust into her one last time and gave in to his release.

He collapsed next to her, waiting for the guilt, the sense of wrongness he'd expected to feel when he finally took this step with Lindsay. But it didn't come. She'd wanted them to feel good, and he had. It was clear from the smile on her face that she had as well.

He hadn't allowed himself to think of his times with Maria. Hadn't allowed memories of her when he was with

Lindsay. They were so different, there was nothing to compare. And he wouldn't do either of them the disservice of attempting to.

He'd loved Maria dearly, but it was time for him to move on. He'd never forget her, but now he realized he didn't have to forget Maria to have a future with Lindsay.

He hoped that would always be the case.

Chapter Thirteen

Lindsay's body was tired and sore from being with Shane multiple times the night before as well as the three nights before that, but as early-morning light came through the window, she couldn't deny she wanted him yet again.

She worried that perhaps something had broken inside of her. That all she could think of was being naked with her husband in the bed they shared. But as he kissed her neck and caressed her hip, she found she didn't mind at all.

If she was to spend the rest of her days just like this, she would gladly embrace her future.

She never wanted to leave his side. She still worried about her fate, as she had before—as far as what might happen when her father arrived and she was not waiting at the castle to wed the laird—but as for that, she'd come up with a plan.

Or rather no plan at all. She would stay right where she was as Shane's wife. She hadn't written back to her father to tell him of her nuptials. Lindsay Wallace was no more. When her father showed up at the castle, the MacPherson laird would report she'd never arrived. Any investigation at the village would yield the news that Randall MacPherson had moved on, and as for his niece… It would be an easy thing to simply disappear. At least until the laird married someone else and she was safe.

The plan wasn't perfect, nor was it without a fair amount of guilt, but it would allow her to keep her husband.

Now that her husband was fully awake, he pulled her on top of him and smiled up at her as his hands on her hips encouraged her movements.

She found she enjoyed this position. Actually, she enjoyed every position so far, but perhaps this one a little more because she was in control and there was nothing more beautiful in the world than seeing the look on Shane's face when he begged her to move faster. She'd never thought she would hold enough power to make such a formidable man beg. But she loved it.

His body pressed up from the bed to get deeper, something she wanted as much as he. He called out her name seconds before he stilled and the warmth from his body pulsed into hers, tipping her over the edge into her own pleasure.

A few moments later, she opened her eyes to see she had collapsed on Shane's chest and his warm arms had wrapped around her body. From the direction of the light, she realized it must have been longer than a few moments. Only the dog snuffling at the door roused her enough to get up. If Tre wasn't let in, she'd start barking, and that would wake her sleeping husband.

"Shh," she told the little dog as she pulled on her new gown and went about starting the fire to make everyone their morning meal. "Let us check the snares while he rests."

Outside, she breathed in the cooler morning air and smiled up at the sunshine coming through the trees, casting everything in a greenish tint. Had the world always looked so lovely and she hadn't noticed? She hummed as she walked along the path behind the cottage. As was normal, Tre ran off to do her own investigating.

Not paying attention, she paused when she saw she'd come across the stone bearing Maria's name. *Beloved wife and friend.* The first night they'd lain together, she'd wondered if Shane had been in pain. She'd asked, and he'd simply smiled at her and said he was fine. She'd searched his eyes for any sign he was keeping the truth from her but found only joy where guilt and pain had been.

She'd never wish for him to forget Maria, but Lindsay was glad he'd found happiness. She was lost in her thoughts until she heard the low timber of voices close by. Her first instinct was to seek out the visitors and greet them, but she kept quiet as she moved behind a tree.

"I was sure I'd seen her go this way. I'm telling you, it's the same lass we caught a few weeks ago."

"The one ye let get away."

"I took a blade to the shoulder, and it still hasna healed right. *You* were the one who left me there to get bashed in the skull."

These were the men who had attacked her the first time she met Shane, when he'd come to her call.

Her heart pounded, and her palms went slick with fear. She had no weapon save the small knife she carried to clean the rabbits they'd caught. She gripped it tight, feeling it slip against her damp skin.

They were looking for her.

Knowing that kept her frozen against the base of the tree until they had passed and she could no longer hear their bickering. It wasn't until Tre came back and she could hear Shane yelling her name that she finally moved.

"I'm here!" she said when he was close. She saw the relief on his face as he came to help her to her feet.

"Are you well? I've been calling for you for some time. I

grew worried when you didn't return."

"I'm sorry. I'm fine." She held up the rabbits, but her attempt to brush off her fear didn't work, as the game quivered in her shaking hands.

"What has happened?"

"The men from that first day saw me. But I hid and they didn't find me. It startled me is all." For her it was a brief scare, but for Shane and the horror he'd lived through, he was more than shaken.

He looked toward the path that led to the river with pure rage. She placed her hand on his arm to stay him from going off to look for the men. She didn't need more trouble with that lot. "I'm fine."

"You shouldn't have gone out without me. It's my duty to protect you." She knew how seriously he took that duty and what had happened when he had not fulfilled it. But it was time he knew he was not at fault for what happened to Maria.

"You can't protect me every moment against everything, Shane."

"It's my duty," he repeated as if it were a spell.

She shook her head. "Nay. I don't expect it. And I'm certain Maria didn't, either."

"Don't speak of her," he snapped, but she reached up and touched the hard edge of his jaw as it jerked.

"I will speak of her. And you need to speak of her as well. This guilt has twisted your grief so it won't allow you to think of her with joy. You need to forgive yourself for what happened."

"I left her. I shouldn't have."

"And what if you hadn't left? What if you'd been there when the French raided the camp? Could you have fought them all and saved her, or would you have been struck down as well?"

He didn't answer.

"Things happen to people we love—horrible things. But we can't stop that sometimes. And turning it upon yourself in this way means she doesn't get the honor she's due."

He looked startled at this but said nothing yet again.

"Maria deserves to be remembered with a smile and love. Not as a way to punish yourself."

He pressed his lips together, and she waited for him to yell at her for overstepping.

It took a few more minutes for him to finally nod and let out a breath. "You're right. I need to do better." He ran both hands through his hair, clenching and pulling slightly before he seemed to release the tension she'd come to expect. "Let's go home." He took the rabbits from her, and with his arm around her shoulders, he guided her back to the cottage.

When she looked up at him, he smiled down at her.

"Thank ye," he said.

She leaned her head against his wide chest and allowed him to hold her close. She understood his need to protect her. To make amends for the wife he'd lost. But it was too much for him to continue to carry.

She'd been afraid today when she encountered the men. Now, she realized she'd never felt so safe as she did in his arms. This clan might not be one she wished to join, and she hadn't wanted to make a home here. But this man was different. She could trust him. Even if he couldn't trust her in return.

・・・

Shane wanted nothing more than to tuck his wife away in the cottage so he could track down the men who'd frightened her, but as he kissed her trembling hand, he knew he needed to stay with her. Going off to fight had been the wrong choice before. He'd not make the same mistake again.

It was in that moment when giving up what he wanted in exchange for what she needed that he realized how dear she'd come to be to him. He'd thought only to provide tangible things like food, clothing, and a safe place to rest her head. Now he felt more than just a duty. Things he wouldn't have thought he had left to give again. When she called upon him, he'd been there for her rather than give in to rage and guilt.

Marriage, he had learned, was not to be one-sided. Growing up like he did, with his father fawning over Deirdre's every whim, dressing her in the latest fashions, and gifting her with gems they couldn't afford, he'd expected to give everything and get little in return. But he'd been lucky both times. Even now, he could tell Lindsay wanted him as much as he wanted her. Though he was surprised to see the fierceness of her need after the events of the morning. He would have expected that after being frightened, she wouldn't want any man's touch.

He'd been wrong. Her hands still trembled as she reached for the belt at his waist, but he didn't consider stopping her. There'd been times in France after a particularly close call that he'd needed to know he was alive. Lindsay had done that for him after a year of feeling dead inside.

"I need ye," she whispered against his bare chest after he'd pulled off his shirt.

He kissed her. "I'll make sure you have everything you need."

She smiled back and then slid down to her knees to take him into her warm mouth, shocking him enough to pull away.

"Where the devil did you learn such a thing?" he asked his innocent wife. He'd known she'd been innocent, had seen the evidence of it on their linens. But this was not a skill of a virgin bride.

"You don't like it?" She tilted her head to the side. "I once saw a maid doing it to a man in the stables, and he seemed to like it. But if you don't…"

He blinked himself back into his right mind. Had he just stopped her? "Bloody hell," he murmured under his breath before attempting to fix the mess he'd made. "I do like it. I didn't think it was something a wife did—more that it was done by…" He couldn't very well say the word "whore" in front of his wife, especially not implying she was doing the act of one. That would be no way to ever have her do it again.

"It's wrong?" she asked, hurt clear on her face.

He couldn't shake his head enough. He feared it would pop off from his neck. "Nay. Nothing is wrong between us. So long as we both agree to it and it makes us happy, it is allowed."

"Did…?" She stopped speaking and bit her lip, but he didn't need her to finish her thought to know where it had been. Had Maria done such a thing? He'd been doing a fair job of not thinking of his late wife while in bed with his present one, but it seemed Lindsay still worried.

"What we do together is between us alone. Do you understand? It must be that way."

She nodded. "Did what I was doing a moment ago make you happy?"

Christ, the lass would kill him. "It made me very happy. So long as it makes you happy, we could…" He gestured dumbly with his hand at his groin.

"We could stop discussing it and get back to it?" she said with a saucy smile on her swollen lips.

"Aye," he answered, but she had already knelt in front of him again and began where she'd left off. As she eagerly brought on his release, he could only think of how this didn't feel wrong like he'd imagined. And how glad he was for that.

Over the next week, they found the perfect balance of seeing to the duties of their home and giving in to their passions. After he'd seen how pleased she was to take him by surprise, he did his best to surprise her with different positions and varying places. His little vixen embraced each one, especially the ones in which she was in control.

He was more than happy to surrender.

He glanced over at the bonny woman sleeping next to him. He couldn't believe this was his life. He was almost afraid to blink for fear she would be gone if he looked away. The familiar fear gripped him, bringing a cool sweat to his spine. He'd felt this way before, and it had caused him a pain so severe he'd barely survived. If he lost Lindsay…

Nay. He'd protect her. He'd not let her fall to the same fate as Maria. But as he tried to calm his pounding heart, he remembered a threat that remained. Something no amount of protection would be able to save them from. His duty as laird.

What would happen when he told her the truth and they moved to the castle? Would she hate him for forcing her into such a life? One she wasn't prepared for. When her eyes opened and a smile pulled across her beautiful lips, he made love to her slowly and purposefully, telling her all the things he couldn't say out loud.

Please forgive me. Please don't leave me.

When he'd claimed her climax and took his own release, they sprawled lazily across the bed until the dog began whining at the door for her morning meal. Lindsay covered her stomach when it growled as well. "I must feed my women," he said with a laugh.

They got dressed, and he smiled when she pulled on the blue dress. He found her beautiful in both gowns, but the blue was his favorite. He went for water at the river while she checked the traps.

"I'm going into the village to trade these two rabbits for a bit of ham. Do ye need anything?" she asked.

"Do ye wish for me to go with you?" He didn't like when

she went off alone, especially in the village, where those men from the guard might see her. But he knew he couldn't smother her, either.

"I'll be fine. You don't need to go to the trouble."

"You are worth a great amount of trouble to me, so make sure ye come back as you are now," he said, unable to help the way his voice cracked.

She frowned and squeezed his hand to reassure him. "I will be back soon." She leaned up on her tiptoes as he bent to kiss her. As with most of their kisses, a sweet peck to say goodbye turned to something a bit more heated. His arms wound around her waist to pull her closer, and his body began to stir.

His moan was met with a laugh, which was not what he was hoping for.

"I must go now, or we'll waste away from all the activity and no food."

"I will just eat you up instead." With that, he nipped at her neck.

"When I return, I shall allow you to feast upon me to your heart's content."

With a sigh of disappointment, he dropped his arms and allowed her to escape. "Very well. Hurry back." He turned to put more wood on the fire and was pleased to hear footsteps coming closer. "Did ye change your mind?" he asked as he turned to see someone standing in the doorway who was not his wife. Not even close. "What are ye doing here?"

It took him longer than it should have to recognize the man before him. But to his credit, he had been no more than a scraggly lad when last they spoke. Alec, his younger brother and war chief, crossed his arms and raised a brow.

"Hello, my *laird*. You don't seem pleased to see me."

It seemed his simple, happy life had come to an end.

Chapter Fourteen

"How did you know I was here?" Shane knew his aunt wouldn't have told a soul, and he trusted Munro.

Alec shrugged, his large shoulders barely moving. "Janet told Tory she thought she saw you in the village. Since we've been expecting you for some time, I decided to see for myself."

It would figure Tory's nosey friend would have told. He couldn't recall seeing her, but he hadn't been looking.

"One question led to another, and soon people were talking of a quiet soldier who had taken over Ronan's cottage. I figured it could only be you, and here ye be. What I don't know is why you're here instead of at the castle, where ye bloody belong."

Rather than tell his brother about Lindsay and deal with the issue of his marriage, he went with his original reason for coming to the cottage rather than the castle. "I wasn't ready to deal with being laird. I only just got done fighting and being called *captain*. Is it too much to want a bit of time to myself?"

His brother let out a huff. "Nay. I guess I understand that. But I hope you've had your rest now, for you're needed in the castle. Deirdre has taken up the running of the clan, and I don't need to tell you it isn't going well."

Shane felt the weight settle onto his shoulders. He'd healed and enjoyed the last few weeks with Lindsay, but now he must see to his duty.

"I'll go with you to the castle and get things settled. But I won't be staying there yet. I have…" He wasn't ready to tell Alec about his wife. "I want to stay here a little while longer. And I'll not be walking through the village with ye and causing talk."

He whistled and waited until Doran came sauntering out of the woods.

"Aye?" he said, taking in Alec.

"Stay here and watch over…things."

Doran nodded and didn't ask why Shane was acting strangely.

With his wife protected, Shane followed Alec. They went through the woods and curved back up toward the castle. It was a longer walk, but it was a fine day and Alec didn't seem to mind being out in it. They walked over a rise that looked out over the farmer's field.

"Why are none of the south fields planted?" Shane asked. With no grain planted, there'd be none for harvest. No grains harvested meant no flour to make food for the people.

"Father increased the taxes on the farmers last year. Once they paid their taxes, there was nothing left to see to the replanting. Many of the farmers left for other clans."

"No farmers? No grain?" Shane rubbed his forehead. "Christ, I'm not even to the castle yet, and I already know I don't want to see any more."

"Do you wish to leave it to Deirdre?"

Shane frowned and continued their journey. For the next few minutes, Shane worried over what to do about the grain. They'd have to buy some from another clan. Did Ronan have extra stores to help? Hell, Shane hadn't seen many cattle or sheep, either. Did his father not realize there'd not be anyone to pay his increase in taxes if the whole clan starved to death?

A few moments later, Alec broke the silence. "Do things look different than ye remembered? You've been away a long time." Alec's low voice had turned sad.

"You mean besides the lack of livestock and crops?"

Alec shrugged, and Shane thought he knew what this was about.

"You've certainly changed." His brother was at least a half foot taller than Shane. When he'd left, Alec had been just under Shane's height. The man was broader as well. Both were expected, since Shane left behind a lad of five and ten, and now Alec was a man at twenty. But those weren't the things that were most noticeable. "What the hell happened to your face?"

"It figures ye would be out with it like that." Alec frowned, making the scar pull his mouth in.

"I didn't realize you and I were ones to pretend something is not the way it is." They'd always shared the truth with each other, though Shane was keeping a sizeable secret from his brother now.

"We are not, but I do blame ye for what happened to my face." Alec shook his head as if he'd shocked himself by saying the words out loud. Shane was equally surprised.

Shane felt his eyes widen, and he stopped walking to stare at the man. "Me? You blame *me*?" Shane was certainly one for taking on more blame than was due. He still felt the guilt of Maria's death. But this? "Surely, I would have noticed if I'd done that to ye."

"You didn't do it, but had you allowed me to go with you and Ronan to fight in France, I'd not have been left here with poorly crafted weapons and forced to be war chief."

"Ah, well if that's to be my offense, I can rest easy, for I'd have allowed ye to come with us. It was da who wouldn't have it. He said one of us must stay behind so he had an heir."

"Well, he almost lost this heir."

Shane nodded. It was clear to see from the scar that was left behind that the injury had not been an easy one. Many wounds of that type turned to fever and ended in death. But it seemed both Shane's brothers were survivors. "I'm glad you're not dead."

Alec grunted his appreciation. "Aye, I'm glad you're not dead as well."

They walked on until Alec turned to him. "How is Ronan? We received your letter he'd been injured. And the other saying he woke from his fever."

"He is in a bit of pain when he walks too far or too fast." Shane looked away, unable to bear the guilt he felt. While he didn't agree he had caused Alec's wound, it wasn't so about Ronan's. Shane had not been at the man's back, where he should have been. He'd let Ronan down.

It was for this reason he hadn't allowed the doctor to take Ronan's leg. Shane was a selfish bastard. Fortunately, his decision had been the right one. Ronan had a bit of a limp, but he had lived.

"I'm sure that stubborn ass walks more than he should just to prove he can."

"Who wouldn't test themselves after such a thing?" Shane asked.

Alec nodded.

"I'm sorry about your face. Does it pain ye?"

"Not as much as it pains others to look at me." He shook his head. "I'm thought of as a trow in the keep. That is what they call me."

"You're rather large to be a trow, aren't you?" Trows were thought to be little yet hideous creatures that aided fairies.

"I didn't say it made sense. I only said that is what they

call me."

"I'll not be calling ye that. Mayhap my first law as laird of the clan will be to do away with such nonsense."

Alec stopped again, glaring at Shane. "Don't even think of doing such a thing. I'll not have you calling attention to me like that."

"I wouldn't do that." They took up walking again. "Once I put Deirdre to rights and take care of things, I plan to sneak off back to my small, quiet cottage." *And my deliciously tempting wife*, he added in his mind. "I'd rather not call attention to myself."

Alec snorted. "As if no one will notice the *laird*." The last word was said with an edge, as it had the first time he'd said it.

"Do ye have something to say about me being laird?" If there was a problem between them over who had inherited the title, it would be best to address it now.

"Of course not, but you're the laird. And ye look the way ye do—the women in the keep will be tripping over one another to get to you." While Shane was becoming accustomed to the marks on his brother's face, he noticed how much worse they looked when Alec frowned or glared, as he was doing then.

"Do they not do the same for the war chief?" Alec held a place of power in the clan and as such would be thought of as a good husband.

This question earned a growl and a glare.

"Women run the other way when they see me."

Shane glanced at him, taking in the scar on his brother's otherwise handsome face. It was daunting, yes. But after one got used to it, it was easy to overlook.

"It isn't that bad. I assume your cock still works?"

Alec gave Shane a shove that nearly knocked him off his feet. "I'll thank ye not to worry yourself over my cock, ye bastard."

They were silent the rest of the way to the castle.

"Ye on the door, open for the MacPherson laird," Alec called up to the guards, who cranked the door open in a matter of seconds. In the bailey, people stopped and stared.

"Are they looking at you or me, Alec?"

"Who knows? People don't know how to keep their eyes to their work and let others go about their own business." That last part was grumbled loud enough for those around them to hear, and Shane thought perhaps the name *Trow* wasn't given to him on account of his face but for his surly attitude.

The bailey looked as it always had, but the frowns on the faces of the people gave the place an air of despair. He'd felt the same on his short trips into the village. How bad had things become? And more importantly, what could he do to repair the damage his father and stepmother had done?

They moved through the great hall, which was vacant except for a few maids cleaning the tables. New tapestries hung at either end. One was of a couple. When he looked closer, he realized it was supposed to be his father and Deirdre. At the other end was an angel. But, once again, he saw it had Deirdre's likeness to it. He snorted a laugh. "An angel?"

"I have no words," Alec said and continued toward the stairs.

No words were necessary. Shane remembered well enough how infatuated his father had been with his Deirdre. No doubt the older man saw his wife as an angel. Shane had thought Maria an angel when they'd first met, and Lindsay had seemed heaven-sent as she helped heal his aching heart. Still, he'd never spend needed money to have their likenesses made into a tapestry that took up the bulk of the wall.

Shane and Alec headed into what had been his father's study. Now, he supposed it was his. Though he had no plans to spend much time in it, if it could be helped. Deirdre's head snapped up when they entered the room, and from the way her lips pulled together it was clear she was ready to yell at anyone who might deign to interrupt her. But when she saw him, her lips pulled into a wide grin, just as false as it had always been.

His stepmother was only pleasant when it suited her and only to those who had the ability to do something for her. Shane expected he now fell into that role.

"Dearest son," she said as she rushed to him with arms held wide. She was, of course, dressed in a fine gown with a choker of emeralds around her neck. The cost of it could have fed a few families. He allowed the embrace, but when he moved to pull away her grin was replaced with tears. "Oh, your poor father so wished he would have lived long enough to see you again."

Instead of stepping away, she drew closer and wept on his shirt. Fake as they may have been, they still made the fabric wet. "I'm just so glad you've finally made it home. As soon as the Wallaces arrive, the wedding can take place as your father wanted."

Unwilling to go into the issue of a wedding that wouldn't happen and get into an argument with his stepmother as soon as he walked in the door, he simply changed the subject.

"What needs to be tended to first? I don't plan to stay in the castle. I'm set up in Ronan's cottage, and for now I wish to stay there."

Deirdre frowned but didn't argue. "How is my sweet Ronan?"

Shane had never known Ronan to be sweet since the day he showed up at Cluny Castle at ten years of age.

"He is well. We parted ways so he could see his grandfather. I imagine he'll find his way here at some point."

"It will be so wonderful to have all my sons home again."

"But just your sons?" Tory said with a snide look as she entered the room.

Shane broke out in a smile to see his younger sister before he picked her up and twirled her about.

"Ye grew into a bonny lass, Victoria," Shane said. She had been full grown at eight and ten when he'd last seen her, but the years had added a maturity she hadn't had back then.

"Put me down, ye big lout," his tiny sister complained at his mishandling of her. But as before with Alec, Shane was the oldest and therefore had the right to devil his younger siblings as he saw fit.

"Verra well, I'll not twist ye about," he said as he reached out and ruffled her hair, which he knew she hated just as well.

She batted his hand away, but he saw the smile on her lips. "Welcome home, brother. It's good to see ye." Her smile slipped as she leaned closer. "Is Ronan truly well?" she whispered.

Tory and Ronan were the same age, and Shane had noticed more than once the hearts in his sister's eyes when she looked at their stepbrother. Shane wondered if Ronan's absence was the reason she'd not yet married. Was she waiting for the heir of the Grants to make an offer for her? There was no reason for an alliance with the Grants, since they were already allies.

But Shane didn't have any plans to marry his sister off to anyone she didn't wish to marry, so if Ronan wanted her, Shane would bless the match even though it made him squeamish to think of his brother and sister marrying. Even if they didn't share the same blood.

"Shane was just getting settled. Tory, would you let the kitchens know the new laird has arrived and have them plan a feast for this evening's meal?"

Before Tory could reply, Shane put up his hand. "No feast. No announcement of any kind to anyone. I wish to ease into my new responsibilities as laird. I've been away for a while, and I'd like time to myself after years spent in a foreign land with men by my side every second of the day and night."

Deirdre frowned but must've realized he wasn't asking for her permission. "Still, I will have my things moved from the laird's chamber so it will be ready for ye when your new bride arrives."

At the word "bride," Shane thought of the woman who was probably waiting for him in the cottage by now. He'd not had ink or parchment to pen her a note telling her where he'd gone, but she most likely assumed he was out hunting. Doran would keep her safe until Shane returned. "Keep your things where they are for now. I'll let ye know when they need to be moved. Is there anything pressing for me to do here today?"

"I'm sure you'll find I have things well in hand," Deirdre said, waving dismissively at several piles of correspondence on the laird's large desk. He couldn't help but notice the way Tory rolled her eyes and the unpleasant sound Alec made behind him.

"Even still, I believe I should like to look over the books."

"You plan to take over the finances?" Deirdre seemed a bit nervous now, which told Shane he would probably not be able to return to his wife in the next few hours.

"It is the task of the laird, is it not?"

"Aye, but as you said, you're getting settled. Mayhap you would prefer I keep the accounting of them until you've seen to other things. There is the matter of the unrest with the MacColls, and the Camerons attempted a raid just a fortnight ago."

"I'll see to those things tomorrow, but, for today, I wish to see the ledgers. I canna very well plan a siege on an enemy until I know what funds I have for weapons. I also saw we have little to harvest as far as grain and not many cows or sheep in the fields."

Deirdre waved her hand dismissively. "Ungrateful barbarians, the lot of them. They didn't want to pay their due and then abandoned the clan before the planting."

"Still, there would've been time to get others to see to it. With no grain, we'll not have anything to feed people."

Another wave of her bejeweled hand. "It will be fine. No need to worry over it."

"That's right, brother—no need to worry." Alec rolled his eyes. "And I can help ye with the books. Ye have little to no funds. It's why me and my men defend the castle with no more than sticks and a few dull daggers." Alec scowled again, and Shane thought it might be the only gesture the man knew how to make.

Deirdre laughed louder than was usual for a casual bit of mirth. In fact, Shane thought the sound bordered on maniacal. "Alec is only jesting. Everything is fine."

"I will see for myself, and if he isn't jesting, we will rectify the state of the armory immediately. If we can't defend the castle, we are limited in what we might do about the MacColls and the Camerons."

The Camerons… He'd hate to have to wage war with his new wife's family. But she wasn't of high enough rank to create an alliance with their enemy clan. If anything, he may anger them even more by having taken one of their women to wed without anyone's permission. He could only hope they would approve of the union when they learned he'd done so to protect her from her rotten uncle. "The books," he said again, more sternly as he moved behind the desk.

Deirdre reluctantly stepped out of the way. "You'll let me know if you have any questions."

"If something seems amiss, you will be the first person I'll see."

The woman's face, still striking, turned pale as he took his seat, hoping things were not as bad as they seemed.

Chapter Fifteen

"Where is he?" Lindsay asked the dog once again. As she had each time before, Tre sat and tilted her head to the side offering no answer as far as Lindsay could tell.

When she'd arrived back at the cottage, she'd found the cottage empty. She'd thought he'd gone hunting, but he'd not taken his bow and quiver of arrows with him. Now it was after dinner, and the sun was working its way toward the horizon.

She didn't think he would leave her alone—he was protective to the side of overbearing, which made her think of something. Going out on the porch, she cupped her hands around her mouth and shouted for her cousin.

Doran seemed to appear out of nothing as he came closer.

"Do you know where Shane is?"

"Nay. Only that he left with a large monster of a warrior and asked me to watch after ye."

She nodded, unsure of the man Doran referred to. "Come in. You're hungry."

By the time they'd finished their meal, Lindsay had grown thin on patience and began to worry about her husband.

What if he'd been injured? What if he'd run into the guards from the first day and they'd overpowered him? She didn't think it likely, but if he'd been caught by surprise, the scraggly warriors could have gotten the upper hand. She was about to go look for him when the dog barked a second before the door opened and her husband stepped in. She rushed forward, looking him over to make sure he was unharmed.

"What has kept ye?" she asked, noting that Shane looked unhappy.

He let out a breath and shook his head. "I was needed up at the castle. The war chief came for me today." He looked to Doran, who gave a nod and slipped out of the cottage.

Lindsay barely kept a squeak of alarm from crossing her lips. It was to be expected. The war chief would want every available warrior to be ready to defend the castle if needed. The thought of sending her new husband off to battle made her heart drop to her stomach.

Lindsay understood Shane had spent five years at war and could no doubt fight well, but she hadn't had to wait at home while he left her behind before and didn't know how she would stand such a thing. How had Maria managed every day when she was forced to stay behind while he faced uncertain danger? "Are ye hungry?" she asked. "I'll make you supper."

"Nay. I am not hungry for food. I just wish to hold ye." He pulled her into his arms and nuzzled her neck below her ear, breathing deeply. "I'm glad to be back here with ye."

"I'm sorry you were called away." She bit her bottom lip, not wanting to know the answer to her next question. "Will you have to return?"

His head moved. A nod. She'd assumed as much, but fear twisted her stomach at the thought of her husband being put in danger. He was strong and brave. But he was a man, flesh and bone, and could be cut down by a blade as easily as any other man. Her arms wrapped around him, holding him tighter as if she could keep him there with her. Safe.

She'd been a fool to think they could hide away in their cottage forever.

He kissed her then, and she felt his need to join with her rise, as did her own. She may not know what would happen in the future. But they had now. She'd not waste a moment worrying about what was to come.

After they'd made love and gained enough strength to get up, he poured them each a drink. She asked him a few questions about the castle, but after each was answered with a one-word response, she determined he didn't wish to speak of it.

"I have to go back in the morning. I'll bring in the water first so you'll have plenty for the day. And I'll check the snares so you'll not need to go out alone. Stay at the cottage. Doran will watch over you, but he's only a lad. I'm not sure when I'll return. I will most likely be late again. There is much to do."

She wondered if the laird had realized she was supposed to have arrived at Cluny Castle by now. Was he searching for her? Even more reason for her to keep to the cottage, where she wouldn't be seen. "I'll stay here."

• • •

The next morning at dawn, Shane brought the water and the rabbits he'd caught home to find his wife was awake. "It's early yet. You didn't need to get up."

"If I won't see much of you today, I'd rather spend the time we have together."

He kissed her forehead and then her lips, making sure it didn't lead to more, as was the way with them. Today, however, there was no time. The books awaited.

After breaking his fast with Lindsay, Shane kissed her and left to return to the castle with Treun following along at his side. "Ye must go back to the cottage. Stay with Lindsay. Keep her from being lonely." He stopped walking and pointed back at his home. The dog let out a huff but turned and trotted back the way they'd come.

He wished he could do the same and shook his head when he realized he'd grown jealous of a little dog. Doran greeted him with a nod, looking like he'd just rolled from his bed.

Shane felt as tired as the boy looked. He'd barely slept last night for worry over what he was going to do. The ledgers were a mess. He could not tell how bad things were yet, but he'd seen enough to know it wasn't going to get better just for having them straightened out.

His father and Deirdre had taken more and more from the people of their clan and spent the funds recklessly instead of investing the money in things that would offer protection. The castle was in ill repair, and the warriors, such as they were, were underpaid and poorly equipped.

Meanwhile, the lady of the castle wore the latest fashions from London while dripping with rubies and sapphires as big as his thumb.

He shook his head as he looked up at the gray clouds above him, threatening a storm. He could smell rain in the air, and he welcomed the turbulent weather as a fine match for the way he felt. He was the laird and would need to take his stepmother's spending in hand. Besides, Deirdre wasn't truly the lady of the castle anymore. Lindsay now was.

How different that would be. No longer a woman dressed in fashion, but one that could sew her own gowns.

A tender smile pulled up on his lips at the thought of his wife as she'd bustled around the hearth, making their morning meal while he assisted. She'd shoved him with her hip, telling him she would see to things herself. As with he and Ronan, standing back-to-back on the battlefield. Shane thought life was better faced with a partner, someone to count on who could count on him in return. A trusted companion. But Lindsay was much more than a companion. She was his wife, and he was coming to see how beautifully they fit together.

He worried about Lindsay now. He felt she was safe enough at the cottage, but what would happen when he brought her to the castle? Would she be accepted? A Cameron lass with no wealth. Surely, Deirdre wouldn't be pleasant. His stepmother seemed desperate for Shane to follow through on the match his father had made. That could only mean she was eager to get the funds provided by the dowry. Shane smiled again at the thought of seeing his stepmother's face when he told her there would be no dowry. Even if there had been, she'd not have seen a penny of it.

It was a shame. The funds would have surely helped his people had he put them where they were needed. But there was no sense thinking on it now. He'd have to find another path forward to set his clan to rights. He certainly had his work cut out for him, especially when Deirdre would continue her attempts to spend what little there was. Perhaps it would be better if he married her off to another clan—one he didn't care for, so as not to feel guilty for setting the witch on them.

Alec was in the bailey with the warriors, running drills. Disgust roiled through Shane at the sight of them. Thin and slow. Weapons rusted and bent. He nodded in acknowledgment to his brother as he stood next to him, watching without a word.

Soon he'd send them out hunting to provide meat for the kitchens. That would take arrows and proper bows, which took coin. And he didn't know how much of that he had as of yet. One thing he could take care of was making sure his wife and any other woman of the clan were safe to walk where they wished. "Line up the men. I wish to address them."

Alec gave a quick nod and called out the order to stand. The men lined up with their chests thrust out for the laird's inspection. Shane searched through the ranks until his gaze landed on the two he'd been looking for.

"You two," he called. He saw the moment they recognized him.

"You?"

"Aye." He turned to a confused Alec and explained. "A few weeks ago, I ran into these two men accosting a woman from the village."

"That's how you received that wound to your shoulder, Horace?" Alec snapped.

The man didn't answer, just stood there with his head lowered.

"It was from my dirk. He's lucky I only hit his shoulder. These men have brought shame to the MacPherson name. Take them to the dungeon. And hear me now. If I find any of you have touched a woman without her acceptance, you'll be joining this lot below the keep. I'll not stand for it. The women of this clan are to be respected. Without them, our clan will wither and die out. They'll be treated as they deserve. Do I make myself clear?"

The rest of the men grunted their acceptance of his words as two of the larger warriors moved Horace and his cohort toward the dungeon.

"Well, you've certainly started off with a heavy fist, brother," Alec said.

"Would you have handled it differently?" Shane needed to know now if his brother allowed this type of behavior. It would pain him greatly to toss his own blood in the dungeon, but he stood by what he believed.

Alec shook his head. "I didn't know of it, or I would have already seen to their punishment. However, it would've been at the end of a rope."

He patted Alec's thick arm, glad they were aligned.

"It is only that you said you didn't wish to bring attention to yourself. This act will certainly have the keep whispering of ye."

"So long as there is no confusion over what will be tolerated and what will not. I do not care if a few people flap their gums." With that, he left Alec to his men and their drills and headed toward his study. But inside, he found Deirdre sitting at his desk, frowning at the books.

"What are you doing in here?" he asked, startling her.

The false smile pulled up, giving her the look of a serpent who had just spotted its next meal.

"I was helping, of course. You're new to seeing to the ledgers, while I have handled them for years for your dear father." Her voice was smooth and silky—no doubt she'd perfected it in order to woo men to their demise. A siren of the land.

He made a noise at that. She could take it anyway she liked. "I have no need of your help. In fact, I don't want you in this room again. Do you understand?"

She gasped in offense as her eyes narrowed on him. For once, he thought this expression might be sincere. He wondered if she even recognized herself when she looked in a mirror. From the very day she'd arrived at Cluny Castle, he'd known the real Deirdre as a conniving wretch. While his father was enamored by her beauty, Shane and his siblings saw beneath her disguise when she'd pulled them aside and threatened to poison their meals if they didn't obey her.

Shane might have disliked Ronan at the time, but it became clear he was treated no better for being his mother's blood child. "Leave now," he said. His own voice had dipped low with the threat.

She crossed her arms and pushed out her lovely, rose-hued lips. No doubt this display had gotten her her way any number of times, but Shane was unmoved. When he turned his attention away from her, she stomped her foot like a child.

"There is the matter of the marriage that needs to take place now that you've returned," she said, giving up the previous ruse.

"There will be no marriage," Shane answered without bothering to look at her.

"But there must be."

Her voice cracked, and he feared she might cry. He just wanted her to leave him in peace with his miserable task. "There will not be. And that is the end of the discussion," he barked, making it clear he was done with the topic. She would've been wise to let it drop, but Deirdre was not wise.

"We canna go back on the agreement." She twisted her fingers, making the rings sparkle in the lamplight.

Folding his hands over the ledgers filled with illegible scratching, he set his most firm look upon her. "I cannot marry, for I'm already wed. You will have to do without whatever bauble or gown you planned to purchase with the dowry, for it is not coming, and if it did, you wouldn't see a single coin of it. Your purse strings have been drawn and knotted."

Rage took over her dainty features, her rosy cheeks mottled with red splotches. Her honey-colored hair had shaken loose from its pins.

"It is *you* who doesn't understand, you ungrateful whelp. For the dowry was already delivered and is spent. Without the funds to repay the Wallace clan, they will come down upon us and take the castle. So, ye had better find a way out of the entanglement you've gotten yourself in so you can do your duty."

"They paid the dowry already?" Why would they do such a thing? Perhaps they'd seen the wealth in the laird and lady's clothing and assumed prepayment would guarantee the deal was done.

"Aye."

"And ye spent it? On what?" Whatever it was would be resold so the dowry could be returned to the Wallace laird.

"A ship."

"A ship?" His eyes went wide, for he couldn't believe such a thing were true. "A ship?" he repeated, for surely he'd misunderstood.

When she offered a sharp nod in reply, he stood and slammed his fists on the books before him.

"You and my father bought a bloody ship when our lands don't touch the sea on any side?" MacPherson lands were located near the center of the Highlands and as such had no access to a port.

"We wished to travel. It has been commissioned by the MacLeods. They've started work on it."

Shane had no words. He was being struck on all sides as if a whole battalion of French soldiers had come down on him at once. The amount paid by Wallace to have their daughter married to the MacPherson laird must have been excessive.

For a moment, he wondered how horrid the lass must be to require a dowry of that size, but it didn't matter, because he wouldn't be marrying her.

He would find a way out of this.

Chapter Sixteen

"Get out of my sight, and if I catch you in this room again, you'll be put in the dungeons." Apparently, Shane was set to put everyone in the dungeon today.

"Perhaps it is time for me to go visit my son," she said while backing toward the door.

"I wouldn't wish that on my brother, but do what you will."

With that, she gave a dramatic huff and swept from the room in a rustle of expensive skirts and displeasure. Shane would see she sold those damn gowns as well. His clan would need every penny. And if his wife, the rightful lady of the house, was content making her own clothes, his stepmother would learn to do the same.

Tory brought him food at midday and sat with him while he ate.

"Deirdre is in quite a fit. You have been well and truly cursed, brother."

"As has she, I assure you." He pointed at the ledgers he'd painstakingly reworked only to have them tell a grim tale. "We have hardly any money. Father and Deirdre have already spent the dowry paid by the Wallaces on a ship of all things. I will have to see what can be done to sell the vessel." He shook his head and rubbed his temples. "A bloody ship." He still couldn't believe the foolishness.

"I knew things weren't as good as Father and Deirdre made it seem, but I had no idea it was this bad." She looked down at her own frock. While not as elaborate as their stepmother's, it was clearly new and expensive. "She purchased my clothes, saying I needed color if I were to attract a husband, for my face would not do so."

"Ye are lovely and could have been married numerous times over. Why did Father not see you settled?"

She shrugged. "I didn't wish it."

Again, he wondered if she wasn't waiting for Ronan to offer for her. He worried for his sister, for Shane had never seen any evidence that Ronan saw her as anything as a sister himself. Tory was in for some pain ahead, and he didn't see any way to avoid it. "Any man would find you bonny, even in rags."

She gave him a hearty hug. "I'm so glad you've returned. Alec doesn't bother to flatter me." Shane laughed, but the smile dropped from Tory's face. "Please tell me we are not so bad as to need to wear rags."

He thought of the dress his wife wore when he'd married her, tattered and too short for her tall frame. He'd like nothing more than to see her dressed in finery more fitting of her station. But he couldn't follow in the path of his father. He needed to do better for his clan. Besides, he rather preferred his wife outside of her clothes, anyway. What good was a fancy gown when a modest one covered the floor just as well? "I will find a way to save our people from the damage done by Father."

"*We* will do it," Tory said, clinging to him tightly. "You're not alone, brother. Not anymore."

He nodded. "Thank ye."

When she left, he settled down at the books once more, hoping to find a way out of their predicament. The money they had wouldn't get them through winter. And it didn't look like much was put into sowing grain last spring, so the harvest would be slim.

Tory's promise was well intended, but Shane knew whose responsibility it was to save his clan. As he worked, the weight upon his shoulders grew heavier until he thought he may no longer be able to stand it. Looking out the window, he saw the sky had turned dark without him noticing.

Alec opened the door and stepped inside. "Deirdre has moved her things. Your room is available to you if you wish to stay."

He shook his head. "Nay. I will be going home."

"Sometime soon you'll need to take your place here. This is your home."

"Aye. But not this night." This night, he would return to his small home at the edge of the woods and to his wife. And for a little while, he could set down the weight of duties and just be Shane the soldier she'd married.

• • •

Shane returned home in much the same way as the night before, exhausted and forlorn. But the smile he offered was genuine, despite the strength it took to put it there.

He drew her close and kissed her. As he was holding her, she picked up the faint scent of roses. The feminine smell drifted from his clothes as if he'd held a woman who wore rosewater. She pulled away and looked him over. He was wearing the same clothes he'd worn when he left that morning, but the fabric did not smell of sweat, as one would expect from a soldier who had been in drills with the war chief all day long.

It had rained that morning, yet he didn't seem to have been wet. Did the MacPherson warriors not train in foul weather? She'd seen the Wallace warriors in the yard every day without fail, come rain, snow, or sun.

"How were your drills today?" she asked, watching for the hint of a lie leaving his lips.

Instead, his lips remained closed and pressed softly against hers. His arms pulled her close again, and she felt the evidence of his attraction growing against her stomach. A man could not feign this reaction, surely. He wanted her, while he wore another woman's scent.

"I asked about your day," she said, pulling away yet again. She was unable to lie with him with these questions circling in her mind.

"I'd rather you save your questions for another time so I might continue kissing you."

"I want to kiss you the same, but I must know..." How should she form the question? To accuse her husband of such a serious offense might shatter the comfort they shared. She had no right to be jealous of Maria, but if he were with another woman now that they were wed, she wouldn't be so generous. She'd foolishly thought she'd be enough, for he seemed pleased with their bed sport. "Are you happy?"

"I am when I'm here with you."

"And when you're at the castle?"

He shook his head. "I'm not at all happy when I'm at the castle."

"And do I please you? When we are in bed together?"

"Aye, lass. Why do ye think I'm trying to get you into our bed right now?"

He laughed, and she felt the truth of his words. He was happy with her.

"I know many husbands find other entertainments outside of their marriage bed."

His smile faded as his brows pulled together and he stepped back to look in her eyes. "Do ye think I would do such a thing?"

She shrugged. It was best to say what she needed to say. Stepping around the subject was not getting the answers she needed. "You're a warrior being summoned to the castle by the war chief, yet you return to me smelling of roses rather than the sweat of physical effort as I would expect. You seem to word things in a particular way. I do wonder why." She looked away, unable to see the disappointment in his eyes that she had such little faith in him. She wished she could take the words back, as much as she hoped he would answer and reassure her with the truth.

He plucked his shirt from his chest and bent his head to smell it. The puzzled look on his face turned knowing as he nodded. "Aye. A woman did hug me today. A relative who was happy to see me returned."

She could've melted to the floor at this quite reasonable response.

"As for the effort, I am spending most of my day inside, toiling over numbers."

This surprised her. "You're seeing to the laird's ledgers?"

"Aye."

"I had no idea you were so skilled."

"I have other skills I have not yet shared with you." His lids drooped into a lustful gaze. "Mayhap, I can show those to you instead of speaking of my boring day spent in dust and ink." At this, he pressed his lips to her neck, trailing kisses up to her ear.

"You have no reason to fear I'd ever spend a minute in another woman's bed—not while I have you. You're everything to me, Lindsay."

That time, her legs did give way, and he pulled her up into his arms and carried her to their bed.

• • •

Shane had barely woken when someone pounded on his door. He'd been lying next to his wife, watching as the light of dawn reached out from the window to touch her midnight hair. He knew he needed to tell her the truth and soon. He'd been careful not to lie to her.

But contorting the facts so they were still true was becoming more difficult with each passing day. Grumbling at whomever had bothered his perfect moment, he slid from the bed and pulled on his shirt before going to answer the door.

The door pushed in as Alec barged past him, muttering something Shane's mind was too groggy to comprehend. He looked toward the bed to be sure his wife was covered. The furs were pulled up past her breasts, but her shoulders were bare and her hair was perfectly messy in the way he loved. Alec froze for a moment before bowing.

"Pardon my intrusion, mistress. I need to speak with my—"

Shane pulled his brother outside before he finished his announcement.

"You have a woman in your bed," Alec said as if Shane had not noticed.

"I know, and I was enjoying being in bed next to her until you came pounding on my door. What do you want? I plan to be up at the castle in a few hours." He'd wanted to spend more time with Lindsay that day, having left her alone so much the past two days.

There was nothing another day of looking at the dusty books would do. It wasn't likely to get any better for him poring over them.

"She's gone," Alec said while running his hand through brown hair the same color as Shane's, just a little shorter.

"Who's gone?"

"Deirdre."

"Aye. She's going to see Ronan. I told her to go. I'm sure he'll be cursing me for it."

Alec shook his head. "Nay. One doesn't take all their belongings for a visit."

"Ye said she moved her things from the laird's chamber."

"Aye, but she didn't move them anywhere else."

"Well, if she has gone, all the better. I'm happy to see her back for the last time." Shane had enough things to worry over. Having his stepmother sniffling around, begging to buy things they didn't have the money for, was something he'd be happy to avoid. It would've been nice to have her jewels so he might sell them.

But Alec was still shaking his head and rolled his eyes as if Shane was missing something important. "She didn't just take her belongings. She took her boxes of jewels, as well as the coin Father kept hidden in his rooms. It seems she took as much as she could carry."

"Bloody hell," Shane said, rushing back into the house to don his plaid and kiss his wife a hasty goodbye. "I'm sorry, but I must go. There's something wrong at the castle, and I must offer my assistance. Someone will be here soon to guard ye."

She smiled, nothing but trust in her dark eyes. "I will see you when you return."

"Aye." With a longer kiss, he was gone.

Alec hadn't come inside but had been standing at the door as Shane gave his wife his goodbyes. His brother's face was a shade of pink he'd not seen in a long time.

"She is lovely," he said as they hurried for the castle.

"Aye." Lindsay was more than lovely, and he was proud

to call her his. There was barely any of her body he had not touched with his lips.

"You'll send a trusted warrior back to her to stand guard," he ordered, and Alec gave a single nod.

Shane was irritated to have been robbed of the jewels and trinkets he might have sold to make a bit of coin for his people, but he couldn't help but be thankful Deirdre was out of his life, no matter the cost—until they arrived in the study and Shane noticed the ledgers had been disturbed from the place he'd left them the night before.

"Alec?"

"Yes?"

"What of the coffers?"

Two strong boxes under the large desk held the laird's coin to be used for the clan. Or rather what was left of it.

"I didn't think to check them. She wouldn't have had a key, and they are too heavy for her to have moved them."

Shane spun around the side of the desk and closed his eyes as if not seeing it would make it less true. The boxes were both hanging open; neither had a coin inside. It was clear Deirdre had enlisted help in robbing them, for she'd not have been able to carry such a heavy load herself.

"We need to find her before she buys another bloody ship," Shane said while slamming his fist on the top of the desk.

Chapter Seventeen

Shane quickly wrote a letter to his stepbrother and had their fastest rider summoned to deliver it immediately with the order to wait for a reply before returning.

In the missive, he told his brother to keep Deirdre at his holding until they could come to claim the items she'd taken. Which, after a thorough investigation, seemed to be everything the clan held of any value and that could be carted off.

"Alec, while we wait for word from Ronan, I need ye to go to the MacLeods on my behalf and explain the situation with the ship. Ask them if they can help us sell it to another party to make the money back."

Alec didn't move; instead, he stood there as if he were a giant carved from stone.

"What is it?" he asked when Alec said nothing.

"I canna go." This was said as if Shane had grown horns and a tail.

"Why not? You are my right hand. You're needed to go in my stead while I sort things out and go to the Grants to retrieve what she's taken."

Alec glared at him while Shane glared right back. It was another minute before Alec finally explained in a tone that made it clear he didn't think it was something that needed explaining. "I've not been anywhere since I've been scarred. No one will want to deal with the devil himself."

"This mark is who you are now, is that it? Because I'll tell you true, I've been looking at your face for the last few days, and it is not so bothersome as you think."

"But it is a shock to others."

"Then they'll be shocked and get over it as I have. I need you to take care of this, Alec. You will go to the MacLeods. Not because I am uncaring but because I care for you enough to force you to do something you don't want to do so you see past these walls you've hidden behind. And most importantly, I'm sending you because I need you, and I know you will not let me down. Would you really fail at completing this important task because you're afraid?"

"Very well. But if they send me away without hearing me, you'll have no choice but to go anyway," Alec blustered.

"If it comes to that, we'll see it done together. But I think you will find this scar is not as big as you think."

With a sound of disbelief, Alec left to prepare for his journey. In the meantime, Tory assisted Shane in listing the things Deirdre had taken with her.

"She took the bloody candlesticks from the library? What value could they be?" Shane complained to his sister.

"You're probably remembering the old candlesticks, not the new silver ones Deirdre had made."

"They hold a candle so you can see to read. Why must they have been made of silver?"

"They didn't just hold one candle. They held a dozen."

Shane slammed his fist on the desk. A silver fixture that could hold a dozen candles could not have been cheap. At the very least he would have been able to melt it down to make arrowheads for his warriors to hunt with.

"She's also taken a number of books."

Shane paused in his pacing and turned to his sister. "Books and very large candlesticks would be heavy. How did she carry them on a horse?"

Tory pressed her lips together and looked toward the ceiling.

"What are you not telling me, Tory?"

"The carriage she had made with the gold filigree is also gone. Along with four horses to pull it."

"When I get my hands on the bloody woman, I may not be able to keep from choking the life from her. I can only hope Ronan will stop me before I do."

Ronan knew his mother as well as the rest of them and would no doubt cheer Shane on in the choking rather than save him from being charged with murder.

"We have to find her."

...

When Shane arrived later that evening in time for dinner, Lindsay couldn't help but notice how tired he looked. And not the tired that comes from a day of hard physical labor, but more the exhaustion that comes with worrying over things with no answers.

She knew the difference because she'd spent the better part of the afternoon alone worrying about what would happen when her father arrived at the castle in a few weeks and found she'd never arrived to marry the laird. And new fear had swirled in to join the rest. If her father found her here, married to a soldier, would he or the MacPherson laird kill Shane so she'd be free to marry the laird as planned?

She hadn't considered how marrying Shane had put him

in danger. Staying here to be found put them both at risk. She now understood the weight of guilt Shane carried around for the mistake he'd made that endangered Maria. She couldn't let anything happen to Shane, no matter the cost of her happiness.

"Is everything straightened out at the castle?" she asked while serving him the stew she'd made, noticing how her hands shook. She put a bit in a dish and set it on the floor for Tre.

"No. In fact, I must return tonight, but I wanted to see you. I'm sorry I've been absent. I have guards watching the house."

She frowned, remembering the guards she'd already met.

"I made sure they were trustworthy. You are safe here—I promise. You know I wouldn't risk leaving you if there was any question."

She'd had guards with her when she'd lived at Riccarton, her father's castle. She didn't want that again. She liked her simple life. "What if we left here?" she suggested in what she hoped sounded casual rather than as if she'd been thinking about nothing else for most of the day.

"Left?"

"Aye. You and I could pack up our things and move on, away from here. Away from the danger of the men, away from the orders of a demanding laird."

Shane laughed, though she didn't think she'd said anything amusing. "Why do you think the laird is demanding?" he asked.

"He keeps you from me when you'd rather be here."

The mirth left his eyes, and he nodded. "Aye. That he does."

"We could leave this place and make our home somewhere else," she repeated. She'd never thought to make the MacPherson lands her home anyway. She'd only changed her mind because of Shane. But Shane was her home now, not this place. Leaving would keep him safe.

Her cousin Meaghan had married a MacKenzie. They could go there and start a new life.

"I am a MacPherson," he said as if she'd forgotten.

"Are you a MacPherson, or are you my husband?" She hated the challenge as soon as she'd spoken it. But it was true. He was being forced to choose between his duty to his laird and her. She selfishly wanted him to choose her, for she was willing to turn her back on her father and his plans for her so she could choose Shane.

He frowned and brushed his rough knuckles over her cheek.

"I'm sorry, lass. I can't leave this place. It's my home. I want it to be your home as well, and that of our children and their children. Running from something rarely solves anything. Most of the time, trouble finds you wherever you might go."

She let out a breath, unwilling to continue this argument, mostly because her husband was right. If they fled, her father would search for her. And he'd only grow angrier for having to track her down and drag her back to do her duty. She was destined to lose this battle. But she feared in losing the battle she would also lose Shane.

Late that night, as Shane slipped into their bed and fell straight to sleep, she decided her fate was sealed. When the time came, she'd do what she needed to protect Shane. And until that moment, she would allow herself to love him with all her heart. During the darkest days, she'd be able to look back on her time with this man and remember the joy she'd felt being his wife.

• • •

Shane was in the bailey the next morning, leading his men in their drills, when the guard on the gate yelled that a rider approached the castle. Knowing it couldn't yet be Alec, Shane wasn't surprised to see the messenger he'd sent to Strathspey, the Grant keep. As soon as the lad dropped from his horse to his feet, he had the missive pulled from his sporran and thrust into Shane's waiting hands.

Shane would have wagons readied immediately to go retrieve the items from the Grants. Hopefully the money was not all spent. What they did with Deirdre, Shane didn't care. He only wanted what belonged to his clan so he could repay the dowry to the Wallace laird. But as his eyes traveled over the letter, he found his mouth falling open in surprise.

"Deirdre isn't with the Grants. Ronan hasn't seen her."

Tory, who'd come out of the castle, sent the messenger into the kitchens for food and drink, then turned to Shane. "Where could she have gone?" she asked as she shook her head.

"The woman is as slippery as a serpent. I should have known she wouldn't have gone where we expected. She no doubt found a sunny rock to slither beneath."

He tapped the useless letter against his thigh a few times as he thought over his next step. He noticed the stable at the far end of the bailey and headed in that direction. Inside the building, he breathed in the sweet scent of leather and horses as he looked about for the stablemaster. "You there."

"Aye?" the man said, looking Shane over before awareness struck. "My laird." The man bowed. It'd been some time since he'd been at the castle, and no formal announcement had yet been made that he had returned.

Shane had no time for such things. In fact, he didn't like that the man had recognized him, but he realized it was bound to get out at some point whether he wanted it to or not. He would need to deal with that soon, but for now he had more pressing problems to see to.

"Lady MacPherson left the castle in her carriage. She must've had a driver and mayhap a few outriders?"

"She's a charmer, that one." The older man rolled his eyes, as if she didn't tempt him.

Shane nodded. It wouldn't have been difficult for his stepmother to have flirted her way out of the castle with a full contingent of riders—such was her way, with a smile and a twinkling eye. At least to the right men.

"One of them must have sent word as to where they were going. Or known ahead where their family could send for them?"

The stablemaster rubbed a hand over his thick, gray beard and called out to a gangly boy who came running.

"The laird is asking where his mother has gone. Did ye hear them say?" He turned back to Shane, his shoulders straight with pride. "This is Luke, my grandson. A quiet boy goes unnoticed as he does his duties. If anyone heard, it would be him."

"I'm sorry, but I heard some of the men asking the lady, and she only laughed and told them they would find out soon enough. I don't know why they would have agreed to go with her. But it was as if the lady was fairy and cast a spell over the men. They were that eager to do her bidding."

A young boy wouldn't have seen the allure of a beautiful woman's smile.

"Thank ye both. If you hear anything from the men that escorted her, please let me know right away."

Tory met Shane as he returned to his study. "I checked with the women in the kitchens to see if they knew where she'd gone. Of course, Deirdre didn't deign to enter the kitchens except to give orders or complaints, so she had no friends there in whom she might have confided." Tory shook her head. "I will say the women were pleased to learn the lady of the castle is no longer in residence."

"They'll not be so happy when we run out of food for them to prepare."

"Is it so dire, brother?" Tory asked. Her green eyes—so much like his—grew wide with worry. He didn't wish to trouble his sister, but he'd not lie to her. He was already keeping enough secrets already.

"It will become dire if we don't make reparations for the dowry Deirdre has already spent."

"You don't plan to marry the Wallace lass?"

"Nay. I can't." He didn't go into the details as to why he couldn't. Fortunately, Tory didn't push him. He imagined, being the daughter of a laird herself, she wasn't in agreement with such an arrangement if it was not wanted.

"I'll ask others. Someone must have heard."

"Not if she never spoke it."

"True."

Deirdre did not get to where she was by being reckless. She would've planned every detail of her escape so no one would find her. Any information they might come across would probably be false to throw them off her trail. The witch was diabolical in getting what she wanted.

"I am going for my bed." *And my wife.* "I'll return in the morning," he said when no other ideas had come to him.

"Brother?"

Shane stopped to wait for her to continue.

"Alec mentioned there was a woman in your bed when he arrived the other morning."

Shane's brows went up. "Our brother speaks of such things to his sister? It's not proper."

She rolled her eyes and shook her head.

"I heard him mention it to Roger, who commented she must be the reason you've not sought the comfort of your role here in the castle."

"The men of this clan gossip like old women." He felt as if there was a hand gripping him tightly around the neck. This world and the one he'd built in the cottage with Lindsay were in danger of colliding. And the risk grew each day.

"Is it true?" Tory pushed when Shane didn't respond.

"Is what true?"

"Do you care for her? I know men seek a woman's company, but the way I understand it, it is only for a night, and then they move on. It sounded as if this one might be more than a dalliance."

"You're not to know of such things, Tory. And I'll not speak of it with you. If you wish to discuss such improper things, I'll bid ye to take it up with Roger. He seems to have an opinion to share on the topic."

With a sigh that spoke of her intense irritation, she turned on her heel and left. He'd been spared for now, but it wouldn't be long before he'd be forced to answer her questions.

Until then, he'd keep his wife to himself.

Chapter Eighteen

Despite Shane's warning not to go into the village alone, Lindsay needed to get a few things, as well as get out of the cottage for a bit. And since he was gone again up to the castle for the rest of the day, she would have to see to the errands herself.

She didn't begrudge his work at the castle, but she did miss him through the day. As she walked through the woods toward the village alone, she spotted one of the guards he'd set to watching her. She glanced down at her faithful companion. Tre wasn't very big, but she would surely defend Lindsay if these guards proved disloyal to her husband.

Her heart calmed when she broke through the trees and entered the village. However, her worries shifted from running into the MacPherson soldiers alone in the woods to running into someone who may be looking for her from the castle.

She brushed it off and went about her errands. It was a beautiful day, and everyone in the village seemed lightened by the sunshine and blue skies. She shared a smile with everyone she met and was surprised to find most of the people offered a smile in return. She'd thought the village to be filled with miserable people like her uncle. When she'd been out before, no one had paid her any attention. But perhaps they all had their weights to carry and some days the load felt more manageable than others.

As she was looking through bundles of yarn, she felt someone watching her. Glancing around, she spotted a young woman who looked away as soon as their gazes connected. The woman was wearing a simple but well-made gown. Something a maid at the castle might wear. As Lindsay moved, the woman followed. Lindsay's chest pounded. Had she been found? What could she do? Run? That meant leaving Shane behind, since he'd refused to leave this place.

She thought of her cousin with the MacKenzies, and the refuge didn't feel as freeing as it had before. She didn't want to have to leave her husband. Moving along to the next stand, Lindsay waited a few moments and then turned quickly, finding the woman watching her yet again. Rather than continue playing this game, Lindsay marched up to the smaller woman and raised her brows. "Why are you following me?" she asked directly, crossing her arms to keep her hands from shaking. It was better to know if she'd been found out than worry herself to death over it.

"Who are *you*?" the other woman asked.

"Who am *I*? *You* are following *me*. Who are you?" It seemed this woman's stubbornness matched Lindsay's own, but eventually, after they stared at each other for a few seconds, the other woman relented.

"I am the laird's sister."

Lindsay was surprised by this. Someone from the castle following her around surely meant they had learned who she was and planned to tell the new laird his bride was living secretly in a cottage with her new husband.

"I am Lindsay MacPherson," she answered, hoping that by using her new surname she could throw the other woman off the trail.

"A MacPherson?" The woman looked her up and down. "I do not know of you. You must have married a MacPherson."

"Aye. Shane MacPherson. I was a…a Cameron before I married."

The woman's eyes grew large. She knew the Camerons were not well liked by the MacPhersons, but that wasn't the cause of the woman's shock.

"You're married to Shane MacPherson?" She nearly choked on the question.

Pity for this girl made Lindsay back down. It was clear this woman knew Shane and was upset to hear he had married. Had she been in love with him and wanted him for herself?

"I am. For several weeks now."

"I see. Well, then. I wish you every happiness." She turned and sped off toward the men who were clearly guarding her.

When Lindsay arrived home, she found Shane rushing from the cottage. When he spotted her walking up the path, he relaxed for a moment before coming toward her, irritation clear on his handsome face.

"What are you doing walking about? I told you to stay in the cottage."

"I only needed some yarn and a bit of cheese. Besides, your guards did not let me out of their sight. Neither did this formidable warrior," she said as she dropped a bit of cheese for Tre.

"What could she do? Bark the person to death?" He leaned down to pet the little dog.

She smiled but shook her head. "The only danger today was from a woman watching me in the village."

"A woman?"

"Aye. The laird's sister was following me." She watched

his face as she shared this news, but he didn't hide his surprise. "You know her."

"Aye," he said slowly, still watching her carefully.

"I think the lass cares for you a great deal and was unhappy to hear of your marriage to me. Whatever she may have been to you, you should have told her. Tender hearts break easily. It's better to be honest." What a shrew she was to accuse him of dishonesty when she was living a life not her own.

"Aye. I should have told her I was wed." Tilting his head, he continued. "Is that all she said?"

"She ran off upset before I had the chance to speak to her. I didn't even catch her name."

"Her name is Tory. If you were to see her again." He gave a nod and looked off toward the castle. "She's family."

Lindsay nodded, happy that he shared this information with her. "You may need to apologize to her."

"Yes. I believe I do. I'll see to it first thing tomorrow, when I return to the castle."

"What are you doing home so early? I wasn't expecting you until later this evening." She was more than happy to see him. But if he was only there for the nooning, she didn't want to get her hopes up.

"I needed some time away from the books. And I wanted to spend the day with you. A reward for keeping my sanity after the mess the books are in."

She pulled him into her arms, and he leaned down to kiss her hair. And then her neck.

"I thought we'd spend the day by the river." He kissed her lips and then pulled back slightly. "But now I only wish to see the inside of the cottage until it's dark."

She smiled and dashed toward the cottage with him quick behind her. Being chased was quite fun, but not as much as being caught. Their laughter soon turned to gasps and sighs as they made love.

As he'd said, it was dark before they were finally sated enough to see to their dinner. They put together a quick meal of apples, cheese, and bread, but rather than eat at the table, they lounged in bed and took turns feeding each other. He even used her stomach to hold his sliced apple, and she giggled when he took a bite of juicy fruit, allowing his tongue to linger on her heated skin.

Since she was sticky, he suggested they bathe together in the chilly river. Goose flesh pebbled her skin until he pulled her close to his hot body.

"How are you so warm in this frigid water?" she asked.

"Thinking of what I plan to do to you when I carry you over to the plaid has me overheated."

"You should carry me out of the water before I turn to ice."

He did as she asked, her legs wrapped tightly around his waist as he held on to her arse to keep her secured to his body. Her wet skin heated, and as he slid inside, she welcomed him with a long moan.

It seemed they couldn't get enough of each other. This new activity had claimed her every thought when he was away and their every moment when he was there.

She couldn't be happier.

• • •

On the way up to the castle the next day, Shane frowned despite the sunny morning. He'd been careful not to lie to Lindsay, but he'd never corrected any of her assumptions or been honest about who he was.

She had no reason to think he was the laird of the MacPhersons. At this point, he'd dragged out the deception so long he doubted she would believe him when he did tell her the truth. Would she be happy to live in the castle and be the lady of the clan, or would she be angry with the burden he'd placed on her?

He had other things to worry about today, like making sure the clan was worthy of a lady such as his Lindsay. He was only in the castle a few minutes before his sister entered the study. She stood by the door, arms crossed tightly across her chest and her foot tapping.

"Good morning to you, sister," he said to put off the tongue-lashing she was sure to give him.

"Don't call me your sister when it is clear you do not think of me as family," she snapped.

Folding his hands on the desk, he nodded toward the chair sitting to the side. "Won't you have a seat so we can discuss this?"

"Nay. I don't need a seat. I need the truth. You are *married*?"

"Aye. You met my wife in the village yesterday, as I understand it."

"Why did you not tell me? Why does she refuse to live in the castle?" she asked.

Shane was equally relieved and irritated that the truth hadn't come out. It would have taken the decision out of his hands. Lindsay would know the truth even then. But however it had come about, his ruse had remained intact despite his sister meeting his wife. He decided to tell his sister the truth, and not just because it would be near impossible to keep two women in the dark regarding his deception.

"She doesn't refuse to live in the castle. She doesn't know it is an option to do so."

"She doesn't realize the lady of the clan gets to sleep in an elaborate room in the castle?"

"She doesn't know she is the lady of the clan. She doesn't know I am the laird. When we met, I was simply a soldier returned from years at war. And she cared for me as that. I have no wish for her to know I misled her, even if I also wish she knew the truth. I can't be certain she would be happy to learn who I am."

"You mean you don't think she will be happy to find out you've lied to her?" Tory clarified.

"I've not lied. Not exactly. I've just not elaborated the facts."

She snorted in a very unladylike way. "You men are nothing more than cowards. You hide away to keep from telling women the truth, even if they would be much better off if you would just come out with it so they might lick their wounds and move on."

Shane may not have been a scholar when it came to understanding women's thoughts, but he was certain his sister was no longer speaking of the situation with he and Lindsay. Rather than pick at that wound, he held out his arms, because he needed to tell her something else she wasn't going to like.

"There is more."

"More? More than you having a wife? What, do you have two wives?"

"Actually, yes."

Shane worried Tory might faint, such was her surprise. He went on. "That is, not at the same time. But I had a wife before Lindsay. Her name was Maria DeLuna. We married in Spain, where she was from. She was killed." His voice dipped on the last word, but he managed to explain what happened to his first wife. Lindsay had been right when she'd told him it would be easier to remember Maria without the guilt getting in the way.

He smiled even as his sister shook her head.

"And you never mentioned a wife in any of your letters home."

"There were not so many letters, and I couldn't speak of

her for some time after she died."

Tory nodded, but her anger had faded. "And you have remarried this Lindsay? A Cameron?"

"I was being forced into a marriage Father had agreed to. Call me stubborn, but I didn't want to make an alliance that would only put more jewels around Deirdre's neck. I wed Lindsay to offer her protection after her uncle had mistreated her, and I do not regret it."

"You're scared to tell her." Tory's eyebrow lifted in that smug way she had when she knew she was right about something.

"Aye. I'm terrified she will not want the burden of being the lady of the MacPhersons. And I'm worried she will not look at me as she does now. As nothing more than a man she has come to care for. Not a laird. Just a man."

"You want her to want you for who you are, not what you are."

"Aye." He was surprised that his sister understood so well. But she was grown. He imagined her lack of company wore on her.

"I can see why you would want that. I'm the daughter and now sister of a laird. I've always expected to be married off as chattel."

"Well, I will not be marrying you off anytime soon," he assured her.

She laughed and shook her head. "Only because you don't have the coin for the dowry."

His lip pulled up on the side. "That might be part of it, but I would at least see you happy."

"Well, I thank you for that. I've never been so relieved not to have a dowry. It means the men only looking for coin will move on."

He let out a breath and nodded.

"Aye. I wish I could move on. Unfortunately, there is the

matter of the dowry for the Wallaces' daughter. It has been paid and already spent. I have nothing with which to repay the laird, since Deirdre ran off with every cent we had. If they come to claim recompense, I have nothing but the castle in which we stand. If he declares war… I will have no choice but to have my marriage to Lindsay annulled so I can marry the Wallace lass as planned to save the clan." He let out a breath, feeling exhausted for having finally spoken his fears out loud. "I do not think I can do it."

"Then we must find a way to keep that from being the only option."

But as he was hugging his sister and hoping for a way to keep his wife, a lad tapped on the door, calling their attention to him.

"Riders approach. It looks to be Alec and his men."

"Lord, I hope our brother brings good news."

Chapter Nineteen

It was clear from the way Alec held his shoulders as he entered the study that he did not bear the good news Shane hoped for.

Tory went to the door to order a maid to bring food and ale for Alec. "What word do you bring from the MacLeods, brother?"

"I wish I could tell you the ship has been sold and my saddlebags are filled with coin, but in truth I don't think it could be so far the opposite."

"What do you mean?" Tory asked.

"When I arrived, the MacLeods welcomed me graciously, but I soon learned it was because he expected me to have the next payment for the ship that sits half constructed in their harbor. When he found out our plans to sell the ship and reclaim the funds for the vessel, he was mightily unhappy."

Shane rubbed his temples, feeling an ache coming.

"You're saying we can't sell the ship to make the money back because first, it is not completed, and second, we still owe money for it?"

"Aye. That is the truth of it. I'm sorry, brother."

"I'll go see about your meal," Tory said as she left the room, probably expecting Shane to launch into a fit of yelling as their father would have.

But Shane didn't yell. To do so would take more energy than he had. He was fairly numb by this point, and yelling would get him nowhere.

"That's it, then. There's nothing to be done. The dowry is gone." Shane went to the window to look out across the lands that belonged to his clan. He could almost envision the Wallace army moving on the castle.

"I'm sorry, brother. But it looks like you'll have to put all the women aside and do your duty."

Had Shane thought he didn't have the energy to yell? "There are not *women*. There is only one woman, and she is my wife."

Alec's shock was evident. He quickly apologized. "I didn't realize. You didn't say."

No. He hadn't. "I wasn't ready to have to give her up. I don't think I can do it. But I must for the clan."

"Mayhap she could—"

Shane cut off his brother's comment before he could finish. He might not have been close to Alec for many years, but he knew the man well enough to know what he was about to suggest. That Shane could keep Lindsay as a mistress while he married the Wallace lass.

He would never disrespect Lindsay in that way.

But to let her go… How could he? He'd known he didn't deserve to be happy, but he had believed Lindsay when she'd claimed him innocent. Now he was being punished yet again. It seemed he'd found his heart in time to have it shattered once more.

. . .

Something was wrong; Lindsay was certain. It wasn't uncommon for Shane to arrive home from the castle after she'd gone to bed. But it was unlike him to apologize when she tried to raise his ardor by placing her hands on him in a way that would normally stoke him to action.

"What is it?" she asked, giving up on her plan to seduce him. If she couldn't make him feel better physically, she would be supportive and allow him to talk about his troubles. "You had a bad day?" She rubbed his tight shoulders where he sat on the edge of the bed with his head hanging.

"Aye. The worst kind of day."

She didn't know all that he did for the laird, but she knew he was seeing to the ledgers.

"Did something not come out right?"

He shook his head and pressed his lips together. "No. Actually, the books are in such a mess, and I don't know how I'll ever fix them."

"Surely the laird doesn't blame you for what happened before you returned. If the books are a mess, it can only be his fault." Once again, she pictured the war chief's snarled face when she thought of the MacPherson laird—her intended. Was he as horrible as she thought him to be? She almost asked Shane about him but didn't want to know.

"It is the fault of Deirdre MacPherson, who has stolen from the clan and ran off to God knows where."

"Then you must find her and have whatever she's stolen returned." Lindsay wondered how far a woman could get alone in the Highlands.

Shane nodded. "It sounds easy but has proven impossible thus far. No one knows where she went."

"Did you check with the stablemaster?" She would have needed a horse or better yet a carriage.

"Aye."

"The kitchens? The women like to talk." She recalled

the women at Riccarton and the gossip they shared while working. They knew all that went on in the castle.

"Aye. They don't know, either."

"Hmm…" She continued to rub the tension from his shoulders as she thought through the situation. She paused. "If she stole something from the clan, she wouldn't want anyone to find her so she'd have to give it back."

He didn't speak. He simply rubbed his temples as if he'd measured every option. But she went on, hoping her words would inspire an idea.

"She wouldn't go to an ally of Clan MacPherson because they wouldn't stand with her if faced with losing the alliance. Which means she would have done the opposite. She would have gone to an enemy of the clan instead. Then, if you came to claim her, they could use her protection as a reason for war."

He blinked. Slowly first. Then a few rapid blinks as if he'd just woken from a deep sleep. He turned to stare at her. His eyes grew wider as he considered her words.

"She went to side with an enemy," he whispered. "That makes perfect sense. I'd thought she would stay clear of an enemy, as she only has a few feckless young men with her. But she has nothing to fear. She's the widow of the MacPherson clan. She is no longer one of us. She can be one of *them*."

"One of who?" Lindsay asked, having lost the trail of his thoughts.

"A bloody MacColl."

Lindsay gasped. She'd heard horrible tales of the MacColl clan. If that's where the laird's stepmother ran, the laird would have a difficult time swaying them to give back what was taken. Not without a fight.

Lindsay wrapped her arms around her husband and kissed his shoulder. If the MacPhersons went to war with the MacColls, Shane would be called to join the army. She wished she could hold on to him forever and keep him there with her, where he'd be safe. But she could not. She would be forced to watch him leave and hope he came back.

...

Shane barely slept the night before. Not just because he was desperate to think of a way to get Deirdre and the money back without having to fight with the MacColls. But also because Lindsay was restless.

Not only had she slept so close to him he could barely move, but when she did drift off, she began thrashing about, calling his name, and crying. She'd apologized but refused to tell him what her nightmares had been about. He didn't need her to tell him to guess she was worried he would be caught up in a war with the MacColls. But she didn't know how caught up he would be.

He couldn't shake the feeling he had brought all of this on himself, with his betrayal of Maria and his deceit with Lindsay. This tragedy was nothing he didn't deserve for his sins. He'd had the good fortune to marry two wonderful women and had found a way to ruin both of them.

All night he'd considered what to do to save his clan, to save his marriage, and he was still thinking about it when he kissed her and left for the castle that morning. He'd come up with no solution that would not end in heartbreak. In his study, he sent a lad to find his brother and send him in.

"What is it?" Alec asked in his normal, unhappy tone.

"I believe Deirdre has gone to the MacColls."

"Why do you think she would have done such a thing? They hate the MacPher— Ah."

"Yes. It's perfect, don't you see? They will offer her protection, and they will give it hoping to draw us to war, where they will most likely win."

"What will we do?"

Shane appreciated that his brother had said "we" instead of "you." It made him feel less alone in this mess. But in the end, it would be Shane's decision. And Shane's success or failure. He couldn't fail. To do so would be to lose his entire clan. The MacColls didn't take prisoners. And they didn't take innocents into their clan—even if they pledged fealty to the MacColls, the MacPhersons would be slaughtered.

"I don't know what to do," he admitted to his brother.

"Is it too much to hope the MacColls will grow weary of Deirdre and simply send her back to us with the things she's stolen from us?"

Shane only lifted his brow. They both knew that wouldn't happen. As much as Deirdre annoyed them, she was a skilled temptress. She was beautiful and knew how to use her gifts to earn loyalty from any man with a working cock. At least those who weren't related to her.

Having called her "mother" for over a decade, Shane, Tory, and Alec knew the real Deirdre. The selfish witch who didn't care who she hurt so long as she got what she wanted.

It would be just like the woman to have the clan embroiled in war so she could keep her useless baubles. No matter how many lives were lost. Meanwhile, if the Wallace laird found out Shane had breached the agreement his father made to marry the man's daughter, Shane could be facing two possible battles with shabby weapons and lazy warriors.

"I have brought my misfortune down on the clan," he said and went on to tell Alec about Maria and how he had been responsible for her death. Alec, like Lindsay and Tory, disagreed. But he knew this was his punishment: to be forced to give up Lindsay because he'd walked away from Maria when she needed him.

"We still have the Grants," Alec reminded him. "Ronan is laird now. He would bring his men and fight with us."

"I'd rather not put our brother at risk."

"Ye may not have a choice."

Shane nodded. He now had more to think about, not less. He accompanied Alec back to the bailey to help with training the men. If they were facing war, it wouldn't do to have the men unprepared. They were a motley bunch, some too thin and small, others too soft and slow. He pushed them hard and taught them how to make quick work of an opponent so they could move on to the next and the next.

Fighting helped to clear his mind of everything but the sound of blade on blade and the sweat on his body. It gave him the opportunity to focus on one thing at a time. He was jumping ahead to thoughts of war. But there was a step to take before that happened. "I must bring charges against Deirdre and request the MacColls return her to us with what she stole to see justice served."

Alec's laughter cut short when Shane didn't laugh. "You're serious?"

"I am. I need to give them the chance to do the right thing before I escalate the matter to the king."

His brother's eyes went wide. "And what do you think he'll do about it?"

"I served as a captain in his army for the last five years. I hope that earns me some regard."

Alec only made a noise to indicate his feelings on the king's regard.

"Just because the MacColls go outside of the law doesn't mean I'll do the same. I'll do things properly so we can stand on the side of right."

"I doubt any of us will be standing at all when this is done." With that, Alec went back to the men. He would rather have had his war chief in agreement with his plans, but he knew Alec would do what was asked of him.

Still, Shane worried if this was the right thing. As he

had come to do when he was unsure of a decision, he went looking for Lindsay after he'd stopped at the river to wash first. He found her in the cottage, playing with a knotted piece of fabric with the dog. The smile on her face creased with worry, and Shane hated that he relied on her so much. But she gave him hope and peace when he needed it most. She came to him, wrapping her arms around his waist.

"What has happened?"

He told her the truth. "Nothing, yet."

She nodded. "I've made a mutton pie, and there is ale. Let's first get you something to eat."

He hadn't realized how hungry he was until she mentioned the food. He nodded and sat at their small table as she brought their meal.

"Go on." She encouraged him to dig in, which he did gladly.

After dinner, Lindsay seemed surprised when Shane led her outside toward the river. Tre ran off to find her own entertainments while Shane clasped Lindsay's hand in his own. He needed air and space and the feel of his wife's hand in his to bring him peace. But as they made their way to the side of the river, Shane realized he wanted more than the touch of her palm against his.

He wanted to feel her body and hear her pant his name as he took her to the edge of pleasure and tipped her over. He'd realized in his plans that he may not be able to get out of the arrangement with the Wallaces. Not knowing how much longer he might be able to call her his wife, he didn't want to waste a moment of the time they had left.

He removed his plaid and spread it out on the soft grass. Their coupling came on quickly and almost rough with the need they both felt. She took control by straddling his body and rocking them both to perfect completion.

"Now, what is on your mind?" she asked as he lay in the

thick grass, catching his breath. She knew him too well, but at the same time, not at all.

He chuckled and turned his head to face her. "Right this moment? Nothing is on my mind. It is completely blank, and I thank ye for it."

She snuggled closer, and he wrapped her in his arms and tucked his plaid up around her before kissing her forehead.

They lay like that for a while, just relaxing and breathing. No sounds around them but for the birds in the trees who had regained their song after their moans of pleasure had scattered them.

Eventually, his temporary peace faded away.

He spoke his plans quickly and waited to hear her response.

Chapter Twenty

Something had been bothering Shane all evening, and even in the desperation of his lovemaking she felt his unease. She looked at him now, hoping he would trust her enough to share his burden. Even if she couldn't help, talking about one's burdens made them easier to bear. "Tell me what has you worried," she said calmly.

He let out a breath. "Tomorrow, someone from the MacPhersons will leave to deliver a message to the MacColl laird. If they don't return Deirdre and what she's stolen, the MacPhersons plan to take the matter to the king."

Lindsay nodded. "While I hope you are not the one sent to deliver the message for the laird, I do see it is the best first step."

"Is it?" he asked.

"Aye. First, it's the best way to determine if she is even there, which I imagine she is. Second, it gives the MacColls the opportunity to do the right thing. If they refuse to turn her over, they will be in the wrong. If the MacPhersons attacked first without giving this option, they would be in the wrong. If the matter catches the attention of the king, the MacPhersons will want to be on the side of right."

He nodded again. "I am quite impressed by your strategy, wife. If ever you bore of spoiling me with your body, you would make a fine laird."

She swallowed, unwilling to tell him how close he was to being correct. She may never be laird, but she was raised to be the wife of one. Her father had never sent her away while discussing matters with his guard, and she had enjoyed thinking through the issues herself and deciding what she would have done and why. But never had so much been on the line before.

"I know you worry about me. But I made it through five years of battles. I will be fine."

She nodded but pressed her lips together. "I've seen the MacPherson guard, and I'm not impressed. Do they even have proper weapons?"

Shane frowned. "We'll hope it doesn't come to war."

She nodded but still worried. The MacColls' answer to any challenge was war. Hopefully, this time would be different.

...

As soon as Shane arrived at the castle the next morning, he sent for his brother as he pulled out a clean piece of parchment and ink.

"Have your senses returned as you slept?" Alec asked when he arrived.

Shane wasn't sure how to answer that question honestly, so he moved on.

"I need you to assign one of our guards to deliver my message to the MacColl laird. Do not send one of the smaller lads—we need a show of strength."

"You want to go through with this plan?" Alec asked with a wince.

"It may seem mad, but we must try to recover what was taken."

"You might as well declare war on the MacColls, for that is how they'll see it."

"Or they may do as requested. They just lost a battle with the MacKays; they'll not want trouble so soon."

"Ye think they will just hand over the money Deirdre stole from us?"

Shane paused and lifted his hand. "Don't forget the candlesticks." He'd meant it to be a joke, but it only enraged his brother further.

"Candlesticks? Bloody hell, brother. Did your brain get sloshed around while you were in France? You're not making sense."

"Actually, I am making perfect sense. It's time I took back what is ours so I can see the clan through the winter."

"You're going to see the clan fall to the hands of the MacColls if you don't stop this madness."

"Better a quick death than to starve and freeze to death." Once again, he attempted to shock his brother into seeing the matter from his perspective.

"And you think the MacColls offer a quick death? You've heard the stories. There is no greater evil than the MacColls. Besides, you're not even certain Deirdre went to them. She may not even be there."

"Aye. You're right. Which is why this tactic will allow us to know for sure." He held out the letter he'd written to the MacColl laird. Shane had toiled over the wording of the letter all night as he slept. After his discussion with Lindsay, he was all the more determined to see this through. "We will give them the chance to do the right thing."

"Go to Ronan. Tell him what has happened. He will

help."

"But at what cost to his own clan? Would we empty his coffers as well? I said I would go to Ronan as a last resort. If there is no other way forward."

"Why are you really doing this?" Alec asked, crossing his arms over his massive chest. His eyes flared as he took a step back. "You are too much like Father if you are willing to put the clan at risk over the happiness of a woman."

"Not a woman, Alec. My wife. I'll be damned if I'll see her regret her life with me. I am not like Father. I don't wish to waste away every farthing on baubles and silks, but I will bloody well make sure she doesn't go hungry."

"If someone must go to the MacColls, it will be me," Alec said.

Shane was already shaking his head, but Alec stubbornly pointed at him.

"If this is what you want, I'll not risk one of my men. I'll go."

"Very well," Shane said, hoping this was the right thing. "You'll leave at first light."

...

With Shane up at the castle on this important day, Lindsay tried to go about her daily chores as if everything was normal. She gathered berries to use to tidy up the lettering on Maria's stone. She checked the traps, finding a plump rabbit in each. She cleaned them and strung them over her shoulder so she could go to the village to trade. All the while, she heard rather than saw the men who'd been sent to watch over her. She knew if she came into trouble they would be there quickly.

Which made her wonder what authority her husband had to order such a thing. He was likely a formidable warrior. Mayhap he would become war chief. She recalled the man acting as war chief now and found him much more terrifying than Shane. Nay, Shane must be a respected soldier. She could see how the laird must be grateful to have him.

She went about her business. Usually, when she visited the village, she would have gone to find a few vegetables or maybe even a tart because her husband enjoyed them. But as she passed the smithy, she stopped. Her cousins were gathered around the large man as he showed them something near the forge. He must have made a jest, for all three boys laughed.

She'd never seen them so happy. And despite working for the blacksmith, they were cleaner than she'd ever seen them, too. She imagined what would happen to them if the MacColls attacked, and her stomach clenched.

"What can I do for ye, miss?" the older man asked.

Lindsay should have continued on as planned, but she couldn't pretend she didn't know the danger they faced. She was worried for her husband and this clan she had never wanted to claim. "I wonder if you could melt down different metal items to make arrowheads?"

The man showed his surprise at her question. "What need do ye have to make arrowheads?"

She came closer. She knew the warriors did not have proper weapons. She wanted to do whatever she could to ensure Shane and the other warriors could not only protect themselves but defend the rest of the clan as well.

"My husband is a MacPherson warrior. He has told me the old laird has left the finances in a bad way. As such, they don't have proper weapons to protect us. I thought perhaps if I brought some things from home, you might be able to melt them down to help. I'd rather not send my husband off to battle the MacColls with sticks and stones."

The man's brows lifted, and he leaned closer.

"Do you think there's a chance we could go to war against

the MacColls?"

She bit her lip, not wanting to worry the man. But while she didn't want to set the village to panic, it might not hurt for them to know what they were facing if they didn't find a way to help. Preferably before it was too late. Fortunately, she didn't need to say anything. Her silence must have told him what he wanted to know.

"We must do something straightaway." He went to the corner of his open shop and clanged two large pieces of metal together.

Lindsay didn't know what making such a racket would do until the villagers began to gather.

"What is it, Munro?" one of the older men asked.

"We're being called on to help the warriors in the castle. Bring me any metal you don't have a use for so it can be melted down to make weapons."

A murmuring went through the crowd.

"What business is it of ours? We don't have enough ourselves, and the castle takes and takes."

"And ye know none of us will even have the chance to carry the name MacColl if it comes to that. You've heard the tales. They don't just kill the warriors when they take over a clan."

The group nodded, and a round of "ayes" went about.

She had only asked this Munro about making arrowheads, but the man took it upon himself to delegate other tasks as well.

"You with children, take to the woods and look for straight sticks and branches, no thicker than your finger. Take them to these men, Roddy and Samuel, and my boys."

Her heart warmed at the way this man claimed her cousins.

"What are we gonna do with a bunch of sticks?" one of the older men asked.

Munro smiled, making him look younger than she'd originally thought.

"Ye men spend your days whittling anyway. You're going to shave them down to arrow shafts." The men frowned but nodded, though Munro wouldn't have seen because he'd turned to a plump couple at the other side of the crowd.

"Hal, we need goose feathers for fletching. Can ye help us with that?"

"If I butcher the geese for feathers, who will buy the meat?" the plump man asked.

"Throw them in the pot to feed us all while we work," Munro suggested.

The man grumbled again but relented.

Lindsay stepped up next to Munro.

"I will put these rabbits in the pot as well to help feed everyone. I know we don't have much to give, and I know in the past the laird and lady selfishly took without seeing the village taken care of."

She received a few nods and kept going.

"But there is a new laird now." The man she was supposed to have married. A man she didn't know and who could turn out to be the same as his father. But she wanted these people to have hope. She wanted to have hope herself. "We have a chance to have better lives if we pull together. If we don't, we may not have any life at all." That got the crowd moving.

Munro continued to order people about, taking several older lads to help him and her cousins in the forge.

"You'll learn some fine skills helping me, lads. The lasses love a blacksmith."

The gawky boys smiled and rushed to do his bidding. Where the threat of death didn't sway them, the possibility of female attention had. Some were sent off with wagons to collect whatever metal would be donated. Some stayed and hauled more wood for the fire.

Lindsay went to meet up with Hal and his wife as they settled a large pot over a fire that was being started. Other women were bringing water and dumped it in as soon as it was placed.

"Throw them in," Hal's wife said with a smile. "It's been quite a while since we've made enough for the whole village."

"Ah, do ye remember, dear Jenny? We met at such a gathering when we were but children. I thought you to be a fairy, for how beautiful you were."

Jenny's rosy cheeks turned darker at her husband's romantic musings. She swatted his arm playfully.

By midday, the whole village was caught up in their duties to make arrows. Lindsay had never considered what effort was involved in such a task. Being the daughter of a rich laird meant she hadn't needed to worry about things like how the warriors would protect the clan. It just was. Not having a set skill, she was passed around to different jobs as she was needed, from trimming down the goose feathers for fletching to affixing them to the arrow shafts with a foul-smelling glue. Occasionally, she would take her turn by the large pot, stirring and adding other ingredients. She even helped Munro by filing the new arrowheads to deadly points.

As the day grew long, she helped serve the villagers who'd come to help and was happy to see a few familiar faces.

"Thank you for helping." She turned to her cousins. "You all look well." She'd seen Doran when he came to watch over her, but the younger boys seemed so happy. Lindsay's heart warmed when they all smiled at her.

"I wasn't sure if you would want to see me, since I caused so much unrest, but if it would be all right, I would like to visit."

Three heads nodded. Robbie came forward and wrapped his lanky arms around her waist in a tight hug. "I miss my ma, and you smell like her."

Tears threatened. Lindsay smelled like her aunt because Lindsay's mother often sent her sister the violet soap they made at Riccarton. To Lindsay, it smelled of home, and now she realized it did for her cousins as well. "You are my only family here. I would love to check in on you and see how you're doing."

"We're not hungry all of the time," Robbie said.

"And we're learning our letters and how to read," James shared.

"We're learning how to make things and run the forge," Doran said. "And Shane says I'll soon be ready to join the guard."

She swallowed down her worry about her cousin being on the battlefield. Shane surely wouldn't allow anyone to put Doran in danger. He was not yet a man. At her youngest cousin's giggle, she turned to see Treun licking his face.

"She likes you. Perhaps you'd like the duty of keeping her out of trouble today."

Robbie laughed again and ran off with the little dog in tow. Her heart was lighter as she went about serving these people, learning the names of the other villagers. She'd never thought this place would be her home, but now with Shane and these people, it might be.

She glanced across the village at Castle Cluny sitting on the hill in all its glory and wondered if they were still awaiting her arrival to wed the laird. With the threat of the MacColls, she hoped they were too busy at the castle to care about the laird's missing bride.

She had plenty of other things to worry about herself.

Chapter Twenty-One

Having no funds to speak of made it unnecessary for Shane to waste any more time studying the books. All it did was frustrate him and make it impossible to catch his breath.

If he was going to be out of breath, he'd do so with a sword in his hand. Alec had left early that morning, so Shane went to the bailey to oversee the drills. He stepped up behind a large man named Fitz as the man was attempting to motivate the warriors of the MacPherson guard. Shane recognized the man by his wide smile. He'd been one of Alec's friends, and like Alec, he'd grown to become a mountain of a man.

"I'll spar with you," Shane offered. "And when I beat you, I expect the next man to be waiting in line to get the same treatment."

Fitz gave Shane a smug smile and shook his head. "You forget I'm not the squeaky-voiced lad you left behind."

"Bigger men canna move as quickly. It means they just make bigger targets."

The men gathered around them, making a circle. Shane guessed they might have cast wagers on the outcome if any of them had more than a coin to their names.

"We shall see."

Shane knew a sound mind was better in battle, so he drew calm around him, blocking out the enthusiastic taunts from the other men. He focused on his enemy and did his best to remember he didn't want to hurt him. Fitz moved first, as Shane expected, and Shane moved so his sword glanced off, then tapped the warrior in the back with his weapon. The men roared in laughter, making Fitz's face turn red. He attacked again and again, and each time Shane was able to defend the attempt.

"You can protect yourself all day, but you will not win that way," the man said.

"Perhaps not, but I also won't lose, and when you have tired yourself out…"

Shane burst into action, spinning under Fitz's thrust to come up at his side with his blade at the man's throat.

"As I said, when you have tired yourself out, I have the advantage."

Fitz laughed and pushed Shane away.

"Bloody bastard with your tricks," he said with no anger.

"Who's next?" Shane called. When no one moved, he decided to tempt them further. "If anyone bests me, I'll give them my sword."

The men looked at their sorry excuses for weapons and then at his claymore, the one given to him by his mother when he was only a lad. It had belonged to her brother, who'd been claimed in battle.

It was as fierce as it was beautiful. A winding thistle pattern could barely be seen on the blade. The same pattern was deeper across the hilt and handle, though the handle couldn't be seen, since Shane had it wrapped in leather to aid his grip.

Another of the larger men came forward. Shane

recognized him but couldn't place the man.

"Get him, Paul!" someone called.

"Paul?" Shane stood straighter. He knew someone named Paul. He'd been a good friend of Ronan's, and his sister…

"Aye, laird. I'm *that* Paul. And I've been waiting a long time to make things right for what you did to my sister."

"Bloody Christ." Shane jumped back as Paul attacked. He was much faster than Fitz and more bloodthirsty.

"We're only sparring, Paul. Don't kill the laird. Alec will be mad if he gets back and finds he's in charge of the clan," Fitz warned.

"The man defiled my innocent sister."

"Do you have another sister besides Ruthie?" Shane asked as they circled each other.

"Nay." Paul lurched forward, and Shane barely kept the blade from catching him in the side. "Just the one, thank heavens."

"I hate to be the one to tell you, but Ruth wasn't innocent when I was with her. She's the one who taught me the way of things."

"How dare you!" Paul's blade clashed with Shane's in a few swipes.

"It's true." Shane used the man's forward momentum to send him to the dirt, then rested his blade on the man's chest right next to his heart to keep him from standing up again. Shane glanced around the ring of men.

"Who else here has lain with his sister, Ruth?" Shane called out, knowing he wasn't the first or the last.

Paul glared as at least a dozen men raised their hands.

Shane thought Paul might go after each of them, but the circle scattered when the gate was opened and a large group of people entered the bailey singing and laughing.

"What is this?" Shane asked the man leading the group. It was Munro, the blacksmith from the village. He gave Shane a wink as he gestured someone forward.

Two men stepped up carrying a large basket.

"A gift for the new laird from the village."

Fitz and the rest of the group parted so Shane was standing before them.

"My laird," the man said, and the other villagers whispered as they dipped a bow in Shane's direction.

He wondered how many of them placed him as the soldier living in the cottage on the edge of the forest. If they told Lindsay… His gaze touched on each person, looking for his wife. He didn't want her to find out who he was—not this way. But he didn't see her among the crowd.

"I'm honored by your gift," Shane said. Whatever it might be was generous, but he doubted it would fill his coffers. If it was food, even that large basket wouldn't be enough to feed his people during the coming winter.

The lads set the basket down before Shane and pulled back the lid, presenting their gift. Shane gasped in surprise. Fitz came closer to peer inside as well.

"Bloody hell," the man whispered. "It's filled with arrows."

Shane looked to Munro in confusion.

"A woman in the village is married to one of your men. She asked if I might help her make some arrows." He turned about as if looking for someone. "Where did she go?" He shook his head. "Anyway, after she mentioned the threat of war with the MacColls, the lot of us decided it was important to make sure you and your men have what you need to protect the clan. We all did our part so you might do yours."

Shane didn't need to ask the name of the woman who'd prompted the village to make so many arrows. It was Lindsay. And his wife just may have saved them all.

• • •

Lindsay couldn't seem to catch her breath as she rushed back to their cottage. She'd tried to refuse joining with the other villagers on their visit to the castle, but they'd insisted. They'd wanted her to accept her proper accolades for motivating everyone to help the clan. While that hadn't been possible, she reluctantly agreed to go with them. She was sure to stay to the back of the group while their gift was delivered to the MacPherson laird.

Or rather, to her husband.

The MacPherson laird.

She'd not understood why he was accepting the gift from the villagers or why Munro called him "laird." And then the truth seemed to punch her right in the chest, stealing her breath.

Inside their cottage, she looked at the bed where they'd shared their thoughts but not their secrets. Had he known all this time she was the woman he was supposed to marry? He'd lied to her. She realized she'd done the same, but she'd done so to protect herself while he'd done it… She wasn't sure. As she paced in the small cottage they'd made a home, other things seemed to fall into place.

The way he'd gone up to the castle to help the laird each day. And how he'd come back to their tiny cottage. Why? Confusion soon turned to anger.

The dog whined at the door until she was let out. Lindsay worried she'd frightened the poor thing. She wasn't certain what she should do next. She was already married to the man her father had contracted her to marry, so she no longer needed to worry what he would do when he arrived.

Lindsay considered getting into bed to pretend she was sleeping so she might avoid whatever was to come next, but she thought better of it. It was the coward's way out. She was the laird's wife. It was time to see to her duty.

After packing her few things, she went to find the dog

so they could move to the castle, where they belonged. The place she'd been avoiding all along.

...

Despite Shane's new arsenal of swords and arrows, he worried.

He'd thought he was doing the right thing. Making a formal request was the way to handle disputes with rival clans. State the infraction and give the other clan the opportunity to correct the situation. Or maybe in this case they'd respond that Deirdre wasn't with them and they'd never met her. But if she was there and they refused to comply, the issue would escalate to the king. And he may do something, or he may not.

This was the way civil leaders acted. And if it were any other clan than the MacColls, it would be understood that Shane had no recourse but to reach out and request justice. But the MacColls didn't fancy rules or care much for the way things were done. Still, he had to at least try to recover what his stepmother had stolen. He'd trust the system and hope it wouldn't lead them to war.

He paced the floor in his study, stopping to look out across the lands that were now his for a sign of his brother.

Fitz came in to report the men had completed a successful hunting trip with the arrows that had arrived earlier that day. The salted venison harvested would help fill their stomachs when nothing else was available.

"Still no word from Alec?" the man asked.

"Nay. I don't know what to think of his delay. Perhaps this plan won't work after all."

"What plan?" Tory asked as she stepped into the study. She may have been the last member of the clan who hadn't heard. He hadn't wanted to share the details until Alec returned. But rather than risk her hearing it from someone else, he let out a breath and told her.

"I've sent Alec to deliver a message to the MacColls. I've asked them to return Deirdre and the money she stole to me so justice can be served."

Tory's face went pale, and her gasp was so loud, he worried she might swoon. But his sister shook off her concern as her face pulled up in anger.

"Why would you do that? You know they might see it as a threat."

Shane put a settling hand on her cool fingers.

"I spent a long time making sure my message couldn't be considered a threat. I was careful with how it was worded so they'd see I was left with no choice in the matter but to seek her out."

"But Ronan—"

"Ronan would help us, aye. But not as much as we would need for the clan to flourish. I'll not empty his coffers unless there's no other way."

To his relief, his sister nodded.

"Aye. I understand. I stand by you always. Ye know that."

He winked at the woman his little sister had become. "Thank you. That means more than you can know." He held out his arms, and she came to give him a fierce hug. He wasn't sure which of them needed the reassurance more. He suspected it was him.

"What of your wife?"

"What of her?" he asked.

"Ye have not told her who you are?"

"Nay. I'm not ready."

"If you get the money back, will it be enough to release you from the contract father signed with the Wallace laird?"

Shane shrugged.

"I'm not sure. I hope so. If not, perhaps I can use some

of it to offer a good faith payment and then repay the rest in grain next harvest. It would be better than nothing."

Since he'd arrived, Shane had faced one problem after another, and he didn't know that he'd solved any of them. Perhaps he was destined to fail his people. All he could do now was keep trying, and at night he'd go back to the cottage he shared with Lindsay and let her distract him until the sun came up again.

His thoughts went to Maria, and he realized he'd not thought of her recently. With everything else to consider, he'd not made time. The familiar guilt came over him, but not as painful as it had been. He had Lindsay to thank for that. In fact, he had Lindsay to thank for many things.

He couldn't repay her by annulling their marriage so he could wed the daughter of the Wallace. He was crossing the hall, heading to the bailey and then for home, when the messenger came rushing in.

"The Wallace laird has arrived. Should we let him in?"

It seemed Shane had run out of time.

Chapter Twenty-Two

Shane greeted the laird and his men as they dismounted. "Welcome to Cluny Castle."

"Are you the new laird of the MacPhersons?" the man asked. His voice echoed against the stone walls surrounding the bailey.

"Aye," Shane answered.

"I'm here to see you wed to my daughter, reclaim the dowry I paid, or take over your holding. The choice is up to you."

Christ. None of those options seemed good. They were already within the curtain walls. There'd be no way to stop them if they decided to attack. A glance over his shoulder at the men who stood willing to die for him gave him the needed push to find a way that wouldn't lead to war. What was his happiness compared to the lives of his men? And what could he offer Lindsay if he was struck down today and the clan taken over by the Wallace laird?

"There was a misunderstanding, for I am already wed. I'll gladly return your daughter's dowry. However, my stepmother has run off with it, and we've had difficulty locating her. As for taking over our holding, I may not be able to stop you, but I'd ask you to hear me out and give me another option."

"I'll hear you."

"Please come into the hall, where we might offer you a meal and drink."

The laird and his men followed them inside, and Tory came forward quickly to see to their guests.

When they sat at the table, the Wallace laird looked at him expectantly. "What is it you are proposing to satisfy the contract between our clans?"

"I wish for more time to recover what was stolen so I can return the dowry to you."

"And if ye can't recover it or not enough to cover it in full?"

"Then I offer a portion of our grain next year."

The man laughed. "Next year? I've already seen your fields haven't been planted for a harvest, but with no funds, how will you plant them for next year?" He shook his head. "Nay. I'll not accept this offer. I will be paid now, or I will take Cluny as recompense."

Shane's men stirred from their seats at the nearby tables. He knew a word from him would launch them to arms, but he couldn't do that. He couldn't lose a single man simply because he was unwilling to do his duty. To give up Lindsay.

He shook his head. "Nay." There was only one choice left, though it was one Shane could barely speak aloud.

He closed his eyes and thought of the cottage he shared with Lindsay. And beyond that the river where they bathed and made love. It didn't seem right that he would have to lose another woman he had come to wed. He'd failed to protect Maria, and now he would fail to protect Lindsay. What kind of a man was he that he couldn't save them?

He would have many memories of Lindsay to savor for the

rest of his days. Lazy moments in bed with her. Her smile. The way the sun reflected off her dark hair. And those dark eyes a man could lose his soul in and not care about getting it back.

Clearing his throat, he managed the words he didn't think his heart would allow him to say. "If you'll give me some additional time, I'll have my current marriage annulled so I may marry your daughter and honor the alliance you made with my father."

Shane watched the other laird, ready for him to draw his sword and launch them into battle right there over their meal, as he had every right to do. The man's longer hair was white with age, and his dark eyes looked upon Shane with disgust.

He imagined he deserved such a reaction. Going against an oath was a disreputable thing to do. The fact it had been his father who had given his word made no matter. Shane was duty-bound to uphold whatever agreements had been made.

Shane knew this all along. He'd realized it could come to this. He'd tried all manner of ways to get out of it, but while he didn't want to think of having to leave Lindsay, he'd known this was a possibility.

And now it had come to pass.

Shane would have to give up the only thing he wanted so he wouldn't lose everything. He just needed to get Wallace to agree, even if deep in his heart Shane almost wanted the man to refuse the offer. The choice of dying there was almost preferred to having to betray Lindsay.

If not for his men and his responsibility to his clan, he might have welcomed the sharp kiss of the man's blade. But this was what was needed to protect his people. He didn't know how he might tell Lindsay. Perhaps when she found out he'd lied to her, she might be glad for an annulment. He'd deal with that only after the man agreed. For a tense moment, Shane wasn't so sure things could end peacefully.

The sound of his heartbeat seemed to fill the space

around them as he waited for the man's reply.

"You'll dissolve your marriage and marry my daughter as promised?" he repeated with his head tilted as if he were testing the words for a trick.

Silently, Shane cursed his father for leaving his clan with such a poor reputation. "Aye. That is my offer—one that will honor the contract."

"I will give you no more than a week to see it done," the man said.

"Two weeks, for we'll have to have the annulment granted by the church and will need time," Shane countered, wanting every second he could manage.

"Nay. A week and not another day more. I've waited long enough for this to be done."

"Very well," Shane said as his stomach twisted in pain. He had no choice. His men would be needed if they ended up in a battle with the MacColls. They couldn't lose a single man if they had any hopes of winning another conflict. But nothing was *well*. Nothing would ever be well again.

He was going to have to give up his wife. Give up the woman who managed to warm his frozen heart, who had saved him when he hadn't known how to go on.

How would he tell her?

How could he hurt her in this way?

• • •

Lindsay wasn't sure how she was still standing. It seemed this day was not through with her yet. After finding the dog, she took him to the stable and entered the castle through the kitchens. The women had been too busy getting ready for the late meal to notice her as she continued toward the hall.

She'd stopped when she recognized the voice in the corridor.

Her father was here.

She'd been ready to step out and call an end to his threats against the MacPhersons, but then she'd been stunned into silence when she'd heard Shane's promise to end his current marriage and marry per the agreement.

Neither Shane nor her father had seen her in the shadows as they clasped each other's forearms and slapped backs as if they were old friends. While the warriors from both sides cheered and toasted Shane on his marriage, Lindsay slipped away toward the steps.

It seemed everything was in order now; however, she was in so much pain, she didn't think she could make it upstairs. As her thoughts twisted to the point of making her dizzy, she only wanted to go back home.

No. Not home. Not anymore. It was nothing but the small cottage on the edge of the trees where she'd once been happy. Where she'd tried to start a life with a man who had wanted her without knowing who she was.

And, apparently, she hadn't known who he truly was, either.

They'd both lied. She couldn't spite him for hiding who he was when she'd done the same thing.

But her heart hurt.

He'd known all along everything between them had been temporary. That he would eventually need to give her up to do his duty. He'd allowed her to care for him, when all along he'd known he would leave her to marry another. She realized the irony, that the woman he was contracted to marry was *her*. They'd married each other to avoid marriage to…each other.

She'd thought he might come to love her someday. She'd seen something true in the way he'd looked at her, and she'd felt it in his touch. But he'd just offered to dissolve their marriage as if it was an easy thing to do.

The dog wiggled in her grip, but she held on to her as she

searched for the room that would be hers. She found a maid, who directed her to the lady's chamber. Inside, she set Tre down so she could look around.

In the cottage, they'd shared a bed, but here they wouldn't. She wouldn't lie next to a man who so easily planned to cast her aside. Breathing in the scents of lamp oil and cloying perfume, she recalled the smells of her home. Baking bread and woodsmoke. She remembered every touch and laugh.

Every lie.

When she wiped her tears away, the little dog whined and Lindsay picked her up.

"He'd planned to leave us all along. This is our life now," she told Tre. "This is my duty."

· · ·

The great hall was full to overflowing with the Wallaces. Tory raised her brows at Shane from across the room. She wanted answers as to what had happened, but Shane couldn't move to tell her.

He was too numb with shock.

When faced with no other options, he'd made the best decision he could to save his people.

The mood of celebration in the hall conflicted with the misery in his soul.

Shane managed to slip out into the bailey and breathe in the cool evening air. Without consciously thinking about it, he called up to the guard on the gate to open it for him so he could go home. He'd put off telling Lindsay the truth long enough. He'd run out of time.

Taking the familiar path to the cottage where he'd learned to live again, he tried to swallow back the tears that threatened. He didn't know what words he'd use to end his marriage, but she deserved the truth. She always had.

He briefly considered how he might keep her in his life while also doing his duty, but he could not disrespect her in that way. He wouldn't suggest she become his mistress, not when she deserved so much more. She should have a full life with a husband who could love her in the way Shane should've been able to.

He worried what man might offer marriage to a woman who'd been cast aside by the laird. And if she returned to the Camerons, would it ruin any chance they had for peace between their clans? He would find a way to help if he could. He had no money, but he'd see she was cared for properly.

His steps slowed and eventually stopped. He dropped to his knees there in the soft, dark earth of the forest and screamed his frustration and pain out to the trees. He'd once thought his heart had been broken and lost in France, but somehow it had survived that loss only to be faced with another.

His anguish echoed back to him, and with it, he heard something else.

Determination.

He shook his head. He could not do this. He would *not* do this.

He loved Lindsay, and he needed her. There had to be another way to keep his marriage without putting his clan at risk. As he knelt there in the darkness, an idea formed. It would not be an easy thing. But weren't the best things in life worth the sacrifice?

He had a duty to his clan, but he had a duty to Lindsay as well. He'd protect her at all costs, like he should have protected Maria. With a new purpose, he stood and headed back to the castle to present the Wallace laird with another option.

In the bailey, Shane ran into Fitz, who was covering as war chief with Alec away.

"Are ye heading back to the celebration?" he asked.

Shane paused and shook his head. He wished Alec was there—not only because he was worried for his brother but because Shane's decision impacted Alec. He had a right to know what Shane planned.

"I've decided what I shall do about the situation."

Fitz's thick brows came down in a heavy crease. "I thought it had already been decided before ye left."

"I can't leave Lindsay ruined."

"Then we go to war with the Wallaces. It would've been better to do so before we invited them behind our walls into the keep."

"Nay. I don't wish to put my men and clan at risk because I'm unable to do my duty. I will abdicate my title to Alec, and I will offer to return to Riccarton to work off my debt to the Wallaces with Lindsay by my side."

Shane watched as Fitz winced and rubbed his chin. "I don't think Alec is going to like this plan. Besides, being laird is your birthright. You are the laird, not a servant."

"I am a husband."

"You would choose a woman over your clan? Ye are more like your father than I realized."

Shane let out a breath and shook his head. "It's not like that. I chose my men and duty over my wife once before, and it ended in bloodshed, guilt, and pain. I'll not do it again. I must choose Lindsay. Don't you see? This is nothing like what my father did. You would have me ruin the woman I married to offer my protection by casting her aside for an alliance I had no part in? Is that what the MacPherson name means to you? Have we no honor at all?"

Fitz huffed out a breath and walked in a small circle before coming back to stand before him.

"You know I'll always stand by you, even if your plan is daft and will lead to catastrophe."

Shane patted the man and turned toward the door to the hall, where Tory was hurrying out.

"There you are. You must come inside at once. Ye are not going to believe what has happened."

Rather than tell him, she simply spun and went back inside, leaving Shane and Fitz to follow after her.

The previous air of celebration had been replaced with anger and accusation. The Wallace laird was blustering to the room at large, and his men had taken on their laird's unrest. A few of them shoved into the MacPherson guard.

Upon entering, they caught the attention of Donald Wallace, who called out his name.

"What has happened?" Shane whispered to his sister. Shane had hoped the man would be in his earlier good mood to hear Shane's proposal.

It was the last chance he had to save his marriage to Lindsay. He'd offer to work off the debt himself as a servant at Riccarton. He didn't think Lindsay would mind, having thought him a poor soldier all along anyway. She'd asked to leave the MacPherson lands, and he'd now honor her earlier request.

After he told her the truth of who he was.

"After you left, the Wallace laird asked for his daughter to be brought to him."

Shane blinked in confusion. "I thought he was bringing his daughter with him."

Tory shook her head. "He says she arrived months ago to help a sick family member and remained at Cluny. He accused you of having her locked in the dungeon until she suddenly arrived. And you're not going to believe—"

She was interrupted from further explanation as the man came closer.

"I didn't know," he told his sister and then lifted his head to face Wallace.

"What is the meaning of this? I know ye have no funds to honor a wife, but to force my daughter into the clothing of a maid?"

"I'm sorry?" Shane meant it as a question, for he wasn't sure what the man was talking about. A maid?

The man shook his head. "I sent a letter to her uncle, and she responded that she had arrived. She'd met some unpleasantness with her maid running off with her things and my blighter of a brother-in-law causing trouble, but you couldn't have provided better for the mistress of the keep? And what is this business of telling me you married another instead of Lindsay? Are ye daft?"

Shane thought perhaps the answer was yes.

"Lindsay?" Shane said, looking between the man and his wide-eyed sister.

Fitz was still standing at Shane's back and whispered, "Bloody hell."

It seemed to take a long time for things to click into place. This man's daughter was named Lindsay. She'd come to help a sick family member. Her uncle had upset her. Shane swallowed and faced the man. But before he could ask what was going on, he heard a familiar voice.

"Father, please calm yourself. I am well. And dressed properly now that I have my trunks."

Shane stepped to the side so he could see the woman standing behind the irate Wallace laird. It sure looked like Lindsay. She had the same dark hair and eyes. She even had the same scar, but she was dressed in a fancy gown, with jewels looped around her neck and hanging from her ears.

She looked every bit like Deirdre, but she was his wife.

He wasn't sure how it had happened, but Shane was married to the very woman he'd been promised to all along. He'd not told her who he was, but she'd not told him, either.

"As it turns out, I'm already married to your daughter."

Chapter Twenty-Three

"I don't understand," Shane's father-in-law seethed. "You said you were married to someone else. What kind of game are you playing?"

"Father, please sit down and take some water," Lindsay said.

"I'll not sit down until someone tells me what is going on."

"It's simple enough to explain," Lindsay said as Shane took another step closer to her. This he needed to hear.

"There was a misunderstanding. Shane and I thought we were marrying different people. Thought we *were* different people. I didn't know he was the laird, and he didn't know I was the woman he was to marry. At least that is what I am to assume." She frowned but went on. "But we are married nonetheless, so the marriage contract has been fulfilled as you wished. Now we will simply move on as we were intended to do." She stared right at him when she added, "There is no reason for an annulment."

Christ. Lindsay knew Shane had offered to end his

marriage to her in order to marry…well…*her*. But what must she have thought, hearing his plans to leave her?

"I can explain," he tried, but she turned and went to Tory.

"I am ready to take over my duties with your assistance. Perhaps you can show me what room is available for my father during his visit."

Tory looked at Shane, then back to her.

"Aye. This way."

"Now that everything is sorted, I suggest we have a dram," Wallace said. Though Shane thought one dram would surely not be enough.

. . .

Lindsay managed to keep her composure until they reached the top of the stairs, and then her shoulders slumped and she had to bite her lip to keep from breaking down into tears—something she refused to do in front of this woman who had most likely known the truth all along and hadn't told her.

"I didn't know," Tory said.

"You didn't know I was the laird's daughter. So it was fine to be part of the deception to a common woman, just not one who would see to the castle? Is that it?" she snapped, unable to hide her anger.

Tory had the decency to look ashamed. "He said he was going to tell you the truth."

"Well, he didn't."

"But you didn't, either."

That was true enough, but Lindsay wasn't ready to concede her mistreatment.

"If we could see to the room for my father. He needs to rest after such a long day, and I'm afraid I wish to retire as well. I managed to find my room with the help of a maid, and my things have already been taken there." She pointed to the room next to the laird's chamber.

"You don't wish to stay with—"

"Nay." She definitely did not want to stay with Shane. *The laird.*

Tory nodded, and Lindsay followed the woman to a room two doors down from Lindsay's new room. "This chamber is set up for guests. If anything else is needed, I can see it done."

"This will do." She nodded.

"It was much more impressive before Deirdre stole a number of items and then Shane had some other things sold off." Tory frowned.

"The bed seems comfortable. That is all he requires during his stay."

As if she'd called for him, her father arrived at the top of the stairs.

"I don't know what the devil is going on, but this place is a right mess."

"I'm sure we'll set things to rights tomorrow. Please rest, and we'll talk again in the morning." Her father relented and went inside.

"I will have a maid sent to you to help you ready for bed," Tory said.

"It seems a waste to have dressed just to change again, but I thought it was the only thing that would soothe my father."

Tory nodded and hovered at the door as Lindsay went in her chamber. "For what it's worth, I'm sorry my brother planned to end his marriage to you. That must have been upsetting."

Lindsay pressed her lips together and nodded.

"I hope in time you can forgive me for not saying something sooner. I'm looking forward to having a sister." The woman smiled, and Lindsay felt her anger slip away. She imagined Tory was only doing what her brother ordered her to do. After all, he was the laird. Everyone must obey the laird.

Lindsay may be forced to obey him as well. She would do her duty as his wife and mistress of the castle, but as for the matters of her heart…that was over.

• • •

Shane went to the laird's chamber and took a deep breath to steady himself before opening the door to find it…empty. Stepping back outside, he spotted Tory.

"Where is my wife?" he asked.

Tory pointed to the room next door. "She's acquired Deirdre's room and asked not to be disturbed for the night."

"She is ordering everyone about already?" Had she known he was the laird all this time? He didn't think so.

"Can you blame her for being angry? She went from being married to a man she thought cared for her to being cast aside by the laird."

"But I wasn't going to. I had come up with another plan."

Tory sniffed. "Too little, too late, isn't it."

"You do understand how ridiculous this is? We're both married to the people we were supposed to be married to. So no harm was done. I don't see the issue here."

Tory glared at him. "If you think that, you're more foolish than I ever realized, brother."

"I lied to her, but she lied to me as well. We were both wrong. Doesn't that count for anything?"

His sister patted him on the shoulder in a pitying way. "I would not go at it like that if you hope to fix things." He might have asked for her counsel, but she shook her head and left him there alone in the hall outside his wife's chamber.

He raised his hand, ready to knock—maybe he'd demand she move into his chamber—but he hesitated. Perhaps his sister was right. She was a woman, after all. She would know better how women thought.

He backed away and returned to his own room. He'd allow her the night to think while he would do the same. Things would be better in the morning.

•••

It turned out he couldn't have been more wrong.

The next morning, Shane found his wife's chamber empty. He didn't find her in the hall or in the kitchen, where Tory was seeing to the morning meal.

"I haven't seen her yet today."

"Am I to look for her or give her more time?" he asked.

"She will find you when she's ready to talk to you."

He nodded and grabbed a few meat pies and a flagon of ale before going to his study. He was already exhausted, and he hadn't been up for even an hour yet. There was the matter of the Wallace laird and smoothing things over with him. The man must think him mad for his behavior.

As Shane had tossed and turned the night away, he'd worried over how to make things right with Lindsay. At some point he began to worry over Alec as well. What if he'd sent his brother to his death, having him deliver his message? He'd been careful not to word the missive as an accusation or a threat. Simply a request from one laird to another to have returned what was taken from him. But in doing so, had he doomed yet another person he cared about? Was he destined to make mistake after mistake until he lost everyone?

"What was I thinking?" he said to his empty study only a few seconds before someone knocked. "Enter," he called, hoping it wasn't the Wallace laird.

A tall lad with fiery red hair came into the room and nodded his respect. "I was told to come tell ye, your brother rides to the castle."

Before the boy had the words out, Shane was on his feet and heading for the door, the youth chasing behind him to keep up. At least this was one worry he could put aside. He only needed to see Alec was well, and then he could better focus on the matter of his wife and how to repair the damage they'd done.

Shane was in the bailey when the gate was raised to allow Alec through. He'd gone five years without seeing him, but for whatever reason these last weeks had felt even longer. "Are ye well?" Shane asked as soon as the man slid down from his horse. When he turned, Shane saw clearly that nothing was well. Not only was his brother's eye blackened and his jaw bruised, but his split lip was pulled into a tight line as tension rolled off him. "To my study."

Whatever his brother needed to tell him, Shane knew it would be better to discuss it in private.

"What has happened?" Shane asked as soon as the door was shut behind him. Alec made his way to the bottle on the desk and poured a dram and then another.

"I thought I'd assumed the worst when I left here. I worried the MacColls would take your message as a threat, but I never considered how horribly wrong it could go."

Shane's stomach dropped. "Do you mean to torment me?" he asked, taking the bottle from Alec before he poured himself a third drink. He'd do no good to Shane if he were too drunk to deliver the message. "Tell me what has happened."

"Deirdre happened. I didn't really believe in witches until now, for she couldn't have such luck. It must have been a spell." He shook his head, and Shane didn't stop him as he retrieved the bottle and downed a third glass.

"They hurt ye?" Shane asked.

Alec shook his head. "I'm fine. Or I will be. Although only for a little while, it seems." He held up his arms and let them fall to his sides.

"She must have been biding her time, waiting for an opportunity to escape. No sooner did I arrive at Collier Castle, greet the laird, and deliver your message, but a maid came running into the laird's study to report someone had run off with Deirdre and the lot of their money."

"And there you sat," Shane whispered, knowing how it would have looked to the MacColls.

Alec nodded. "They called me a distraction and took to trying to get me to confess that it was the true reason I'd come. To distract them while other MacPhersons came in and took what belonged to him. Namely, his coin and his wife—aye, Deirdre has married another laird. It seems she has the knack for it."

Shane poured a dram of whisky for himself. He didn't think he'd make it through the rest of this tale without a bit of fortification.

"When I refused to tell them what they wanted to hear, they locked me up for a few days and tried again. When I still didn't confess, they planned to take me back to the dungeon, but I overpowered the guards and escaped."

"And they think we've stolen their money and kidnapped the laird's wife?" Shane said, knowing he had the right of it but hoping for anything he had misunderstood.

"Aye. And I don't have to tell you they're planning an attack on Cluny. I would wager we only have a day or two to prepare before they arrive."

"Bloody hell." Shane ran a hand through his hair and tugged at the longish locks.

He'd known it was a risk but thought he had the law on his side. With the way things stood, he couldn't reach out to the king to decide the matter, for the man could very well believe the MacColls and side with them.

A knock at the door disrupted Shane's pacing, and the Wallace laird came in after Shane bid him enter.

"What is this?" Alec asked.

"This is Donald Wallace. He came to see me wed to his daughter as our father agreed."

"Bloody hell," his brother whispered. "And you're married to your Lindsay in the village."

"Nay, I'm married to Lindsay, this man's daughter. They are the same." Shane might have laughed at the absurdity if he could scrape together even a shred of humor under the laird's irritated gaze.

"Christ," Alec whispered. "I think I may have preferred to stay in the dungeon at Collier."

Chapter Twenty-Four

Lindsay frowned at the beautiful blue sky above her as she walked toward the village. It didn't seem fair that the day was so lovely when her heart was in such a state. She'd rather a dreary day or perhaps a storm to match her mood.

She frowned at the maid and the two guards that followed as well. Not that they had done anything, but that they were there. A reminder of what she had lost—her freedom.

She'd had a guard many times, but it had been different. She'd allowed herself to think it was the way Shane showed how he cared when he wasn't there to protect her himself. To make sure she didn't suffer the same fate as his beloved Maria. Now she saw it was just what he was accustomed to. The laird's wife must be protected at all times.

As if sensing her mood, Tre looked up and barked. "I don't know what to think," she told the dog for what seemed like the hundredth time that morning. She wanted nothing more than to go to her rock so she could sit by the running river and think. But the mistress of the castle wasn't expected to sit about on a rock when there were things to be done at the castle. And, besides, it wasn't her rock any longer. She'd given it to her husband. *The laird.*

Instead, she went to visit her cousins and Munro. Munro had taken up her challenge to the villagers to assist with arming the warriors. He was in his forge, melting down something to create a sword. The boys were gathered around but stayed back when he warned them of the heat.

She was happy the boys had found a new home, one that was safe and would help them grow into good men.

"Swords today, I see," she said with a smile, though it felt as if it was in danger of breaking on her lips.

"I should have a dozen or more ready to bring up to the castle by the evening meal. I reckon I will see you there, *my lady*," Munro said, giving her a knowing grin. So he had learned who she was. That meant the rest of the villagers no doubt knew as well.

Her simple life was over.

• • •

"What is going on?" Donald Wallace demanded after looking at Alec and taking a step back. Whether it was the new wounds or the old scar, Alec had managed to make the man pause at least. Still, the news was grim. He thought of telling the man it was none of his business, but his daughter was in danger, so Shane relented and shared the dismal truth.

"The MacColls plan to attack us."

As expected, Donald Wallace sneered his disgust at the name. "Why?"

Shane gave a quick explanation, and the Wallace laird let out a sigh. "I didn't bring my full army, and it would take too long for them to get here, but I'll add my swords to your lot. It won't do to leave my daughter here if Cluny is forfeit."

If Shane had hoped the man would make him feel more

confident, that surely didn't happen.

"I thank ye," Shane said instead.

"You'll need others to join us if we're to win."

Shane nodded and pulled out a clean piece of parchment and his ink. "It may take Ronan too long to get here to help us, but the MacIntoshes are our closest allies." He turned to Alec. "Summon your fastest riders. We'll send one to the Grants as well. And the Camerons."

"The Camerons?" Alec sniffed. "They are our enemy. They won't help us."

Wallace smirked. "It's an old strategy but a sound one."

Shane explained. "They are our enemy, but they hate the MacColls even more than they hate us. They will come and fight if they know we have a chance to win. They'll want to see the deed done by their own swords."

"The enemy of my enemy is my friend," Wallace said with a nod. "And the MacColls won't expect you to ask for their help. It gives us the numbers and the upper hand."

Shane handed the missives to Alec. "Send off the messengers and take to your bed. You need to be rested and ready for what comes tomorrow."

Alec left to arrange the messengers, leaving Shane alone with his father-in-law.

"Lindsay explained what happened, and it seems you are both at fault. Though I'm not sure she has come to see it that way as of yet. But she will. She knows her duty. She'll see it done and be a good wife to ye as she was raised to be."

The man seemed to think that was the end of the matter. Did he care nothing for her happiness? Duty was one thing, but a marriage—the kind he'd had before—was not bound by duty. He didn't know what kind of future he might have with Lindsay, and at the moment he needed to focus on having a future at all. "I will make things right with Lindsay. After I settle things with the MacColls."

"Or you'll be dead and it won't matter," the man said before shrugging and leaving.

"Good God," Shane said while hanging his head in his hands. But he got no reprieve, for Tory entered without even knocking. She was out of breath.

"Alec told me what is happening. How can I help?"

"Have you seen my wife?"

Tory frowned and shook her head. "I haven't seen her since last night, when she called me out for lying to her."

"She was angry with you?"

"If you were her, wouldn't you be? She told me she was your wife, and I told her I was the laird's sister. In truth, neither of us lied, but that doesn't matter, does it? Not really. We all knew well enough what the truth was, yet we said nothing. I only hope she'll grow to trust me again someday. I was so happy to have a sister." She pressed her lips together before adding, "Not that I don't like my brothers, too."

He stayed her with his hand. "Ye don't need to twist the truth to spare my feelings, sister. I know how you feel and how it would be nice to have another woman here for you to be friends with. I hope I haven't hardened her heart against the lot of us."

"Do ye think she will leave?" Tory asked.

It wasn't until the question was voiced that he began to think of that option. He wanted to say no, and say it loudly and confidently, but he wasn't sure.

"I don't think so. She doesn't seem the type to give up on things."

"I hope she doesn't give up on us." She pointed at him. "Don't even think to have me keep anything from her again."

"I won't. I swear it. I believe we've all learned a valuable lesson."

She helped him sand and seal additional letters requesting warriors to help defeat the MacColls for good. With enough people, they could defend Cluny and then attack the MacColl stronghold and take it over. These messages were dispatched to the Gordons and the Campbells as well. Any clan within a day's ride was contacted. By the time he went down to the hall for the evening meal, Shane was still worried but hopeful. They had a chance.

What he wasn't sure was if he had a chance with his wife.

Lindsay was already seated at the high table in the place next to his. She was wearing another beautiful gown with a different strand of gems at her throat. Would she expect such gifts from him?

Anger flared in his stomach, though he wasn't certain if he was upset that she might want such things or that he didn't have the means to give them to her. In her fancy clothes, she looked different. Beautiful in the way other ladies were.

He found he missed the plain dresses she wore when she'd just been Lindsay. He nodded to her as he took his seat. "Wife," he said in greeting and nodded at her father, who was seated next to her.

"Husband," she answered coldly.

"I missed you today." He'd hoped saying as much might coax her into telling him where she'd been, but mostly he'd said it because it was true. He found he rather missed being able to go home to their little cottage, where he could tell her his worries and she would listen and offer her advice.

"I went to the village. I wanted to check in on my cousins and see to some other things. Munro is working on more weapons for your men."

"They couldn't come at a better time."

"Why? What has happened?" Lindsay asked.

But it was her father who answered her.

"Nothing for you to worry over. The men will take care of things."

She nodded stiffly but said nothing else. Shane hadn't

known his wife well. He surely hadn't known she was the woman promised to him. But the Lindsay he'd known, the one he'd married, had not been one to sit around and let men handle things. She'd roused the village to make arrows.

It may have been a topic to be discussed in private, but there was no time, and she deserved the truth. She's always deserved it. But now he was going to do better about providing it, and not just because Tory's earlier question was still teasing at his thoughts.

Will she leave? He'd certainly given her no reason to stay as of late. "My brother returned with bad news. The MacColls plan to attack us. We may only have a few days before they arrive. They think we took Deirdre and their money."

Lindsay gasped, but not in the way that he worried she might swoon. This was simply surprise.

"That woman is a menace," she said angrily.

"Aye, that is a kinder word than I have used."

"What can I do to help?" Shane noticed she had lowered her voice. Perhaps so her father wouldn't put her off again. Still, he didn't want her to feel obligated. This was his mess.

"You have done plenty already. You don't need to worry."

He could tell he'd said the wrong thing as soon as the last word left his mouth.

"Have I not proven myself to you? Am I to be the *laird's wife*, a fixture at your table to be paraded about in my finery solely to make you proud? Should I put all my efforts on bringing forth a *male* child so I might finally prove my value and my reason for existence?"

"I, uh—" No words would come, and definitely not the right ones.

She interrupted his stammering when she stood. "Please excuse me. This silly dress is set to suffocate me."

He rose, but she was already gone and was halfway across the hall. He knew he'd done wrong by her, keeping his identity a secret for far too long and forcing her to live in a tiny cottage with simple gowns and food. But he didn't think this outburst was his doing. Or at least not completely.

"Women," the Wallace laird said. "They don't wish to keep to their purpose. Always wanting more."

"I don't know about all women. But that one certainly deserved more from me."

She surely had deserved the truth. The truth he kept from her was far, far worse than her not revealing her truth to him. He was the laird, and he had failed even before he began.

• • •

Lindsay couldn't be bothered with a maid. She tugged at the gown until she could get it loose enough to twist herself out of it. Next, she removed the necklace and tossed it on the dressing table. It wasn't that she was ungrateful for the things her father had bought her and brought to Cluny for her. It was just that in his mind, that was all she was. A decoration. Good for nothing more than to show his people how generous he was. She and her mother spent every evening looking pretty and saying nothing. And now it seemed her new husband had the same mentality, which really struck her as unlike him. Perhaps she didn't know him at all.

He didn't want her help.

When she'd been a simple woman, it had been fine that she helped in the village to make weapons, but now…she was the laird's wife. That was all. She would no longer be his confidant or the person he shared his worries and concerns with.

This was the very marriage she had wanted to avoid. Except perhaps Shane wasn't a monster. Though now that she thought back, she realized how much the war chief and Shane looked alike. Because they were brothers. Another wave of irritation washed over her as she tugged on one of her older, more comfortable gowns. The one she'd made, from that other life. That rare bubble of time where it was all so sweet and perfect. Before they knew the truth of it all.

She didn't answer the first knock at her door—or the second. She didn't know who it could be, but it didn't matter, for she didn't want to see anyone. She shouldn't have been surprised when her husband opened the door and came in anyway.

"Am I to be called on to do my wifely duty so soon?" she asked as she pulled the jeweled comb from her hair with a yank.

He frowned at her. "I know we didn't know what seems like the most important part of who we are, but I don't think that's true. We did know things. Mayhap, even things no one else knows. And you damn well know I would never force ye to lie with me if you didn't wish to. Not ever."

She let out a breath and nodded. "Aye. I know it." She was so angry it seemed to leak out of every word and breath. "Why have you come?"

"I didn't doubt you'd be able to handle whatever it is I might say. I only wished to spare you from worrying over something not your responsibility."

"I am a MacPherson, am I not?"

"Aye. You are." He paused and then paced in the room before coming back to stand before her. Then he began to speak and didn't seem able to stop until he'd told her everything about Deirdre stealing from the MacColls and their impending arrival as early as tomorrow.

"As you mentioned, Doran delivered another load of knives today, and not a minute too soon," he said.

"Do you need me to go to the village tomorrow to see to the people there?" she asked, wanting to do something useful.

When he frowned again, she raised her chin, ready for him to tell her she wasn't needed, like her father had said so many times when she'd been eager to learn something or help in some way.

"You are the mistress of the castle now, but Tory can see to things here while you see to the villagers and whatever else needs doing to prepare them. I will send a guard with ye, and if ye get word of trouble, you will come directly back to the castle."

"And bring as many of the villagers with me as I can," she said.

He nodded. "Have them ready to move. It will be safer here in the castle. We hope to head them off in the field to the south, but there's still a chance we could be overrun, and if that happens…" He didn't need to go into detail. Everyone would be better protected behind the high walls.

"I have heard tales about the MacColls. I'm sure I'm not the only one whose sire threatened to ship them off to the MacColl clan if they didn't obey as a child." It must've been a common threat among the Highlands. She only hoped they weren't as bad as the tales said them to be.

But Shane was no fool. He knew standing against the MacColls alone was dangerous, and that was why he'd sent messengers in the hope of getting other clans to join them. He'd not been too proud to ask for help to ensure a victory. Even her help.

"I will do what I can to defend the castle and the people inside," she said.

"Thank you." He nodded before leaving.

Lindsay didn't get much sleep that night. She lay in her strange new bed, thinking of the night before, when she'd been so angry she'd wanted to run from the castle and not stop until she found a new home. But now she was preparing to protect this home. And her husband was depending on her for more than making his table lively.

He'd been prepared to leave her, but perhaps he did see her as a capable person, someone he could count on and trust. When he'd been telling her what had happened and his plans, it had felt like before.

When the sky lightened with the coming dawn, she went downstairs to help Tory feed the warriors who would go to fight this day. She knew not all of them would come back. Her gaze caught on the man at the high table, who nodded to her in what she guessed was approval. Lindsay went to him as he and her father were planning.

"We'll be in position when they arrive. We'll wait on high ground to fight them off. And thanks to Lindsay and the villagers, we have a brace of weapons to ensure victory." Shane smiled as her father disregarded his mention of her efforts.

Shane made the whole business sound far too easy. She didn't think it would be. The men moved to the bailey, and she paused, unsure of what she should say. Things were strained between them. But if this were the last time she saw him… She swallowed back the tears that pricked her stinging eyes. "Please take care," she managed, though her voice came out hoarse.

"I shall return soon enough." He turned his horse and left, leading the men to battle as their leader.

Lindsay needed to busy herself with the tasks of the day so she wouldn't worry. With her faithful four-legged friend at her side, Lindsay went into the village to gather some last-minute supplies. Everyone was hurrying about, making final preparations as well. Children and animals alike were loaded into wagons to make the journey to the castle.

She stopped at person after person, offering them an invitation to come to the castle for protection. Some were reluctant, but a little before noon, a messenger arrived.

"Scouts have reported the MacColls have entered our borders. They should be upon us in a few hours. Please return to the castle straightaway. The gates will be shut and not opened again until the MacColls are defeated."

"And what of our warriors? Are they ready to protect us?" a man asked from the other side of the gathering.

A rumble went through the crowd, and the messenger looked uneasy. Lindsay moved toward the front of the group.

"Aye!" she shouted. "I spoke to my husband this morning. They are ready. Thanks to your hard work, the warriors are fitted with proper weapons that should see them safely through the battle. On behalf of my husband and his men, I thank every one of ye."

"It's true it has been many years since these twisted fingers have held a sword in defense of the MacPherson crest, but I hope ye don't think to keep those of us who can fight from standing beside our men on the battlefield."

Lindsay stood on tiptoe to see the older man who spoke. He was one of the men who'd helped shave down the arrow shafts. She looked to Doran and thought of the people here who wanted to help, and how it felt to be passed over as too weak to be useful.

"I'm sure they'll welcome anyone who wishes to join them." She pointed to Doran. "See my cousin, Doran, and he will lead ye to the other men. But please be safe and come back to us."

Doran grinned as he beckoned the men forward. "Come see me if you want to be certain you won't miss the fun."

"Fun," Lindsay muttered before pulling the lad closer. "Ye will stay out of the fighting and do what the other men tell ye to do. They shall need runners and the like. A person need not carry a sword to be a hero. Remember that."

The boy nodded and trudged off with a few of the men following along, including Hal, the butcher.

His wife, Jenny, came to stand next to Lindsay. "I have never understood why the Lord saw to make the dumbest of his creatures so brawny."

While she didn't think a battle with the MacColls would be fun, she was glad to see the men's spirits so high. And every man who stood next to her husband offered a greater chance he might come home. She may not be ready to forgive him for casting her aside and agreeing to end their marriage so he could marry another (her in the end), but she didn't want him harmed.

That thought made Lindsay lean over to the other woman. "I must gather supplies for the healing of wounds."

Jenny bit her bottom lip but nodded, and the two of them skirted around the other villagers to find a healer named Bess who seemed to recognize her even though Lindsay had never seen her before.

"Last I saw ye, you were sleeping off the damage caused by your uncle."

Ah. Shane must have called on this woman to help. "Thank you for caring for me," Lindsay said.

"Shane cared for ye, so it was easy for me to do the same. I hear he married you."

"Aye."

The woman smiled widely. "I am his aunt. Ye have a fine man."

Lindsay didn't argue, and not just because as his aunt she would most likely defend him to the death, but because she had seen his worry for his people. He was a fine man and even a fine laird. She just wasn't certain he was a fine husband.

They went about helping with bandages and herbs. Lindsay took everything out to the wagon and was shocked to see it was gone. She turned to see the line of villagers had made it all the way to Cluny Castle on the hill.

"We must hurry," she called to the other women, but she

heard the chains let loose and felt the thump of the heavy gate as it crashed to the ground.

"It's too late," Bess said. "We're trapped outside the gates."

Lindsay put her hand on Jenny's shoulder as the woman began to panic.

"We will be fine," she said in a voice more confident than she felt.

Chapter Twenty-Five

Shane assigned a few of his best archers to stay behind to defend the keep. The rest of his men and a few of the men from the village stood ready. The clanking of weapons and the shifting of horses reminded him of his years fighting in France. But this was much more personal.

The men suiting up for war were his family. His clan. Their blood would be on his hands.

Alec rode up next to him. Their horses were fitted with armor. "I sent two more men to guard your wife," he said with a frown. "Though, I'm not sure why they were needed inside the gates." Alec hadn't agreed with sparing more guards for such a task, but then, he didn't know what could happen. He'd not choose his men over his wife again. He'd learned that lesson in the most painful way and wouldn't lose Lindsay as he had Maria.

Lindsay may hate him for his deceit, but he'd see her protected, no matter what. And he'd care for her as a husband does, though they may not ever have a love marriage. That was the chance he took.

The sun was high in the sky as they held on the field to wait for the MacColls to arrive.

"It looks like we'll have a busy day ahead of us, men. Rest assured, your families are safe in the castle," Alec said.

Shane had wanted to keep the battle well away from Cluny, where his wife and his people waited for them to return. "We'll head them off here in the meadow between the border and the river," Shane said, leading the way.

If any of his men responded with more than a nod, he didn't hear it. Maybe that was because he could barely hear anything beyond the rushing of blood at his temples. It was always this way when he went into battle. His nerves would rise up as if determined to take him down themselves. But as soon as it began, there was nothing but peace that came around him as he did his work to defeat the enemy.

It seemed they'd go to war with the MacColls alone. The warriors from the other clans had not arrived in time to offer aid.

It was just his clan against the monsters he'd heard tales of since he was a child.

On the opposite hill, he saw them, their weapons gleaming in the sunlight. The mass of men pulsed with anger and anticipation. Shane could already see they were outnumbered.

"We are fighting for our loved ones, our lives, and our home, men. Fight well."

. . .

Lindsay paced in the small cottage. While Bess seemed calm, Jenny was a mess with worry for Hal as well as them.

"We don't even have a blade between the lot of us," the woman fretted.

"No one will expect us to be here. It's not like they'll

come looking for us."

She shared a glance with the older woman. Lindsay wasn't accustomed to battle, but she knew if the MacColls won, they'd come to the village straightaway to claim their spoils. And here sat the three of them and a little dog, who just then went to the door and barked.

"Shh, ye wee beast. You'll tell them where we are!" Jenny scolded louder than the dog had barked.

"What is it?" Lindsay asked the dog, not expecting an answer, but she followed Tre to the front of the cottage when she came to sit by the door. Lindsay peeked out the window and saw three men entering the clearing where Bess's home sat. Their plaids were red and similar to the MacPhersons' tartan, but she looked closer and noticed the differences.

"MacColls." Their name passed her lips like a hiss.

Both Jenny and Bess gasped behind her as Lindsay continued to watch through a slit in the curtain. If the MacColls had already set on the village, did that mean the MacPherson soldiers had fallen? But when she peeked out again, she saw it was only those three soldiers. Blood marked their once white shirts. They seemed to lean upon each other as if holding one another up. One held firmly to the banner showing two stars and an arrowhead.

She moved to the other side of the window to see another man leaving on horseback, the MacColl banner waving behind him. The other two men now sat together, holding a white flag of truce.

She looked to the dog next to her, who whined, and then back to the women. "Do they need help, or is this a trick?" she wondered out loud, and once again, the dog offered no help. She just cast her brown eyes on Lindsay as if asking what she should do.

So many questions and no clear answers.

"They are injured, holding a white flag," she told the

others. "I wouldn't trust them if they told me the sky was blue. But they are in need of help."

"Let them rot," Jenny snapped. "It could be a trick."

Lindsay looked to Bess as if waiting for the woman to break the tie. "I've never been one to turn away a person in need. If I'm wrong this time, God will surely see me avenged."

Lindsay nodded in agreement. She needed to do the right thing, and she knew if she left them to die, it would haunt her the rest of her days.

"If it was a MacPherson bleeding outside of the MacColl holding, they would let us die," Jenny said. She wasn't wrong.

Bess answered, "Which is exactly why I am not going to do the same. I hope to say I am better than the MacColls. Don't you?"

Lindsay nodded, though fear had clogged the words to reply. Instead, she gathered her things into a basket. Bandages, thread, and clean water. She also tucked a carving knife inside, just in case. Which made Jenny roll her eyes. It may not have been a proper blade, but it was better than nothing.

Her heart pounded as she opened the door. "You two stay here and bar the door until I return."

"Nay. I'll not tell my nephew I stood aside and allowed his wife to face this danger alone."

"And there is no reason to put us all at risk. I will go. You stay here."

Rather than give the woman a chance to argue, Lindsay stepped out and shut the door behind her. Snippets of things she'd heard over the years flashed through her mind. The MacColls ate the hearts of their enemies, even the children. But as she moved closer, she realized these men were not monsters. There were no fangs or claws to be seen. Simply ordinary men who needed assistance.

The man on the right set down the white flag and stood to

come closer on unsteady legs to help her, as she would expect from any proper gentleman. She paused. Perhaps he planned to pull a dirk and cut her throat. She couldn't yet be sure. She only knew if these men wished to harm her, she'd be ready. She wouldn't go down without a fight.

"Thank ye for yer aid, mistress," the man said, taking the basket to ease her burden.

"I will see to your wounds if you promise no harm will come from it."

The other man laughed roughly.

"The lot of us have been trying to find a way out of the MacColl clan for a few weeks now. Our laird has left the clan in shambles, and it wasna all that great to begin with. He took in a demon witch who twisted his heart against his people."

Shane had told her the same had happened to his father, who had spent the clan's coin on baubles for his needy wife.

"Aye," the other man agreed. "I'd wager we'll all starve this winter anyway, so why not change allegiance to the MacPhersons? At least we might live to see spring."

Lindsay chose not to tell them the MacPhersons weren't so well off, either. Instead, she went to work. She stitched and dressed two wounds and gave them water. As they drank and rested, she returned to the cottage to inform the women the men were harmless. The other ladies and Tre returned with her to help the men into the cottage.

They'd all stay there and then go up to the keep as soon as the battle was over. Lindsay wondered how long that might take. How long until she knew the fate of her husband?

• • •

The battle started with a volley of arrows. The bolts, provided by Shane's clan, soared through the air and met their marks as if guided by the hopes of his people. Men in the red tartan of the MacColls littered the ground before they'd even engaged.

Lindsay's father spat on the ground and nodded that he and his dozen men were ready.

But it wasn't enough. They were still outnumbered. If only another clan had been able to join them… As if Shane had summoned them by thinking of them, the Camerons poured over the hill from the west. Their chief said nothing, just gave a nod as he called out a battle cry and descended onto the field.

When the armies converged against the MacColls, many of their enemy's warriors dropped their weapons in surrender—whether it was because it was clear they'd now lose or because they didn't want to fight for the wily bastard they called laird, Shane wasn't certain. Still, enough others fought that Shane frowned at several MacPherson bodies lying in the grass. They'd be mourned later. Now, Shane needed to fight so there wouldn't be more of his clansmen's blood spilled. Shane lost himself in the pulse of battle. His sword swung around as if an extension of his own arm as he slayed any MacColl that engaged him.

He didn't raise his sword to anyone who'd dropped their weapons. He didn't understand the reason they chose not to fight. All he knew was that every MacColl who defected meant less of a chance he'd lose someone else today. While he surveyed the battlefield, he spotted two MacColls moving on a smaller man. When he looked closer, he recognized the boy. Doran.

He hadn't realized he'd come to fight. He was getting better with his moves but was in no way ready for such a battle. And to engage two large warriors would mean instant death for his wife's young cousin. He couldn't imagine having to tell her the news.

"Alec!" Shane yelled and pointed.

As if it were no more than a minor inconvenience, Alec

stepped behind the men and cast his sword in a long arc, cutting them both down in one swipe.

The boy swayed for a moment but didn't swoon. Shane was impressed to see the lad shake off his fear and jump right back into the fight, picking lone warriors and using the moves Shane had taught him. Shane might have sent him home if the battle hadn't slowed to just a few smaller fights between the clans. In the middle of the chaos stood a large man with no fewer than six retainers at his side.

Laird MacColl.

Shane whistled, and Alec looked to him right away. His brother glanced between them but understood well enough. It wasn't the same as fighting with Ronan, but they were brothers and there was still a bond there. Alec gathered Fitz and a few other men to come with them as they went to meet the other party. The men spread out to a half circle around the laird as Shane grew closer.

"I am Shane MacPherson, laird of Clan MacPherson. You attack us on our lands at your peril."

"You stole my wife and money, and I'm here to take back what is mine. Give me my wife, or prepare to surrender your own in her stead. Otherwise, we end this with blades."

Shane shook his head. "I do not have your wife or your money. I'm afraid you've fallen victim to Deirdre's tricks. She did the same to my father. What money she didn't squander, she stole when she fled our keep to go to yours. Now she did the same to ye."

"Lies. I think I'd know my own wife."

"You mean our stepmother? I've known her since I was twelve summers and know her better than ye think," Shane said.

The retainers blinked and looked to one another. Finally, the laird shook his head. "She said marrying her would align the MacColls and the Grants because her son was the laird of the Grants."

"That he may be, but his mother is no one to speak for my stepbrother. The Grants would side with the MacPhersons if they'd had time to arrive. Of that, you can be sure."

"Uncle, we are alone against the Camerons and the MacPhersons. We're outnumbered. We must retreat."

The laird glared at the younger man. "Don't be a coward, Bacchius. MacColls do not retreat. So long as there is breath in my body, I will fight."

"Bloody hell," Alec said, sounding almost bored as he stepped closer and drew the sword from his back. "Let's get on with it, then, so we can have our supper."

Shane and Fitz did the same, and the fight began. Shane faced off with the other laird. At the first cross of their blades, Shane knew his opponent was weak with age and laziness. But the fire in his eyes was still strong. He'd not give up even if he knew he'd lose.

Shane hoped his own pride would never be his downfall, like it was to be for this man. Shane would not play with the man. Defeating him would likely lead to a quick surrender and fewer lives lost.

A feign to his left and a strike to his right, and the man dropped to his knees. Shane lifted his sword to finish his enemy, but he gasped at the sharp pain in his back. He turned to see the laird's nephew staring at him with wide eyes of surprise, his skin as pale as milk.

Shane watched as Alec bore down on the man, severing his head from his lanky neck. Turning back to the laird, Shane tried to raise his sword again, but the pain stole his breath, and he stumbled back. Fitz moved in and ended the laird in one slash of his claymore.

Shane saw the remaining men drop their swords as soon as their chief fell. The war was over. No one else would be harmed today. As he gasped for air and gave in to the fire spreading through his back, he thought of Lindsay and then Maria. He would be with one of his wives today; he wasn't yet sure which one.

He hadn't wanted to say goodbye to Lindsay for fear it would bring ill luck. He wished now he had said more to her. He should have told her he was sorry. That he hadn't wanted to leave her but was only doing what he thought was best in that moment.

"Ye have grown lazy," Alec said.

Fitz reached out and smacked Alec. "What is wrong with ye? You don't speak to a man who might die like that." Shane wanted to thank Fitz for his loyalty but needed to focus on moving air in and out of his burning chest.

"He isna gonna die. It's but a scratch. And look at his mouth. He's not bringing up blood from the lungs. If we get him to a healer so he doesn't keep flooding the field, he should be fine by morning."

Alec's words—harsh as they seemed—put Shane's mind to ease. The war chief had certainly seen his share of mortal wounds and knew if Shane's was serious or not. Shane hoped he wasn't wrong.

The men loaded him into a cart and began the bumpy ride back to the castle. The sky swirled above him, going in and out of focus. Light sparkled at the edge of his vision. He didn't have much time left before he succumbed to sleep. And he wasn't sure if or when he would wake up again.

"Alec?"

"Aye? I'm here."

"Take me to Bess's cottage."

"She will be at the castle. We must take ye there."

Shane shook his head and hoped he could hold on long enough to speak clearly so his wishes were heard. "Take me to her cottage and bring her to me. If ye are wrong and I die, I don't want to do it at the castle in front of my people." In front of Lindsay.

"Aye, laird. If that's where ye wish to go, I'll see you there."

He remembered something else he needed to tell his men. "Send word to Ronan that we have prevailed so he doesn't worry."

"I will see it done, brother."

Shane must have faded, for Alec leaned over to pat his cheek painfully.

"But know this—you will not be leaving any of us. I have no wish to be laird. Do ye hear me?"

Shane attempted to nod, but his head felt too heavy to move. He had no desire to leave anyone, especially Lindsay. But he couldn't fight the need to close his eyes and let the quiet darkness draw him in.

...

Lindsay had known no greater fear than seeing the war chief jump off the back of a wagon at Bess's cottage. Another man close to his size stood with him, but there was no sign of her husband. That must mean… Were they coming to tell her he'd…

Nay. They didn't know she was there. As they got closer, she picked up on part of their conversation through the open window.

"…that blighter nicked Shane in the back like a coward," the large war chief was saying.

"Aye, but the bastard got what he should. His body missing his head," the other man responded with a grin as if something was amusing. "Did ye see how I did it, Alec?"

She'd known the war chief's name was Alec—her husband's younger brother—but somehow hearing it said while he was there made him less intimidating. A man instead of the monster she'd thought him before. And when his lips tipped up in a smile, she was almost shocked he was capable of such a thing.

Certainly, they wouldn't speak like this with smiles on their faces if Shane had been mortally wounded. "Where is he?" She looked between the men and the wagon as she rushed out to meet them.

Alec glared at her, and she remembered why she'd thought him frightening.

"What the bloody hell are ye doing here? You're to be up at the castle. Where are your guards?"

"We were left behind as we were gathering supplies to tend to any wounds. We are fine, and I have two injured MacColls inside that will need to be taken up to the castle."

"Bloody hell," the man repeated. "Shane told us to bring him here and fetch Bess to stitch him up."

"Bring him inside," she said, though her voice sounded far away as they lifted Shane from the wagon. Dizziness caused her to sway and blink. Alec grasped her upper arms and gave her a tiny shake to drive it away.

"Don't worry, lass. He's one for dramatics when he's injured. He'll not die today. I've seen the way a man looks when death comes for him, and Shane will live. I swear it."

She shook off the lightheadedness and nodded. "Quickly. It's not that I don't believe you, but I need to see him myself."

He nodded. "Aye."

The dog followed him as Alec carried her husband into the cottage. His legs dragged behind them in the dirt. Alec held a bundle of bloody rags to his back.

"He's bleeding like a stuck pig," he said, matter-of-factly, as if it was a common thing. Perhaps for men of war it was. Would Shane have acted as casually had it been one of the other men bleeding?

She thought of Maria and wondered if the woman had

been as cavalier, having seen the efforts of war every day. Lindsay said a little prayer to the other woman. *Please, help me save him.*

"He'll be fine," Alec said again.

Lindsay knew a man only had so much blood to let before there was no more. But a man could also die without a drop spent if the bleeding occurred beneath the skin. She set to work with Bess at her side, while the other men argued about the severity of her husband's wound and what to do with the sleeping MacColls.

She cleaned the wound and began stitching up the gash so the bleeding would stop. She paused a moment when her hands trembled.

"Do you want me to do it?" Bess asked. "My eyesight isn't what it once was, but I can shut a wound."

"Nay. I can do this," Lindsay said quietly, more to herself than in answer to Bess.

"Do ye need a dram of whisky to settle your hands, mistress?" Fitz asked while holding out a flask.

She considered for a moment but then shook her head. Plying whisky wouldn't help her in the long run. She needed her wits about her to help Shane. She focused on one stitch and then the next and next. God, there were so many needed to seal up the large wound. She could only hope he hadn't lost too much blood. There was no way to know for sure. His body was cool to the touch, but he didn't shake, which was a good sign. The bleeding slowed to a trickle and then a stop. Bess coated the whole mess with honey to help with the seal.

When Lindsay finished bandaging the wound, she placed a kiss to her fingers and lightly touched it over the tied cloth. It was a silly thing. She didn't know what would come next. There was still much unsettled between them, but she wanted him to wake up that instant.

Alec and Fitz were speaking quietly but urgently out on

the porch. She guessed they were in a disagreement over what was to be done next. With a deep breath to steady herself, she went out to face the men.

"How is he?" Alec asked anxiously. For all his bluster before, it was clear he'd actually been worried.

"The bleeding has stopped. I don't think anything vital was damaged. He is resting now, and he's cool but not shaking, so while he's lost a good bit of blood, I'm not sure yet if it was too much. It's up to him now."

She stood to the side as the men discussed traveling to the MacColl stronghold to take the castle while it was weakened. Lindsay thought it was a good strategy, though she couldn't care when all she saw when she closed her eyes was her husband lying inside.

Once the men agreed on a plan, they turned to her as she stood there numbly. Her hands shook.

"Did ye hear me, mistress?" Alec asked, closer to her now.

She startled and shook her head.

"Ye are in charge of the clan until he wakes. There's much to be done."

She could only nod as Alec and Fitz loaded the injured MacColls into the cart and came back for Shane to take them all up to the castle, where she would be in charge of the clan.

Chapter Twenty-Six

Shane had been injured once in France. When he'd woken in the hospital, he'd been surrounded by the groans of injured and dying men. He'd wished his wife was by his side.

He was thinking of that when he tried to open his eyes to ask for water. He swallowed and forced the word from his throat. "Agua," he asked in Spanish. "Por favor."

"Uh. Water? That's what you asked? I'm sorry, my Spanish is not good," the woman said.

Lindsay. He recognized her voice, and everything came flooding back. He was in Scotland, not France. He'd been in a battle with the MacColls, and his clan had won. His eyelids fluttered open as he forced himself to look at her, eager to make sure she was well.

"Are you…?"

"All is well. I'm glad you've chosen to wake up."

Her voice trembled on the last word, and he reached out for her hand. For all the anger and confusion and mistrust they'd shared, he was heartened to see she'd worried over him. She cared. Her warm palm pressed against his cooler one. He felt a small, warm weight against his opposite hip and managed to look down to see the dog sleeping against him on his bed in the castle. If he'd had the strength, he may have shooed her away. But he imagined he wasn't in any condition to argue at the moment and let the little dog rest.

"Alec?" he asked.

"He is well. He's seeing to things with the men. The MacColls have been defeated or surrendered."

"How many men did we lose?"

"I-I'm not sure. Some. I will ask my father when he returns." She frowned, and he thought maybe she'd heard more but didn't want to tell him. He didn't press; he wasn't certain he was ready to hear the tally anyway.

Whatever the number, every life lost was his fault, as if he'd drawn his blade against their throats himself. He should have anticipated his letter would lead to war. He'd felt like it was the best way to recover their losses, but now…

He remembered something his father had told him after catching him ordering his brothers around as the heir—that being a good leader wasn't about ordering people about and sitting on your arse while others serve you. Every order given should be thought out fully. Every ruling had a repercussion. And every decision had the opportunity to be a mistake. Wise words from a man who'd abandoned the idea of leadership and being responsible for his clan. Shane remembered them.

He was now the laird of the MacPhersons, as well as what was left of the MacColls who had pledged loyalty to him, and now, while the MacColls had surrendered, he'd go to Collier to claim the castle as his. But it would mean he had two clans to feed and see through the winter with no money. He hadn't anticipated that outcome. It seemed like everything he did as laird turned out to be the wrong thing—including the secret he'd kept from his wife, that he was indeed the very laird.

When he asked to stand up, she offered her support as

he took a few steps. His body was stiff and the stitches pulled with each movement, but he was up and moving about.

"You scared me last night," she said as he stretched a bit. "Your skin turned warm, and I thought for sure you'd start a fever, but then a few hours later your skin cooled, and now you've woken up."

"You must have done a fine job of cleansing the wound. That's what Bess has always said." He smiled at his aunt hovering by the door.

"She used all of my whisky," his aunt complained with a smile.

"As the healer from my clan taught me."

Shane tilted his head, thinking the method odd, not to mention a waste of good whisky, but he couldn't argue the results, so he shuffled along toward the door with Tre and the two women following along.

"Ye should rest," Lindsay said.

Shane nodded. "I will. But there's something I must see to first." Shane made his way to the steps, stopping twice to put a hand on the wall when he swayed. It seemed he'd lost a lot of blood, which was surely missed. Slowly, he made his way downstairs and into chaos.

Tory met him as soon as he entered the hall, which was teeming with people. "You're looking recovered, brother," she said, though her wince made it less convincing.

"What is all this?"

"Many of the MacColls from Collier have already come here in the hope of finding better living conditions. I set the warriors to hunting to keep us in venison, pheasants, and rabbits so we can feed everyone. They brought a wagon near to full of turnips to pay loyalty to you, and the kitchens are making good use of those. We just need homes for them. Until then, I shall set them up in the great hall and the bailey."

"Thank ye, sister, for taking to the running of things

while I was away. You've done well."

"Nay, it wasn't me. It was Lindsay. Between carrying for ye and advising me, I don't think she's slept at all." Despite her anger with him, she'd tended him and ran the clan while he'd been abed.

"I see you're up," the Wallace laird said.

"Thanks to your daughter, things have been seen to while I was down."

The man frowned and went on without a word of acknowledgment that his daughter was capable of such things. Was this how Lindsay had lived, with a man who refused to spare a word of encouragement or pride?

"What are ye to do with all these mouths to feed?" Wallace said.

"I'm not sure. I only just now found out they had come here. Let me think on the situation, and I'll come up with a solution."

The man snorted and walked off.

Tory glared after the man. "He doesn't think a woman can do anything but sit by and smile. I'm not sure how Lindsay endured it." Their own father had always said Tory didn't need anything inside her head so long as her face was bonny.

"It seems to be the way of lairds to underestimate their daughters."

"If ye are blessed with a lass, make sure you don't do the same," she said before heading off to see to a young couple who'd just entered the hall.

Shane knew better. He knew how well Tory looked after things until he was forced to stay at the castle. He also knew how clever his wife was, and he would seek her advice to select the best path forward.

"Where is Alec?"

"He's gathering the MacColl warriors and sorting them

as to their loyalty."

"Dare I ask what he's doing with the men who still pledge fealty to the MacColls?"

She scrunched up her nose. "So far, I've not heard of any who have."

While Shane was glad the war seemed at an end, it meant more people to care for and still no funds. He needed to get to Collier and see what was there to salvage. Surely, Deirdre hadn't been able to leave with everything.

Tory pointed toward the door. "He's out in the bailey."

Shane nodded and headed in that direction, not sure what to take care of first. He felt overwhelmed and wished he could return to the small cottage on the edge of the village and talk to Lindsay until his worries drifted away in kisses and heat. Those days were likely over in exchange for the cold marriage of a laird and his lady. He didn't want that, but what did she want?

In the bailey, he found the gates standing open. Through them, he spotted small camps of people. More of the MacColls he was now responsible for. He didn't yet know what he would do with everyone, but Collier Castle still sat unclaimed, and Shane was going to take it and any spoils it held. While he didn't look forward to sitting a horse or a long ride in his state, there was nothing for it.

He needed to leave straightaway.

"Alec, gather half the men and get them ready to leave for Collier within the hour. We will claim the castle."

"Will you be joining us, brother?" Alec frowned at the blood staining the side of his shirt.

"Aye. I need to see what is there. I can better prioritize what's needed after seeing the holding and claiming it for the MacPhersons."

Alec was still frowning but gave a single nod before shouting the order for the men to line up. A second order went to a boy who ran off to the stables to inform the stablemaster the mounts needed to be brought to the bailey.

Shane went inside to look for his wife. He wanted to commend her for all she did and tell her he wanted to talk out their troubles when he returned, but he didn't see her in the hall and didn't want to use up his strength to return upstairs.

Wallace headed him off as Shane looked for Tory to give her a message for Lindsay. "What will ye do?" he asked. "Ye've even more people now and still no way to provide for them all."

"Aye," Shane said. He wanted to roll his eyes. Did this man think him so daft as to not see the trouble he was in? It seemed everything he did was the wrong choice. Every step he'd taken north from France had been fraught with wrong decision after wrong decision. But it was too late to retreat. He could only go forward. "I will find a way. That is all I can do."

It seemed simple enough, though Shane knew it was truly impossible. Unless they could find Deirdre and their money, they wouldn't make it through winter. So that was what he'd do. Assess Collier and then turn every resource on finding Deirdre.

The other man scoffed, and Shane didn't blame him for his reaction. This man's daughter was at risk if Shane couldn't find a way to save the clan. If ever he became the father of a lass, he'd wish for the same thing as Wallace: that she be protected and cared for. It was the smallest thing a husband promised his wife, and it seemed neither of them were certain he'd be able to manage it.

"I must go. Tell Lindsay…" There was so much he wanted to say to his wife. Yet no words came to his lips. "I will return."

And with that he left the hall, the castle, and his land in search of a miracle.

...

Lindsay was assisting the other women in getting as many rooms ready as possible. In this situation, it hardly seemed right for Lindsay to take up a room that could be used for others when she could surely share one with Shane, as they had previously. And if that thought gave her stomach an odd twist, she ignored it in favor of focusing on her work.

In the hours she'd tended to him, it had been easy to remember the man he'd been. The one who was given to fits that ruined his sleep. The ease with which he'd slumbered had worried her, but he seemed well enough now.

She'd seen the way he'd looked at her earlier as if he wished to say something but wasn't sure of the words. She felt much the same. There was so much standing between them. All their lies, their duties—and then there was the matter of his heart. He'd given it to another, and what pieces might be left had not been offered to her.

"Lindsay!" She heard her name bellowed from the hall.

"In here, Father."

The Wallace laird filled the doorway, startling the other maid, who scurried away as soon as the opening was clear.

"What are you about, doing a maid's work?" he grumbled.

"If you've not noticed, there are many heads downstairs in need of beds. I'm doing what needs doing."

He shook his head. "This was a mistake. I had no idea this clan was in such a state. I'd never have sent you here had I known. I should have taken your letters more seriously. I don't think your mother would forgive me if I left you here. We will leave in the morning for home. I'll have this farce of a marriage dissolved, and we'll find you a proper husband— one who can take care of ye the way a husband should."

Lindsay's first thought was joy. It was what she'd wanted all this time, and she was pleased to hear her father regretted marrying her off, which she guessed would be as close as she would ever get to an apology.

But after the words sunk in further, she found herself clenching her hands, ready to protest. Had the MacPhersons become her home? Her family? Did she want to leave?

As if expecting an argument, her father cut off what she opened her mouth to say. "The man has gone off to claim Collier Castle, as if he will find the answers to his problems there."

Her father shook his head, but Lindsay was shaken by his words. "Shane has gone?"

"Aye. With all the things to do here, he rushed off to pile more onto his already large heap of problems. Nay, I'll not leave you here to be worked to the bone and grow sick with hunger."

"Can you not help set Cluny to rights?" She knew he'd already paid her dowry and that those funds had been spent or stolen. But her clan, while not rich, was well-funded. *Her clan.*

Again, he shook his head.

"I already paid the dowry, and it's gone. I'll not receive the goods promised in exchange and will need to use my funds to feed our own clan after such a loss. The best I can do is not demand what is owed back to me. I'll not take the castle." He sniffed as he looked about with disdain. "The last thing I need is to take over this clan in the sorry shape it's in."

"But I might be able to help," Lindsay said.

Her father laughed. "You owe him nothing."

Was that true? She was interrupted from saying anything else when Tory entered the room after knocking lightly on the door. "A letter has arrived for you."

Tory's green eyes seemed to say something as Lindsay grabbed up the note and flipped it over to see the seal. Disappointment and anger rushed through her. It wasn't from Shane.

"Did Shane leave a note or a message?" Lindsay asked, hating the desperate edge to her voice.

"Nay. I didn't know he'd even left until I went looking for him a little while ago." She frowned before saying, "Mayhap he was afraid we would tell him he shouldn't be riding yet."

Or mayhap he didn't care enough to even tell his wife he was leaving. Unsure what to think, she opened the letter and began reading, only vaguely hearing her father dismiss Tory with a "That will be all."

Lindsay read the letter quickly and let out a small squeak of surprise at hearing her dear cousin was with child and would deliver in the next month. She asked Lindsay to come visit before cold weather descended on the Highlands and they were both stuck where they were until spring.

Lindsay considered asking Shane when he returned if a visit to the MacKenzies would be prudent and then remembered how her husband had gone off without consulting her or so much as saying goodbye. "I'll be ready to leave in the morning," she told her father.

・・・

After a fitful night's sleep, Lindsay rose shortly after dawn and dressed. She still wasn't sure how long she'd be gone or if she ever planned to come back. Just in case, she'd packed her trunks, and as her father saw to having them loaded in the carriage, Lindsay took Tre to the village to leave the little dog with her small cousins.

She paused at the path that would have led her to the cottage. She longed to go there, to continue living that life. But it had been nothing more than a lie.

In the bailey, her father was mounted and ready to go.

"I should say goodbye to Tory," Lindsay said.

"Nay. I'm ready to go. We leave now."

Lindsay sighed, and after deciding the other woman was probably busy in the kitchen, seeing to the morning meal, Lindsay decided she wouldn't risk her father's mood another moment.

The sun painted the horizon pink and purple as they rode for the MacKenzie stronghold. Looking back over her shoulder, Lindsay wondered if she would ever return. Her father had offered the very thing Lindsay had wanted weeks ago, but everything had changed since then, and then changed again and again.

What she knew was she needed time to heal from the wounds Shane had caused, first with his plan to end their marriage, and then with his silent abandonment. He'd not left so much as a note, so she'd done the same, leaving with no promise to return and no words to know what their future might hold.

A few days later, they arrived at Castle Leod, and Lindsay paused to take it in. She'd hoped for some sign to tell her this was the place she was supposed to be, but it was just a gray stone castle, much like the one she'd left.

"Are we to stand here or move up to the gate?" her father snapped after they'd been standing on the rise for some time. His mood hadn't improved when he'd learned of her desire to visit Meaghan, but he'd accompanied her all the same. Hearing his disapproval of Shane had forced Lindsay to defend him, which had caused a great number of arguments along their travels until they'd both resolved to stay silent.

She needed only to ride down the small hill, and they would let her in. Her cousin would welcome her with open arms, and she could start a new life here if she wished to. No longer with her husband, but not with her father, either. It was what she thought she'd wanted that morning, but now she wasn't so sure. If given her choice, she wished she could go back to the time before she knew who her husband was. She wanted to live in oblivious happiness once more.

But that wasn't an option, so she nudged the horse into movement and went to face her future.

As expected, Meaghan was pleased to see her. Her husband, Joshua, was a pleasant fellow, just as big as Shane but with blond waves instead of Shane's sable locks. She shook off the comparison and forced a smile on her face as the couple welcomed them inside the keep to meet a few of her friends.

She was given a room in the castle while her father was pleased to visit with the MacKenzie laird. They'd missed the nooning; a tray and a bath were brought to her room. It was a lavish welcome, and she was grateful, but she missed taking a quick dip in the frigid river with her husband to get clean. She was dressed in a fancy gown from her trunks and was surprised how it seemed her life with the MacPhersons had almost been wiped away.

"You look much better," Meaghan said as she came to check on her before supper. Lindsay was not looking forward to eating in the hall with the rest of the MacKenzie clan. She was a new guest and would therefore be stared at as some oddity. She said as much to her older cousin, who laughed.

"You are not the only guest among us, though the other will not be a guest for long. In fact, if you've come from the MacPhersons, ye may know her already."

Lindsay tilted her head as Meaghan went on.

"Lady Deirdre MacPherson has stolen our laird's heart. They'll be wed in a fortnight. She is the late MacPherson laird's widow, we've been told."

Lindsay's eyes widened in surprise, and she pulled her cousin to the side of the corridor.

"Deirdre MacPherson is here?"

Chapter Twenty-Seven

It'd been a long week for Shane and Alec to fix what needed immediate attention at Collier so they could return home. In that time, Shane had nearly healed, making the trip back to Cluny easier to manage than his trip had been in getting there.

They arrived home late, when everyone was already in bed. After pilfering some food from the kitchens, Shane went to his study to see to any correspondence. He lit a lamp and sorted through the messages on his desk. The first missive held the Cameron crest on the seal. Shane worried if the clan that helped them win against the MacColls was now sending a bill for their services. If it was so, they'd be disappointed.

Shane didn't have two pennies to rub together. A familiar throbbing began behind his eyes as the pressure of his new role began to build. Collier had given nothing of great value that a poor laird could sell to feed his people.

He'd found a village in worse shape than at home and fields that had been planted but poorly tended. There wouldn't be many viable crops to harvest next month.

Laird,

I thank you for the opportunity to fight beside you to destroy our common enemy. We have proven we are an unstoppable force when we work together. Perhaps it is time the MacPhersons and Camerons stop raiding each other's lands and create an alliance. Let us consider building each other up instead of breaking each other down. Our fathers have held on to this hostility between our clans for far too long. I doubt they even knew why they hated each other. It was simply done because their fathers had acted the same. Let us stop it with us. If you are interested, I look forward to discussing it.

The letter was signed by Robert Cameron himself. Shane read the letter again, scouring the words for tricks and finding none. Could it be? A bit of good news after months of nothing but more and more impossible situations?

Alec entered, looking as tired as Shane felt.

"I thought you would have gone straight to your bed."

"I may have, but there is a woman and three bairns in my bed. So I came here so as not to disturb them."

It made sense that Tory and Lindsay would have made use of every available bed, with the castle overrun by needy families looking for a safe home. Shane and Alec discussed strategies about what to do with everyone, and Shane was impressed by Alec's ideas. They must've dozed off, for Tory woke them when the sun was shining through the window.

She held out yet another missive, despite the remaining ones on his desk that still went unopened. One of them was from the MacLeods, and he could only guess that they demanded the remaining balance on a ship he would never use.

Tory frowned at them. "I see you've returned, even

though you didn't deign to tell me you left."

"I'm sorry, Tory. I'd not wanted to hunt you down and be lectured about my health. As ye can see, I'm fine."

"Are ye?" she said with a shake of her head and a sniff. "Fine? Ye don't even realize how far from fine you are at the moment."

"What has happened?" Shane tilted his head before asking after his wife. "Where's Lindsay?"

"That's a good question," his sister said with a shrug. "I imagine she is nearly home with her father. I expected this might be word of your annulment, but it's from Ronan."

"She left?"

"I would point out, you left her first. What did you think was to happen?"

If he thought his sister would have his back in all things, he'd been mistaken.

"She was new to the castle, a stranger to everyone, thrust into taking over for ye when you were wounded and then abandoned. All this after she'd heard you plan to leave her to marry another. What did you expect would happen? That she'd feel welcomed and loved and wish to stay? Ye are daft."

"I didn't have to because I was already married to her! And I changed my mind almost immediately after agreeing to that foolish plan of annulling my marriage to her," he said. "I thought it would be the right thing but realized right away it was not. I am not without faults, you know."

"Well, ye won't be married to her for long. I overheard her father offer to take her home and end your marriage, since you're unable to care for her the way ye should, and she leaped at the chance. I can't blame her."

"She saw I wouldn't be able to clothe her in the fine garments and jewels she was accustomed to and decided to find someone else who could offer her more."

Tory laughed but not with humor; instead, she glared

at him. "Men! Ye think ye know everything, but ye are as helpless as a newborn babe." She reached into the bag tied at her waist and pulled out something that shimmered in the light. As she slammed the jewels down on his desk, Shane realized it was the necklace he'd last seen draped around his wife's neck. "It's the only thing she left behind. My guess is it was her way of helping in the only way she could. In a way you don't deserve."

Shane stood holding the emeralds and rubies as he watched his sister storm away out of his study. He'd made yet another mistake.

"Aye," Alec said beside him, making Shane think perhaps he'd said it out loud. "Look at this."

He held out the missive Tory had brought in—the one from Ronan that Shane hadn't realized he'd dropped. He was still reeling from what Tory had told him.

Lindsay had left him.

Hadn't he already worried he wouldn't be able to take care of his wife as he should? That his clan would grow lean over winter and go without because they had no money?

He'd already decided he'd do whatever was necessary to make sure Lindsay got the life she deserved. He didn't realize he only needed to stay out of her way and she would see his promise fulfilled.

Alec frowned when Shane didn't move to take the letter. "Should I send someone to bring her back?" Shane might've laughed at his younger brother. Surely, he didn't know much about women if he thought that was an option. As if Lindsay were a child that had wandered off and needed someone to bring her home.

"Nay. Tis true, I have nothing to offer her here. I will grant her freedom and wish her well, wherever she is."

His words were met with silence. Of course he didn't expect Alec to have any grand plan for winning his wife back.

Instead of waiting any longer, he nodded toward the letter still in Alec's grip.

"What word does our brother send? I pray it's not more bad news. I'll not be able to bear it." He slumped back in his seat.

"He has good news. He's found Deirdre. One of his men has a daughter who married a MacKenzie. He reported that Deirdre is living there and a wedding between Deirdre and the laird is being planned. I'm not a friend to the MacKenzie laird, but no man deserves to be swindled of all his money."

Hearing this stirred him to his feet, his earlier fatigue gone. If he could recover his funds, he might have a chance to get Lindsay back.

"Let us ride. The sooner we get there, the better chance we have of catching her with our money." They prepared quickly, and Shane put his angry sister in charge while he was away.

It was quite a thing to see the laird, the war chief, and the ten soldiers in their entourage leave the castle to chase down one small woman. But Deirdre was wily and not to be underestimated.

• • •

Lindsay did not get to meet the laird her first night at Leod, and the next morning she slept late in the day. So it wasn't until that afternoon that she found her cousin.

"You must take me to your laird," Lindsay demanded. "This woman he plans to marry is a conniving witch. I must warn him."

Meaghan shook her head. "Ye said as much last night, but I canna believe it's the same woman. She is beautiful and poised."

"As is the most venomous serpent."

"But you can see how much she loves the laird when she looks at him."

"She sees only the gifts and riches he can give her." Lindsay doubted she'd sway the laird if her own cousin didn't believe her, but she had to try. She couldn't remain quiet while Deirdre ran off with yet another clan's funds.

Meaghan's brow creased, and she blinked a few times. "She has commissioned a number of expensive items. Her chamber has been elaborately decorated. The bed coverings are made of the finest silks. Her gowns. Her jewels. The laird has lavished her with many gifts. And just this morning, she asked him for a carriage." She shook her head. "You say she did this to the MacPherson laird?"

"Aye." Had Lindsay not slept so late, she might've been able to stop the woman sooner. "She did the same with the MacColls, though she stayed with the MacPherson laird for many years because he continued to treat her as a queen."

"Come, then. We must tell him. Whether he chooses to believe us is another matter." Meaghan led her to the study and whispered to the guard next to the door. Lindsay only heard the words: "… of the utmost importance we speak to him alone."

The guard slipped inside the room as Lindsay's heart pounded. How would she convince this man, who thought he'd found love, that his would-be bride was nothing more than a lying monster?

She knew well enough the pain that came from thinking one was in love only to find out the other person had different plans.

The guard returned to the corridor and held the heavy door open with a nod. Lindsay forced her feet to move forward, grateful Meaghan had stayed with her for this important conversation.

The laird was younger than her father, but the white hair

at his temples spoke to his age.

Lindsay dipped into a curtsey. "Thank you for allowing me to stay at Leod while I visit my cousin, my laird." Her voice shook slightly.

"You are quite welcome." He looked to Meaghan in question, and Meaghan in turn looked at Lindsay.

"Allow me to introduce myself."

"It is not necessary. Your father already told me. You are Lindsay Wallace." He nodded regally toward her but paused when Lindsay shook her head.

"Nay. I am Lady MacPherson, wife of Shane MacPherson, the new laird of Cluny." At least for the moment. It sounded odd to use the title she never planned to have and didn't yet know if she planned to keep.

His brows rose, and a smile pulled at his lips. "Ah. I didn't realize the MacPherson laird was here as well. It is very good to see some of my bride's family has deigned to attend our wedding after all. She said everyone from Cluny rejected her. I'm glad to see you've had a change of heart."

Lindsay swallowed loudly in the silence that sat between them. What could she say to convince him? She decided it was best to just wade in.

"My husband is not here. And I'm afraid you have been misled, my laird. You see, Deirdre fled Cluny after stealing the clan's funds. From there, she went to the MacColls and married their laird only to do the same thing, leaving them with nothing but empty coffers. And now she is here, most likely planning to do the same with you."

"What madness is this? Do you think I don't know the woman I intend to marry?" Any hint of pleasantness had fallen from his face. She couldn't blame him. No one wanted to believe such things about the person they loved.

Lindsay may not have believed Shane planned to abandon her if she'd not heard him say it with his own lips. The pain of that memory sent a shiver down her spine. She pleaded with the MacKenzie laird. "I'm sorry, but you do not know her. Not the real Deirdre MacPherson."

The man blustered about as the door opened. Joshua came in, asking his wife what she was doing.

"This woman thinks my Deirdre is planning to empty my coffers and leave me. She brings unbelievable tales about a diabolical siren who captured the MacPherson and MacColl riches."

Joshua's brows shot up as he looked to Meaghan.

Lindsay worried she'd risked her cousin and her husband by speaking the truth, but she couldn't stay silent and allow another innocent clan to fall victim to this woman. Rather than go with Joshua, Meaghan came closer to stand next to Lindsay.

"My laird, I have seen the things she has purchased. The gowns, the jewels. It makes me question her intentions," Meaghan said as Joshua gasped and begged the laird's forgiveness for her accusations. But Meaghan wouldn't have it. "What reason would Lindsay have to lie about such a thing? She only wants to warn you to save us from the same fate as her own clan."

The man was looking at Lindsay now as if he was considering locking her up in the dungeon for heresy against his bride. It was a testament to how numb Lindsay's emotions had become that she didn't really care if she ended up in a cell. The man needed proof, and she had none. But that didn't mean they couldn't get it.

Lindsay held up a hand. "I have an idea—one that will allow you to know for certain if I am telling the truth."

The laird dropped his crossed arms. "Go on."

Lindsay quickly explained her plan, which flowed from her lips while she was making it.

"And you see, if I'm wrong, no harm will be done. But if

I'm correct, you'll have your answer."

The man walked back and forth behind his elaborately carved desk. Finally, he nodded to Joshua. "I'll write the letter. Tell no one else of this. Once we confirm this is untrue, I'll not have my betrothed think I didn't trust her."

"Yes, my laird," Joshua said before leaving the room.

"Now we will see the truth," the laird said.

Lindsay nodded, wishing someone had been able to save her from giving her heart to someone who planned to toss it aside. Love was a treacherous wave that carried one far from the steady ground on which they'd once stood. She worried she might already be swept away to the sea with no land in sight.

Chapter Twenty-Eight

Lindsay tried to control her breathing and adjusted the maid's clothing she wore as she served the head table. Meaghan thanked her when she filled her cousin's glass with more wine before shakily moving to her father's. It was so like the man to not realize it was his own daughter who poured his wine. Servants were beneath his notice. He shoved in another bite of food as Lindsay moved to the laird next, then Deirdre's glass.

Even if Deirdre had looked at her, she wouldn't have recognized Lindsay, as the two had never met, but Lindsay was nervous.

As was the plan, the laird announced he'd sent off a messenger with an invitation to Cluny.

"I know you said they rejected your invitation, but I want you to have your family here for our wedding. I want them to share in our happiness," he told her.

Lindsay watched as Deirdre's face went pale.

"I told you I didn't need them. I only need you." It was clear the woman struggled to keep her annoyance reined in.

The laird smiled and kissed her temple. "I only want you to be happy, dearest."

The quickness in the way the woman's expression transformed was otherworldly. Lindsay thought perhaps she truly was an enchantress with the speed at which she shifted into the guileless bride.

"You make me happy. But I have a bit of a megrim and should like to go lie down."

"Of course. I will escort you myself."

"Nay. You have an important guest. Stay and enjoy the entertainment this evening with Laird Wallace. I understand Ranald will be playing. I do know how much you enjoy his talent."

She bowed quickly and left the hall.

Lindsay watched as something akin to worry came over the laird's face when his betrothed fled to the stairs. It was obvious he was plagued by doubt. The next part of the plan would make everything clear.

He excused himself from the table, and Lindsay's father continued devouring his meal with no more than a grunt of acknowledgment as she moved toward the stairs.

"I'm sure we will find this to be a waste of time," the laird said as he joined Lindsay in the alcove across from his study. They pulled a tapestry across the opening to hide and wait.

"I hope it's a waste of time. I do not wish to cause you the pain her deceit would bring. I want to be wrong more than you can know," Lindsay said, but she knew she wasn't wrong.

They only needed to wait a few minutes until Deirdre arrived at the door to the laird's study. When the laird gasped, Lindsay feared Deirdre would hear and change tactics, but the woman was not to be distracted from her plan.

"I'm sorry. I don't believe we've met," Deirdre told the guard, her voice silky and the bodice of her gown tugged down to reveal her heaving bosom.

"I am Roger, mistress."

"Roger," she purred and drew her finger under his chin. "The laird has gone off riding this afternoon, and I fear for his safety alone. Would you see that he is safe?"

Joshua had told the guard to leave his post if approached by Deirdre, so the man gave a quick nod and left his place in front of the door. When Deirdre went inside, Lindsay cast a frown at the laird. His gaze remained on the heavy door as if he tried to see through the thick wood to what was happening within.

Lindsay had her suspicions and knew they wouldn't need to wait long to see if she was right. In a matter of minutes, Deirdre would reveal herself as the feckless thief Lindsay had predicted and this man's heart would shatter. She wished she could save him from that, but at least she could spare him from losing everything. This way, his happiness may be forfeit but he'd be able to feed his clan.

The door creaked open slowly. Deirdre's head popped out first, looking in both directions to make sure no one lingered in the corridor, before she stepped out and closed the door behind her. She grunted with the effort of handling the leather sack that clinked when she shifted it to her other arm.

The laird stepped out from the shadows of their hiding place, and Lindsay joined him. "Deirdre, what are you doing?"

The woman was so startled she dropped the bag. The weight of the coin broke the ties, and gold spilled out onto the stones, some rolling on their sides to scatter into the shadows.

If Lindsay had expected the woman to give up and confess her crimes, she'd been wrong. Deirdre had spent her life perfecting her lies, and like a devious spider, she wove another tale with a blink of an eye.

"You have invited my stepson to the castle. You don't

know him like I do. He will raid your coffers while you're distracted with the wedding. I thought only to protect your assets. I will always look out for you, my love."

"You mean you will always look out for yourself." Lindsay couldn't help but speak her mind. "Shane would never steal from a clan he calls an ally."

Deirdre sneered at Lindsay and turned a coy look back on the laird. "This woman clearly doesn't know my stepson as I do."

"I believe she does," the laird said, crossing his arms and frowning at the woman.

Seeing her ruse was crumbling, Deirdre turned on him. "What are you doing with this serving maid, hidden away in the shadows?" she screeched. Tears overflowed her stunning blue eyes, trailing down her cheeks as she sobbed. "You have already turned to another and forsaken me. I thought you loved me. I thought you would love only me."

"This woman and I were hiding to witness as you proved yourself false."

"You planned to steal from him as you did the MacPhersons and the MacColls," Lindsay said.

"Who are *you* to tell my betrothed such lies?"

"I am…" She swallowed and forced the words out, even though she suddenly felt she had no claim to them. "I am Lindsay MacPherson, Shane MacPherson's wife and the lady of Clan MacPherson, and you will give me back what you've stolen from the MacPhersons and the McColls, as it rightfully belongs to my husband."

The woman gasped and stuttered a denial that Lindsay ignored. The laird tilted his head and said only, "How could you do this?"

Deirdre glared at him. Lindsay thought they might finally be seeing the real Deirdre. Lindsay stepped closer. "As you can see, this woman is a thief. Please have a guard come and hold her. I'm sure my husband will wish to have her charged for theft."

Deirdre's face went pale for a moment before she stood taller. The gesture was unimpressive, since she was much shorter than Lindsay. The laird bellowed for a guard, and Deirdre's expression changed to that of a trapped cat. She spun away. Lindsay made to grab her, but the woman ducked out of her grasp and ran for the steps.

She pulled down an oil lamp from the wall and threw it to the stones, catching the dry rushes on the floor to flame. Lindsay grabbed a pail of water and quickly put them out, but the corridor was filled with smoke and she couldn't see where the woman had gone.

The laird ran through the cloud of smoke, and Lindsay followed, waving her hand and coughing. But they were met on the stairs by the guards coming up.

"Where is she?" the laird asked.

"She didn't come down the stairs," Joshua said.

"But she ran this way and did not come back up," the laird said.

"Christ save us, the witch moves like a specter," the other guard said while crossing himself.

Lindsay didn't believe such a thing. She tried to think of what Deirdre would do next. She must have slinked past them in the hall while they were dealing with the fire.

"Where is her chamber? She won't want to leave the rest of the money."

Lindsay followed the man down the corridor toward Deirdre's chamber as Joshua ordered the warriors to search every room.

Halfway down the corridor, she saw Deirdre fumbling with a key in a door. Lindsay assumed it was her bedchamber. Of course she would have kept the room locked. She wouldn't have trusted a maid to clean it and find all the loot she'd hidden inside. A thief afraid of being robbed. It was poetic that it kept her from getting to the money herself.

Lindsay rushed forward with the laird and the guard pushing closer. She saw the fear in the woman's eyes when she realized she wasn't going to retrieve her spoils. She raced in the opposite direction, just as Meaghan stepped out of a room at the other end of the corridor.

Pulling a dirk from her waist, Deirdre grasped onto Meaghan and held the blade to her throat. Meaghan's hand went instinctively to the slight bump of her stomach where her child grew.

"Stay back or I'll have no choice but to kill her," Deirdre said as Meaghan stared past Lindsay with fear in her eyes.

Joshua gasped and held his arms out, blocking anyone from moving forward. "Hold. She has my wife."

Lindsay watched in horror as a drop of blood welled on her cousin's neck when Deirdre attempted to pull Meaghan toward the steps on the far side of the castle. They had to get Meaghan away from her before she was harmed. Deirdre was desperate for escape, her eyes flicking from side to side as if searching for a way out.

Lindsay remembered her training with her father's retainers. When they'd left Riccarton for Cluny, her guard had told her to fall or fake a swoon if she were captured. It was more difficult for someone to lift dead weight.

"Meaghan, I hope you don't faint!" Lindsay shouted her hint to the other woman.

A warrior behind Lindsay sniffed as if she had lost her mind. "Why would ye say such a thing? It's clear she's already frightened."

But Joshua understood and nodded.

"Aye. Should you need to swoon, I'd understand," he called.

Awareness flared in Meaghan's eyes, and with a quick

nod, she went slack and slipped down Deirdre's body to slump on the floor. Deirdre tugged at her arm, but when Meaghan didn't move, Deirdre realized her only option was to flee. She turned to run as Joshua flicked a blade through the air. It caught Deirdre in the arm, causing her to cry out, but she kept running. The men continued on down the stairs after Deirdre while Lindsay stopped to see to her shaking cousin.

"Are you hurt?" Lindsay asked.

"Nay, but I was so afraid I'd be killed." She pulled in air, her eyes pooling with tears. "All I could think about was the babe." She placed a loving hand on her stomach.

As she held her cousin and tried to soothe her rattled nerves, Lindsay considered her own situation. Seeing her cousin rounded with child had caused a small flare of jealousy, but it was quickly pushed away by her joy for Meaghan and Joshua. But now she thought of the last time she'd had her courses. Could she be…?

Lindsay was helping Meaghan to her feet when Joshua rushed to his wife.

"Are you hurt?" he asked, his eyes frantic.

"Nay. I'm fine. Did you get her?"

He shook his head and fisted his hand in anger. "She must've been prepared for a quick escape. She slipped away into the woods. We found a place that had been dug up."

"The money," Lindsay whispered. "I must check her room."

Joshua called for a man to send the chatelaine, who pulled the chain of keys from her waist and made quick work of opening the door. Lindsay coughed from the smog of heavy perfumes in the room. It looked like the room of a queen. Ornate gilding, jewels, and silks gave the impression that someone of great wealth stayed there rather than a vicious criminal.

They searched the room.

Under the bed, Lindsay found two leather bags, heavy with coin. She closed her eyes in relief. She guessed it wouldn't all be recovered; some of it had surely been buried in the hole they'd found in the woods. But to recover anything pleased Lindsay. The money would be returned to the MacPhersons so the clan would have enough food for the winter. Did that mean she'd be returning to Cluny as well?

One of Joshua's men came in to give him a report. "She stole someone's horse and ran. Six warriors are giving chase."

"She's a snake," Lindsay said, remembering what Shane once said about the "laird's stepmother." She now knew Deirdre was his own stepmother. What a fool she'd been to not put it together.

She knew Shane would want the woman found so she could be held to face justice, but if that didn't happen, at least they had some of their money back.

"What is all this?" the Wallace laird asked as he entered the room, looking at her.

"Your daughter has spared my people a devastating winter and myself a great amount of pain."

Her father laughed and looked about as if waiting for someone to tell him it was a jest, but when no one did, he straightened his shoulders and gave her a nod. "I am happy you've a sound head upon your shoulders."

She detected something she thought might be pride in his words and could only stand there blinking until the laird called everyone to the hall to finish their meals.

• • •

The next morning, with the MacPherson money secured in her own room, Lindsay went down to the hall to break her fast. Many eyes were on her as she entered and made her way to the high table.

"My honored guest," the laird said, gesturing to the seat on his left that had up until today belonged to Deirdre. The man frowned as she sat.

"Thank you." She offered a smile, and she could see the pain in his eyes. Was her own pain as easy to see? Perhaps it was only noticeable to those who knew what heartache looked like. "I wanted to say how sorry I am for how things turned out. I know it hurts a great deal to learn someone you loved had other intentions."

He tilted his head as he studied her. She thought maybe he did see her pain, for he nodded once, and then, with a deep breath, he brushed off her sympathies.

"I owe you my gratitude for saving me from the same fate as the other lairds in Deirdre's path. You'll be rewarded for your efforts."

"Restoring what was taken is all the reward I need," she said, though she wondered if she shouldn't ask for more.

If she was with child, she'd need to make sure she could provide for her and the bairn.

"I wonder if I might stay here longer than just a visit?"

He smiled. "Nothing is more important than having a home."

"If ye are looking for a wife, mayhap we can arrange something," her father said.

Lindsay pressed her lips together to keep from bursting into tears at his words, but the MacKenzie laird was the one to answer.

"I believe it's much too soon for such things." He turned back to Lindsay. "While I'm not able to offer marriage, I'd be pleased if you wished to call Leod your home."

Lindsay's lip trembled. She'd not planned to make a home with the MacPhersons, but she missed it a great deal. Her dog, their cottage, but most of all…Shane. She did miss him, no matter how much he'd hurt her. She loved him.

"We do not need to speak of such things now. Let us take some time to heal a bit before discussing such tender topics," the MacKenzie laird said.

"Thank you, truly," she said but was unable to stop a single tear from escaping.

. . .

Shane seemed to live in a daze. He knew he sat on a horse next to Alec and Ronan. They'd met up with their brother the day before, and he was accompanying them to Castle Leod.

Shane also knew they were headed to find Deirdre. He knew when to eat and when to sleep and when to press his lips up in the form of a smile, but everything happened without his heart playing a part in any of it. He was as numb as he'd been after losing Maria, but at least he knew Lindsay lived.

Still, he was lost without her. The more he thought of her, the less he believed she'd left him because he had no money. She'd never cared for trinkets or fancy gowns, even when he'd tried to purchase them for her. But he did worry that she didn't trust him to provide for her.

If he was able to get his hands on Deirdre and recover the money she'd stolen, he'd be better able to take care of Lindsay, as well as the rest of the clan. Perhaps his wife would forgive him and agree to come home if he proved himself capable. He'd need to find her first.

The men sitting around the fire had gone quiet, and when he looked up he found himself in the familiar situation of being spoken to and not realizing it. "I'm sorry. What was said?"

"Never mind. I'm not going to repeat the entire conversation because you weren't paying attention." Alec rolled his eyes.

"It seems you're only with us in body, brother. Your mind

is elsewhere. I had hoped being home would have healed ye," Ronan said with concern.

Ronan knew everything. He'd known Maria, had been standing next to Shane when he'd said his vows. And he knew how heartbroken Shane had been after her death. As Shane had struggled with his pain, he'd lashed out at Ronan, blaming him for pulling Shane away from the camp and leaving his wife. It wasn't true. Shane had made the choice to leave Maria unprotected. Ronan had nothing to do with it.

Ronan shook his head. "I'd never have thought you'd marry again. I expected the duty of heirs would fall to Alec."

Their younger brother grunted and shook his head. Shane decided to confide in these men who were his family. "I think of Lindsay all the time. I try to come up with ways to get her back. She returned to Riccarton, to her home. She and I are still wed. But I worry that when I return from this errand, I'll find annulment papers waiting. It would mean the last thread connecting us will be severed."

The flames from their fire cast the other men's faces in harsh shadows, making their laughter seem sinister.

"Perhaps I'll never go back home," Shane said. Then he'd never get such a message and never have to end his marriage.

Alec's eyes went wide. "Ye must return home. I've told you. I have no interest in becoming laird. The clan needs ye."

"You're lucky, brother, that no one is attempting to steal your birthright." Again, Ronan's face turned grim.

"Are you having troubles with the Grants? You have only to ask, and my sword is yours to command," Shane said.

"I thank you, but I'm dealing with things on my own. I just don't always know who to believe."

Shane nodded. "I'm blessed with Alec. I'd trust him if he told me the sky had turned green rather than blue. There's something reassuring in that, even with everything else in chaos."

For Shane, everything hinged on finding Deirdre and getting back his money. Then he might find Lindsay and beg her to remain his wife. He was more certain than ever that he needed her by his side. She was unlike any other woman.

Tomorrow, they'd arrive at Leod, where he hoped to find the woman who had caused him so much trouble. And he could start to put things back to rights in his life. And in his heart.

• • •

Shane and his men were greeted the next morning by the MacKenzie laird himself as they rode into the bailey. When Shane introduced himself and his brothers, the MacKenzie laird held out his hand and clasped his strong grip along Shane's bracer as if they were old friends reunited after many years apart. But Shane knew he'd never met the man—Gillen MacKenzie.

"We've just finished the noon meal, but come inside and I'll have food brought for ye and we can discuss why you've come."

Shane nodded and followed the man inside his empty hall. He spoke to a woman who startled at something he'd said before scurrying away as if frightened. Gillen was still smiling as he sat himself in the center of the high table and offered the seats next to him to Shane and Ronan.

"Tell me why you have come." The laird got the conversation underway as soon as the ale and bread were served.

"I was told Lady MacPherson has come here. I need to speak with her." He needed to hang her scrawny neck from a rope, but if this man intended to marry her, he didn't want to show his hatred for the man's betrothed.

"Ah, yes. There were actually two Lady MacPhersons

visiting. One ran off after I caught her trying to empty my coffers, though, thanks to your wife, I didn't lose anything but my pride from the short relationship."

"My wife?"

"Lindsay MacPherson. I understand she's married to you?"

Good God, his wife was here. He'd have his chance to make things right. Shane stood and looked around, not wanting to waste a second. "Where is she? I must see her right away."

Gillen laughed again, then tilted his head.

"You didn't know she was here, did you?"

"Nay. But I still want to see her."

"I sent her cousin to bring her down. But know this—her father has gone on. And I've offered her use of my home for as long as she wishes to stay. It will be up to her if she wants to return with ye."

Shane wanted to bristle at another laird telling him what he could and couldn't do with his wife, but the man was right. Shane could only thank him for seeing his wife safe. He'd not be able to throw Lindsay over his shoulder and take her back to Cluny. No matter if it was the way of the past, he wasn't a monster.

If she was happier here with her family, he'd not ask her to leave.

When the laird looked toward the stairs, Shane followed his gaze as Lindsay and the other woman who'd been in the hall earlier came into view. Lindsay looked beautiful, dressed in a lovely gown of gold and green. Her hair was set on her head in a proper manner, and all he could think was how much he wanted to release her midnight tresses from the tidy coiffure.

She paused. He didn't know what to expect. She swayed as if deciding if she wanted to run toward him or away.

"Lindsay," he said and took the first step to bring them together. To his relief, she stayed where she was. When he was close enough to reach out, he lifted his hand to touch her but let it drop before making contact, unsure if she'd want him to pull her into his arms and kiss her as he wished to do. Things were broken between them. He needed to fix them but wasn't sure how to start.

"You've come for your money. I'll have it brought down so you may return home."

"My money?"

"I was able to recover it from Deirdre's room after she ran off. She got away with some of the coins she'd hidden in the woods, but it appears most was left behind."

He watched her, feeling like he was getting a rare gift to just see her again. He knew how silky her dark hair was. He knew how soft her lips were, how she fell apart in his arms when he made love to her. The sounds she made when she reached her release and held on to him so tightly, he'd thought she'd never let him go.

But she had, because he'd been willing to give her up and she knew it. He didn't know what to say. Didn't know any words that could tell her how sorry he was. Instead, he watched her as she spoke, telling him the story of how they'd set up a trap for Deirdre so the laird would know if she was unfaithful.

Women came in from the kitchens, bringing food for them. Lindsay stepped back and turned as if she planned to leave.

"Please stay," he begged and didn't care who knew.

She shook her head. "I should get back to the solar. When you're done eating, please send your men to carry the bags down."

He nodded and watched her walk away. When she was gone, Shane slumped back in his seat and let his head rest on his fists. The pain of seeing her was more than he could bear. If he'd had any question before of what he was to do, he knew the answer now as clearly as he knew his own name.

"I've lost her."

"I can't turn her out of my keep. For what she was willing to do to spare me and my people, she will always be welcome here. But I hope for your sake you can win her back."

The laird waited a moment before whispering, "Tell me your plan."

Shane explained that he'd thought Lindsay had left because he had no money.

The man laughed. "Did you really believe that?"

"After months of failing, it seemed reasonable, until I looked in her eyes just now. Now I'm certain it wasn't about the money." He shook his head.

"No. It wasn't," Gillen said. "So, what will you do?"

Chapter Twenty-Nine

Shane was there. Lindsay couldn't believe the pain she felt when she saw him standing in the hall. He'd come for the money, not for her. She knew that, but still she'd had to fight her body's instinct to run to him and allow his arms to protect her from everything that caused her pain.

The way he looked at her didn't help. He reminded her of Gillen. A man trying to get through his pain the best way he could. To her surprise, it was the other man who'd arrived with Shane and Alec who entered the solar first.

"I've not had the honor of meeting my brother's bride. I'm Ronan, his better-looking stepbrother."

Lindsay couldn't produce more than a small smile at the man's jest.

"I'm sorry. I wasn't trying to make light. He told me what happened. It bothers him."

She nodded. The situation bothered her as well. She didn't know what to do.

"You've come for the money. It's in here."

She led him to her room and pointed under the bed,

where she'd hidden the MacPherson and MacColl coins. Though with Deirdre gone, she knew it was safe enough now.

Ronan glanced at the small coat she'd been knitting for a babe. He looked back to her, startled.

"Are ye...?"

She waited to see if he'd be able to form the question. When he simply stood there, red and unable to meet her eyes, she realized her brother-in-law couldn't manage the words "with child."

"I think I might be," she answered. She had planned to tell Shane when she knew for certain. She didn't know how he'd respond, but she knew she couldn't keep their child a secret from him. If there was anything she'd learned over the last few months, it was how damaging secrets could be.

"I plan to tell him," she added quickly.

"There's something you should know."

She frowned. Had Shane sent his brother to sway her?

He raised a hand. "Please, hear me out."

Reluctantly, she nodded and waited.

"I know what you heard. When he said he'd annul your marriage. But what you don't know is that he couldn't go through with it."

"Because he found out he was already married to the laird's daughter."

"No. Before he knew who you were, he'd returned to the castle with another plan. He was going to keep you as his wife and offer to work off the debt at Riccarton. Alec thought it was an absurd idea, but Shane told us you'd go with him because you'd loved him when you thought him just a soldier."

Tears pricked at her eyes. "I had."

"But do you still? Because he chose you, Lindsay. When it came down to it, you think he chose the clan, his duty, but he chose *you*."

She blinked back tears, but more came in their place.

"I was with him in France when he lost Maria. I thought he'd never forgive himself enough to find love again. But he loves you. And I don't think he'll be the same if you don't come back."

"I love him. I just…" She just what?

They had both lied to each other. But was it possible that they were both willing to give up everything to stay together?

"I don't know if you realize this, but it seems clear to me that fate brought you together. Mayhap it did so before it should have, before you knew the truth, but you met and fell in love just as you would have if you'd met on that field as planned. I've always heard that a person can't escape their destiny." Ronan shrugged. "Shane is your destiny."

With that, he took the bags of money and went back to the door. He offered a roguish wink and left.

That night, she lay in her bed, thinking about what might have happened if she'd gone to the castle to meet him when she was supposed to. If she'd met him and gotten to know him as the new laird of the MacPhersons rather than Shane, one of the laird's warriors. If he'd known she was the woman he was to marry. She realized with a start it wouldn't have mattered. He was still the Shane she knew and loved under the title of laird.

She threw off her blankets, and after pulling on a robe, she hurried for the door. She knew what room he was put in. Meaghan had shared the information that evening. She went to his door and tested the latch. It opened, but as she held out the lantern she'd brought with her, she saw him thrashing on the bed, calling her name.

She went to him, and while sitting on the edge of the bed she stroked his cheek. "I'm here," she said encouragingly. "I am safe, and so are ye."

His eyes fluttered open, and he blinked a few times before

whispering her name. He reached for her hand. When she didn't pull away, he must've been heartened, for he tugged her closer to rest her palm on his chest and placed his hand at her hip. He looked up into her eyes, and she couldn't look away.

"Is it true you were willing to be a servant for my father so we could stay together?" she asked him.

He blinked and then looked away before answering with a short nod. "At the time, thinking you were a maid, I believed it would be the best way for us to stay together. It seems ridiculous now, knowing who you are. To think you would have agreed to such a thing." He shook his head.

"I would have agreed," she said without even having to take a moment to consider it. "Of course, it wouldn't have come to that, but if my only choice was to return to Riccarton as a servant's wife or lose you, I would have picked whatever life allowed us to be together."

"And now? What life will you choose? The one that allows us to go home and be laird and lady together for the rest of our days—or do you prefer to stay here? You should know, if you choose to stay, I might very well ask to be hired on as a servant so I can stay close to you."

She smiled at his determination.

"I love you, Lindsay. It doesn't matter what I have to be. So long as I get to be with you. I choose you."

She smiled and leaned forward to kiss him.

"I choose you, too."

They'd both misled the other and made a mess of things. But in the end, the only thing that mattered was their love for each other.

"No more lies. No more secrets. Just us. Forever," he promised.

She nodded but remembered the final secret she was still keeping. "I was going to tell you tomorrow—I just wanted to be certain first. But I'm pretty sure I'm with child. I only realized it after I arrived here."

His eyes glistened, and he kissed her again, long and slow and full of promises she knew he would always keep. "A babe."

She nodded.

"Is that the final secret between us?" he asked. She made a show of tilting her head as if she was thinking it over, but then she nodded again.

"Good. Will you stay so I can show you how much I've missed you?"

She nodded and linked her fingers through his.

• • •

Shane kissed her, pouring his heart into the press of his lips to hers. He wouldn't hide anything from her again. He'd make certain she wouldn't have any reason to doubt his love for her.

He savored every touch and kiss, knowing he would always choose her no matter what was to come. He'd learned much from his loss and would never take love for granted.

"I am meant to be yours. Whether we'd met that day in the woods or later when the contract forced us into marrying, we'd be together," she said.

He considered her words and nodded.

"Ronan thinks it's fate and there was no escaping it," she added.

Shane was surprised not only that his brother had thought of things such as fate and destiny, but that he'd speak to Lindsay on Shane's behalf. He'd have to find a way to thank him.

"Do you wish to escape?" he asked while kissing a path between her breasts.

"Nay. There's no use trying to defy fate." She sighed

loudly as his lips passed her navel. "I happily surrender."

He kissed her most intimate places, and along with his touch, he felt her body respond, tensing tighter and tighter until finally he pushed her over the edge of passion. While she was still catching her breath, he moved above her. Her slim legs wrapped around his hips, pulling him closer. He didn't try to resist as he thrust inside her, claiming her as his. She was his wife and would be the mother of his child. He'd wanted to avoid the match his father had made for him, but now he'd thank the man if he could.

When she roused late the next morning, he kissed her awake until her lips pulled up against his in a smile. He'd happily wake her up that way for the rest of their lives.

"Mmm… As much as I would like to stay in bed with you all day, we should get ready."

"Ready for what?" he asked with a groan. He wasn't in any hurry to get up.

She rolled to her side, and he placed his hand between them on her stomach where their child grew.

"We need to get home, as there is much to be done," she said with a content smile on her face.

"Home? When we first met, you told me you'd never call my clan home." He offered her a cocky grin as he recalled their first meeting in the woods after they'd teamed up to take down their enemy. He knew as long as they stood together, they could face whatever came next.

She shrugged and pulled him close. "You're my home, Shane MacPherson, soldier. Wherever you are, that is where I shall be."

With Lindsay by his side, he planned to make Cluny a home for his people, his wife, and their family. However large it may become.

Epilogue

After saying their goodbyes to the MacKenzies, with promises between Lindsay and Meaghan to visit after their children were born, Shane sent Alec back to Cluny with the money they'd recovered and news of the laird's return with his wife.

The money they recovered would keep their clan going through winter and allow a good planting in the spring. Lindsay was happy to see how relaxed Shane was now that there was hope for their clan. At both castles.

Ronan had left earlier that morning to return home. Shane had worried over both his brothers.

"Ronan has seemed haunted by something since the morning we met to leave for France. Whatever it is, he hides it deep," Shane said as they rode to meet the chief of the Camerons.

"Perhaps you should just ask him."

"Aye." Shane smiled. "You're very wise, wife."

While the welcome wasn't exactly warm at the Camerons', it was peaceful. And Shane had told her it was beyond time the two clans put their issues behind them in exchange for peace.

"I didn't get the chance to thank you for coming to our aid against the MacColls. If there is anything we can do to repay you, please let me know," Shane said while Lindsay sat next to him at the dais in the great hall.

A small feast had been prepared in their honor.

"I believe it is time our clans united in blood," the Cameron laird explained.

Dear Lord, Lindsay didn't need to be a laird to know what he meant.

Marriage.

Shane nodded slowly.

"I would be amicable to such an alliance; however, as you see, I am already married. And we're expecting our first child in the spring."

The man nodded and held up his glass in a toast. "I wish you much joy in the building of your family." After they drank, he set his glass down and leaned closer. "I'm sure there's something that can be arranged. We shall discuss it further in my study over a dram." It was common for men to keep their business from their wives, but Shane told her everything that night when he slid into bed next to her.

The next morning, they said their farewells and headed for home. It had been a short delay that had ended with an unexpected alliance, and now she and Shane smiled at each other as they crested the hill with Cluny Castle on the horizon.

Home. She was excited to become the lady of the keep and start their life there. "Are you going to tell Alec about the arrangement you've made with the Camerons?" she asked.

He twisted his lips to the side. "Not yet. We don't need to worry about it until the spring. I'd rather not hear his griping all winter if I can help it."

Lindsay laughed. "You think he'll be displeased?"

Shane let out a breath. She'd often thought he carried

the weight of the world on his shoulders, and now she saw it wasn't the whole world—just their small part of it.

"Alec has told me more than once that he doesn't wish to be laird. I think he uses the scars on his face to hide away from everyone. From life."

Lindsay nodded. When she first saw the war chief, she'd thought him to be the trow everyone called him. But now that she knew the man he was, she saw the kind man he tried to hide from everyone. Perhaps even himself.

Shane offered a smile. "I can only hope the arrangement I made for him turns out as perfectly as the one our fathers made for us."

"You mean the arrangement we were both too stubborn to allow?" she reminded him.

"It all worked out in the end, did it not?"

"Better than I ever hoped," Lindsay said. She was happier than she ever thought to be as one of the MacPhersons.

The gates opened as they rode up to the castle. The bailey was filled with people eager to welcome them back. Lindsay felt her cheeks turn pink as Tory entered the bailey. As soon as she got down, she went to the other woman and apologized.

"I can't blame ye, for my brother was acting like an arse. I would've done the same thing."

Lindsay told Tory how excited she was to have a sister and was interrupted by a small dog hopping around at her feet. She bent and picked up Treun, who licked her chin happily.

Her cousins came over to greet her. They offered a smart bow before looking back at Munro for his approval. He winked, and the boys smiled. It was wonderful to see them so happy, not to mention clean and well fed.

"Will you take the dog back?" Robbie asked, his earlier smile gone.

James nudged him. "You shouldn't have reminded her.

Now she will for certain. She might have forgotten."

Lindsay knelt so she could speak to them easier. "I think—if it's all right with Mr. Munro—that it would be nice if you could keep her with you. And I'll see her when I come to visit you."

The boys turned again to Munro, who nodded, making the boys run off cheering.

"I received a letter from the MacKenzie war chief. He's offered to foster Doran there for a bit," Munro said. "I've agreed until next year. Let him fill out before bringing him home to join the MacPherson guard."

Shane clapped the man on the shoulder and nodded in agreement. "Allow the other clan to bear the cost of feeding a boy of that age."

The men laughed as Lindsay smiled at her husband. It was wonderful to see the joy in his eyes instead of pain and guilt. She looked around at the people who had come to greet them. She had a family here, both by blood and in name, and the love of this man.

"You should know—with all the MacColls we've taken on, your room has been given away. It means you'll have to share a bed with me."

She laughed as she took his hand and allowed him to lead her into the hall filled with the scents of roasted meat and berry tarts.

She had done all she could to avoid becoming the lady of the MacPherson clan, but today she gladly accepted the title and the man who came with it. And with that, she looked up into her husband's happy face and allowed the love of this place to surround her.

She was home.

Acknowledgments

Thanks to my editor, Alethea, who stuck with it on this book when it refused to be wrestled into submission.

About the Author

One very early morning, Allison B. Hanson woke up with a conversation going on in her head. It wasn't so much a dream as being forced awake by her imagination. Unable to go back to sleep, she gave in, went to the computer, and began writing. Years later it still hasn't stopped. Allison lives near Hershey, Pennsylvania, and enjoys candy immensely, as well as long motorcycle rides, running and reading.

Also by Allison B. Hanson…

CLAN MACKINLAY SERIES

HER ACCIDENTAL HIGHLANDER HUSBAND

HER RELUCTANT HIGHLANDER HUSBAND

HER FORBIDDEN HIGHLANDER HUSBAND

LOVE UNDER FIRE SERIES

WITNESS IN THE DARK

WANTED FOR LIFE

WATCHED FROM A DISTANCE

Discover more romance from Entangled…

Her Forbidden Highlander Husband
a Clan MacKinlay novel by Allison B. Hanson

Daughter of the Laird of the Stewart clan, Evelyn is expected to perform her daughter's duty, including marry for the better of the clan…even if that's against her will. But upon learning her father plans to trade her to an unknown clan in exchange for cattle, she will do almost anything to escape the future set out before her—including running away and marrying war chief Liam MacKinlay.

Highland Surrender
a Sons of Sinclair novel by Heather McCollum

With his family's honor on the line, Nordic Viking Erik Halverson must follow his destiny—and royal command—to sail to Scotland, find his enemy's weakest link, and *abduct* her. Their mistake was thinking Highlander Hannah Sinclair wouldn't fight back. Now Norway's greatest warrior has a Highland hellcat on his hands, and *Odin help him, he can't resist her.* But with the brutal Sinclair brothers coming after them, Eric must choose between duty and passion…

Printed in Great Britain
by Amazon